A STRANGER IN TOWN

The Stranger sat, looking out the windows of the truck. No guards or sentries stood watch outside the town, no lookouts to warn Kemp. The town of Billington sat unprotected and at his mercy.

A vision began to form in his mind, surely a message from the trunk of secrets, because when he closed his eyes to concentrate there was blood everywhere. He saw himself walking through streets stained red with the life juices of his enemy, rivers of gore running in the gutters, and dead bodies of innocent people piled on the sides of the road like sacks of foul-smelling trash on garbage day. In his hands, he carried the severed head of Wilson Kemp, his ultimate prize in the coming fight. It was a wonderful revelation, a harbinger of things to come and it pleased the Stranger immensely.

"Man, I can't wait. This is gonna be so much fun."

Other *Leisure* books by Gord Rollo:

CRIMSON
THE JIGSAW MAN

STRANGE MAGIC

GORD ROLLO

LEISURE BOOKS NEW YORK CITY

This one is for my children: Amanda, Andrew, and Emily.
Forgive me for always writing you cool cats in as characters in
my books. Couldn't resist!!!

A LEISURE BOOK®

January 2010

Published by

Dorchester Publishing Co., Inc.
200 Madison Avenue
New York, NY 10016

ISBN 10: 0-8439-6333-6
ISBN 13: 978-0-8439-6333-5
E-ISBN: 978-1-4285-0798-2

The name "Leisure Books" and the stylized "L" with design are
trademarks of Dorchester Publishing Co., Inc.

Printed in the United States of America.

10 9 8 7 6 5 4 3 2 1

Visit us online at www.dorchesterpub.com.

FRIDAY, SEPTEMBER 18

THE STRANGER, THE DRUNKEN CLOWN, AND THE PERVERTED PEEPING TOM

CHAPTER ONE

THE STRANGER

As with most things wicked, the war of the magicians began in darkness. Dark thoughts. Dark prayers. Dark secrets. Dark deeds. All overlapping shadows locked tightly within the Stranger's ruthless cold heart. No guns were fired, no trumpets sounded, no armies charged but the countdown to inevitable violence had surely begun. Silence for now perhaps, but Wilson Kemp's luck was finally running out . . .

The final night of the Stranger's hunt was bitterly cold, the sky filled with storm clouds as black as his ever-wicked mood. Only the light from one small flame in the middle of a damp wooded clearing fought valiantly to hold the stygian darkness at bay.

It was losing the battle.

Once, not long ago, the fire had blazed with the blinding strength of a hundred armies, causing the night to panic and retreat to safer distances. The entire clearing had been visible then; out to and including the ring of tall, sturdy pine trees encircling the small fire like an indestructible fort wall. Inside the coniferous battlements was an area roughly twenty feet across with an uneven grassy terrain that reeked with the fragrance of fresh pine. A couple of dirty dishes and some soiled blankets lay strewn beside an old antique travel trunk on the left side of the clearing. The king of the light, the raging fire, sat almost in the dead center of its natural kingdom, seated upon its flaming throne. It had cockily dared the night to take its best shot.

The darkness had been smarter than that, choosing to hold back, contain its fury, and play the waiting game. It surrounded the insolent light, cutting it off from its supply lines; then waited for the inevitable. The fire had started weakening, its armored circle shrinking by the minute. The trees were no longer visible, and with the battlements down, the night had rushed in to bombard the fire with frequent sneak attacks. It would attack, then withdraw; attack, then withdraw, slowly driving its weakening enemy to its knees. Soon the night would move in for the kill.

Heavy footsteps sounded in the nearby woods, foretelling the arrival of someone new to the fray. Like magic, a man appeared out of the gloom into the fading circle of light. He carried an armload of sticks and broken branches over beside the campfire and set them down gently.

He was a tall, sinister-looking figure, maybe six foot one and rake thin. Everything about him was dark, from his jet-black hair and scruffy beard to his full-length black wool overcoat that hung low over his dirty black cowboy boots. The taut skin on his bony face and hands was the sickly white pallor of someone unaccustomed to spending time getting to know the sun. His eyes, though, were the darkest things about him, peering out from deeply recessed optic cavities like twin black holes in the white galaxy of his face. It was hard to pin down his age. People would guess the Stranger to be somewhere between forty-five and fifty, but they would be wrong. His frail-looking body was far more powerful than it looked and many a man had foolishly underestimated him.

Silently, he stood and watched the fire die. He considered tossing a few branches onto the flames, helping it in its fight, but decided not to. The fire wasn't his ally; he was a friend of the night—a kindred nocturnal spirit of sorts.

Besides, he liked to watch things die.

Ordinarily, he took great pleasure in observing death, but apart from an occasional crackling hot ember, this sadly inadequate blaze offered no comfort. It was depressing the Stranger. For him, death was a powerful ally, a close friend, and something to be treated with respect. There should be frightened prayers, and anguished crying. There should be desperate wails of despair, and high-pitched screams of unbearable agony. There should have been at least some begging for mercy. Unfortunately, there was none of these, so the shadow-shrouded man conjured up screams within his disturbed mind and enjoyed what he could from the fire's final struggles.

In the dying light, his dark eyes gazed around his makeshift campground. *Campground* was too strong a description for this barren place: *refuge* was better. The tall Stranger basically had nothing to his forgotten name, save for the dirty dishes and crumpled tattered blankets, but that didn't bother him in the least. The only thing in this world that meant anything was the antique trunk, which his eyes locked on and lovingly caressed.

The trunk itself wasn't spectacular. It was nothing

more than a 72"×30"×24" wooden traveling crate, fancied up with wood stain, leather straps, and some colorful brass buckles thrown in for show. The buckles had tarnished long ago, losing their shine; the wood stain was cracked and peeling. The cheap mahogany frame was rotting and long past its prime, but the thick leather straps were as strong and unblemished as they'd been when first put on. On the trunk's front side, in fading red letters, a shaky hand had painted a crude sign. Barely legible now, the sign read:

FIRE AND ICE
The Greatest Show on Earth

The Stranger's thin lips curled into a cruel grin as he slowly, almost reverently, reread the familiar words. He walked over and gingerly sat down on the trunk's domed lid, his frail weight enough to cause the rotting wood to slightly sag. The deteriorating condition of his beloved trunk didn't trouble the Stranger, since the trunk itself meant nothing at all. It was the trunk's contents that were important.

Inside was something so wonderful, just thinking about it sent a chill down his spine. It held such priceless treasure, such an incredible secret, and he was the only one who knew about it. The power he sat on top of thrilled him and he thought of it often, but tonight he had other important things to think about. He yanked his thoughts away from the trunk and let them drift to darker places.

A mental image of a man began to come into focus. Anger began to boil within the Stranger, as always, wiping the smile from his skeletal face.

"Wilson Kemp!" he said, hissing the name between clenched teeth, fighting to control his sudden fury.

The tall man literally shook with hatred for the imagined man. Kemp wasn't his real name, but a reliable source had informed him that was the name he'd been using for a long time now, hiding from the world. No matter—the Stranger could hate him equally as much, regardless of what he called himself. The Stranger had been searching for Kemp without success for over a year now. It had been a year of bitterness and lonely, near-intolerable frustration.

"Why can't I find the bastard?" he asked the darkness. "Where can he be hiding?"

The disappointment was driving him mad, and only the strong belief he was getting closer to his enemy kept his reason intact. He had to be close now; he just *had* to be. The search had been exhausting, covering the better part of the northern states. He'd started out last August near his hometown in New York State, traveled east to Maine, then slowly swung across the central states to end up in Washington. From there, he'd started east again, along the rim of the country, to where he presently camped. This unusually cold early Friday morning was his 389th day on the hunt.

The wooded clearing in which he sat was just off U.S. Highway 80, about a mile and a half from the community of Warren, Ohio. Warren, located in the northeastern corner of the state, was less than twenty miles from the Pennsylvania border. The Stranger had traveled nearly full circle. He was sure he was getting close though; he could feel Kemp's presence burning like a white-hot poker embedded in his cold heart.

A lonely owl broke him out of his stupor with its

annoying, repetitive question those of his ilk always seem to be asking.

"None of your goddamned business who I am," he shouted at the unseen inquirer.

As quick as the bird had come, it was gone, reducing the noise in the forest to a quiet hush. This suited the Stranger just fine; he liked the quiet of the early morning before the sun broke the horizon. The peace gave him time to plot his revenge on Kemp—and what blissfully sweet, painful revenge it was going to be.

"If only I could find the bastard," he muttered.

Again his train of angry thoughts was derailed, this time by a small stray dog approaching out of the dark woods. Dogs always wandered around him in search of a handout, or at least to warm themselves by the fire. This particular mutt was real mangy, small and pathetic-looking. At first glance, the Stranger thought it looked a bit like the famous old movie dog Benji, only this little guy lacked the Hollywood pampering—its black and brown hair tangled and knotted with burrs and clumps of dried mud.

The Stranger hated animals of all kinds and usually would have reached for a large jagged rock. If he had a good shot, and luck was on his side, maybe he could smash the worthless piece of crap's skull on the first throw. More often, he'd simply send it away whimpering and limping into the night.

He reached for a fist-size rock and was about to throw it, but suddenly changed his mind. He felt close to Kemp and that made him feel good. Charitable even. Maybe it was this satisfying feeling of nearing his enemy, maybe it was because this mutt resembled Benji, or maybe he was just going soft but regardless of the reason, he allowed the stray to curl up beside him and the ever-dying fire.

The dog sighed contentedly, having finally found a warm place to ward off this unusually chilly night. It appeared to be cold, sad, and lonely. These were feelings the Stranger couldn't understand; such emotions were alien to him. He didn't feel the frosty wind blowing around him at this moment, nor did he notice the damp, musky-smelling clothing he was wearing. He didn't even feel the heat cast from the fire. Lighting the fire was more symbolic than anything, just something he always did. There were many reasons for having a fire each night, including the fact he liked to watch the flickering flames perform their dance before disappearing into the night air, but it was definitely not for the heat. He was beyond such meaningless comfort. His volcanic anger for Wilson Kemp kept him warm. Hatred was the only feeling he could relate to now.

The dark man scratched the mangy dog behind its ears as it settled into a contented dream about whatever it is mangy dogs dream about, his own thoughts drifting back to Kemp and his plan for revenge. It was then the antique trunk on which he sat began speaking to him. It spoke no audible words the outside world could hear, but the message was clear in the Stranger's head.

The trunk had located Kemp.

Finally.

The trunk was the Stranger's secret weapon, his reliable source that had somehow found out the name their enemy was hiding under. Now it was telling him the bastard was hiding in a town called Billington, in Pennsylvania. He quickly pulled his old, torn, dirty map out of his inside coat pocket.

"Where . . . where?" he asked, his long, pale finger tracing up and down the entire state of Pennsylvania.

Just as his frustration level hit the boiling point, he found it. Billington, Pennsylvania. On the map, it looked like a decent-size town in the northwestern part of the state. Billington lay on Highway 62, right where the Allegheny River crossed. It was about halfway between the cities of Pittsburgh and Erie but a little off to the east. He found the scale of the map, and quickly determined how far away he was.

He was close. Real close.

If his calculations were accurate, less than ninety miles separated him from Kemp. *Ninety miles!*

The tall Stranger was pleased, so pleased in fact, he actually reached down and tenderly stroked the dog's sleeping head. His thin, icy lips started to curl into an evil grin and the feeling coming over him was the closest to joy he'd experienced in a very long time. He laughed out loud and snapped the small, fragile neck of his new pet with one quick clenching action of his powerful fist. The mutt let out a tiny yelp and as its legs twitched for the final time, the last of the embers in the fire died.

The battle was over; the darkness had won.

The Stranger sat in the dark, petting the dead dog and smiling happily until the sun rose to wake up a rooster on a nearby farm. The overzealous rooster continued to crow with annoying regularity, which ordinarily would have sent the Stranger into a rage but not today. No, today for the first time in a year, he actually whistled as he gathered up his meager belongings. He placed the dishes and blankets into the antique trunk and then as an afterthought, also placed the corpse of the recently killed dog and gently laid its broken body on top of the blankets. After closing the trunk and lovingly buckling it up, he took great care to make sure all traces of his stay in the clearing were erased. He made sure the fire was fully extinguished, then covered the pit with dirt, sticks, and pine needles.

He took one last look around, eyeing the clearing critically, acknowledging he'd done a good job. No one would ever know anyone had spent the night there, which was just how he wanted it.

The rooster was singing his song again off to the dark man's left. He noted the direction. He intended to find that rooster because where there was a rooster there was a farm, and where there's a farm there's transport. He had ninety miles to cover before he got his hands on Wilson Kemp and he sure didn't feel like walking them.

Hoisting up one end, he dragged the trunk of secrets into the thick foliage of the woods. Within moments, the Stranger was gone.

The black and rust-colored rooster on the fence post crowed yet again, perhaps for the hundredth time this morning. It apparently liked to hear itself sing because almost immediately, it began huffing and puffing to prepare for a new rendition.

"Shut up, Ricky!" Duke Winslow screamed, throwing a handful of dirt and gravel in the general direction of the bird. "I've been up for hours already, so shut your trap."

Ricky the rooster, obviously offended, jumped down from the fence and strutted defiantly off to find a more receptive audience.

"Finally," Duke whispered, adjusting his Cincinnati

Reds ball cap back down near his thick, bushy eyebrows, where he always wore it.

He'd worn his hat like that, low and tight, for so many years now he actually had a permanent crease on his forehead to mark its position. Of course, with Duke just turning eighty-one years of age, the hat crease was only one of many lines on his wrinkled, barely noticeable brow.

"Damn bird. Gets more sleep than I do, then has the nerve to harp on for hours. Stupid thing would sing all day if I didn't shut it up."

It had started this nonsense about two years ago, just after Duke's wife Jenny passed away, finally losing her battle with cancer. She had always come out and talked to Ricky, telling it what a pretty bird it was. Now the bird continued to sing, not realizing Jenny wasn't coming to talk to it anymore. Duke knew exactly how the bird felt—he missed Jenny something fierce too.

Ricky strutted around the side of the barn and Duke went back to changing the oil in his 1997 Ford F-150 pickup. He wanted to get it finished because they were calling for rain today. Dark clouds were already rolling in, the heavens getting ready to let loose.

From the looks of things, he still had time before the clouds burst, if he didn't dawdle. His truck's red exterior was a bit chipped and rusty, but under the hood the engine still purred like a happy kitten.

"Proper maintenance, that's the ticket," he muttered to himself as he labored to crawl beneath the oil pan to tighten the nut back in place.

It took him the better part of five minutes to work himself into position, his age not so much the problem as his ample belly. The lifelong protrusion stuck out over his belt, stretching his green shirt, pants, and his favorite red suspenders to their limits. Sweat poured down his face, soiling his white mustache and beard, despite the chilly morning breeze. He knew he was dangerously overweight but to hell with it. He'd been heavy all his life, why worry about it now?

A heavy scraping noise down by his feet startled him. Lying beneath the truck, he was unable to see what was making the unusual sound. He tried to peer between his feet but his belly was in the way. He wiggled around a bit to the left just in time to see a pair of dirty black cowboy boots come into view. The well-worn boots walked up to the side of the truck, less than a foot away from him, then stopped.

"Who's there?" Duke asked. An ominous silence started the old man's heart racing.

"I said, who the hell's there?" Duke was trying to sound tough but was failing miserably.

For thirty seconds, nothing happened: neither man spoke, nor moved. Then the black-booted man walked around to the back of the truck. Duke heard that strange scraping sound again and decided he'd better get his fat ass out from under the truck and see what was going on. There was no fear in his decision; he was far too old to be scared. He was more curious than anything. He pushed and pulled, wiggled and squeezed, and finally stood up to see a dark-clothed man starting to heave a large trunk up into the back of his pickup. Duke noticed the trail leading to his truck from the woods. Obviously he'd dragged his trunk from that direction, which explained the weird scraping noises he'd heard, but didn't help him the least in understanding what was going on.

"Hey, mister, can I help you with something?" Duke asked, his curiosity getting the best of him.

The Stranger set one end of the trunk onto the bed of the red pickup and left the other end on the ground. It wasn't until he was sure the trunk was well balanced and wouldn't fall that he turned to face the sweaty old man.

"How you doing, Duke? Long time no see," the dark man cheerily said, instantly turning on the charm. The trunk had whispered to him the fat man's name.

"Ahh . . . okay, I guess," Duke answered, thoroughly puzzled as to how he knew his name. "Excuse me if I'm being rude, but do I know you? Can't seem to place your face. Course, my memory isn't as good as it used to be."

The Stranger gave the old man his best-friend-in-the-world smile, while listening to the voice in his head.

"Sure you know me, Duke. I used to help out here on the farm. I was a friend of your wife. Used to help Jenny out in the fields."

The dark man knew he'd been reaching with that last lie but the secret trunk was never wrong, so he'd gone with it. He knew he'd pushed the right button and the lie would work the second he'd mentioned the old man's wife. The aged farmer's face lit up instantly, glowing with pride. The Stranger wasn't even sure if he'd heard the rest of the lie but no matter, he knew this old man wasn't going to give him any trouble. Through clenched teeth, he forced himself to keep smiling.

"You knew Jenny? Well, why didn't you say so?" Duke beamed, always happy to talk to anyone who'd known his beloved wife. This guy was a bit weird-looking and Duke still couldn't remember seeing him around, but any pal of Jenny's had to be okay. He stuck out his hand to the tall visitor, who shook it eagerly.

"Pleased to meet you, Mr. . . . ?" Duke paused in mid-shake. "Don't remember your name. What was it again?"

"You can call me Mr. Black if you'd like."

"Mr. Black it is," Duke said amiably, although he thought to himself it was a bit formal for his liking. Around these parts, most people liked to be known on a first-name basis, but to each his own. "You can call me Duke, everybody else does."

With the formalities taken care of, Duke steered back to his original question. "Now, can I help you with something?" he asked, nodding in the direction of the large travel trunk sitting on the edge of his truck bed.

The Stranger cranked up his fake smile as high as it would go, really laying it on thick. He said, "Yeah, matter of fact, you can. I'm really in a big hurry and I don't want to bother you, but I'd sure appreciate it if you could give me a lift into town. This trunk's hard to travel with and I could sure use a break from lugging it. I'm not as young as I used to be."

"Makes two of us, partner," Duke laughed. "A lift? Sure, no problem. I was heading into town anyway. You'll have to give me a minute though; I was just in the middle of changing the oil. Won't take long."

"No problem, take your time," the Stranger replied. Things were moving along just fine, just fine indeed. He waited for the old man to top off the oil and slam the rusty hood back into place before moving on with his plan. His *I'm your pal for life* smile was back in place. "Sorry, Duke, but could you help me back here for a second? This trunk's not so bad to drag, but it's a bit heavy for one guy to lift. Can you give me a hand?"

"Sure I can." Duke smiled as he grabbed an end, happy his new friend didn't consider him too old and useless.

"Man, you're not kidding, this thing *is* heavy. What have you got in here?"

The Stranger tried to act surprised; as if that wasn't the exact question he'd been waiting for.

"Well, I don't know if I should tell you, Duke. You see, it's kind of a secret." He paused for a moment, strictly for dramatic effect. "You any good at keeping secrets?"

"Secrets?" Duke asked, noting the fading sign on the side of the trunk advertising "The Greatest Show on Earth." That got his curiosity really cranked up and running wild. He'd always enjoyed a good secret. Mind you, he wasn't too sure he was good at keeping them. With his fingers crossed behind his back, he quickly replied, "Yeah, sure I am. No worries. What's in the trunk?"

"Something wonderful," the Stranger purred in a dreamy whisper. "Let's get it all the way up on the truck and I'll show you. Deal?"

"Sounds good, let's do it."

Together they labored to move the trunk into place at the front of the truck bed, just behind the passenger-side cab window. It was too long to fit straight on sideways, across the truck, but still wedged snugly on an angle between the side rails tight enough that it wouldn't tip or slide around anywhere.

"There," Duke wheezed, wiping sweat from his brow again. "That ought to do it. Can I have a look in it now?"

His fake happy demeanor was now replaced with a genuine smile of pure evil that spread across the dark man's face. He said, "Sure, Duke, be my guest."

Duke seemed to shed about seventy-five years of age as he began undoing the thick leather straps on the antique trunk. He worked at them in a near frenzy, an excited child unwrapping his biggest Christmas present.

In seconds, he had the trunk lid open and was peering inside. His childish grin vanished from his face. He was disappointed.

"Hey, what's going on? This crate's got nothing in it. It's empty."

"It's *what?*" the Stranger gasped in mock disbelief, ever the showman.

He knew the trunk was far from empty. He knew for a fact he'd put his dirty dishes and blankets in there less than an hour ago. Somewhere in there was also a small dead dog probably looking less and less like Benji by the minute. There was another magnificent thing in the trunk too, but like the others, it was somewhere else at the moment. Not to worry, the Stranger was sure it would make an appearance fairly soon.

"You see?" Duke said. "Empty."

"Well, so it is," replied the dark man pretentiously. With a flare, he held up one skinny finger, as if an idea had just occurred to him. "I know what's going on. You opened the lid wrong. You forgot to knock."

"I forgot to what?" Duke asked, confused but curious once again.

"To knock," the dark man said, closing the lid of the trunk as he spoke. "You have to knock on the lid three times before you open it up."

Duke thought his new friend might be a bit odder than he first thought, but again his curiosity got the best of him and he soon found himself knocking on the wooden lid like he'd been told. After the third knock, the tall man gave him the nod to open the trunk again. When he did, his eyes almost popped out of their sockets. The trunk was no longer empty.

"How in hell . . . ?" was all Duke could manage to say

as he stared down in awe at the collection of things that had seemingly appeared out of thin air.

The Stranger smiled at the old man's reaction, amused by the look of wonder on his wrinkled face. It was only his blankets and dishes back again, but to the farmer it must have seemed like something amazing had just happened. He was just starting to wonder where the dead dog was, when he spotted it in the far corner. It had changed. The small mutt had been completely stripped down to the bone. Every ounce of hair, skin, fat, and blood was gone, leaving only a few greasy muscles and tendons to hold together the skeleton's shape. The bones of the small, broken-necked skeleton were so incredibly white they almost looked bleached. Its appearance even caught the Stranger off guard, so it was no great shock when the old farmer noticed the bones and gasped in surprise.

"What's that thing?" Duke asked, pointing with a shaky finger toward the small skeleton.

"What thing?" The Stranger played stupid, closing the lid of the trunk again.

"Right there in the . . ." Duke started, but left the sentence unfinished as he opened the trunk to find it completely empty again.

"You forgot to knock again," the dark man giggled. He was actually starting to enjoy this.

Duke wasn't enjoying it nearly as much. He was confused. Taking a step backward, as if a wider view might aid him, he stopped to think this through. Here in front of him was a trunk that, according to the sign anyway, was from "The Greatest Show on Earth." Inside the trunk, things could appear and disappear right in front of his eyes and beside him stood a mysterious dark-clothed man. Although Duke was old and maybe a few ticks slower than he used to be, it didn't take him too long to add these things up.

"Hey, I get it. You must be some kind of magician or something. Right?"

"Something like that, yeah."

"Can you do it again for me?" Duke asked excitedly, pointing back at the trunk. This was by far the most excitement he'd had in ages.

"Do what, Duke?" the Stranger asked, back to the showman routine. "I didn't do anything. It was you who knocked on the lid, not me."

This really started Duke's juices flowing. He literally pounced on the lid of the trunk, showing more energy than he had in decades. He rapped loudly on the lid, bruising his knuckles in the process, but was too excited to notice. He threw the lid open without the slightest hesitation and laughed like a loon when he saw that, indeed, the magic trunk was full of dishes and blankets again.

"Well, if this isn't the best goddamnedest trick I ever seen! I never even saw you move. You didn't touch the trunk, did you?"

The Stranger gave him one of those *I can't reveal my secrets* kind of shoulder shrugs, but said nothing. Duke returned his attention to the trunk and remembered the tiny skeleton he'd seen in the corner earlier. It was gone.

"Say, where'd that skeleton go? You know . . . the little thing in the corner, kind of looked like a dog or cat maybe. It was fake, wasn't it?"

"It's still there, Duke, you just haven't looked hard enough." The magician pointed at a lump underneath the. dirty blankets slowly moving up and down. "See what I mean?"

"Holy cow!" Duke shouted, truly amazed. "Now I get it. First you show me a fake skeleton. Then, somehow you swap it for the real thing. I've watched these live animal tricks on television before. I'll bet there's a puppy or something underneath that blanket, isn't there?"

The dark man offered no response, and Duke didn't wait for one. He tore off the dirty blanket with one strong yank, a grin spreading across his face that would have made a great white shark jealous. His smile never did fully form though, his lips freezing in place like a department-store mannequin. Moments later, he started screaming.

Under the blanket was definitely *not* a puppy.

Under the blanket was something so hideous Old Duke Winslow's mind began to snap. Insanity was a far more attractive alternative than trying to deal rationally with the nightmare his eyes beheld.

The Stranger had been waiting eagerly for this moment. He waited a few seconds to let the true horror of the moment sink in, then rushed at the farmer's turned back. He hit him with all his strength, a two-fisted hammer blow on top of his head, driving the screaming old man down and on top of the impossible monstrosity lying in the trunk.

In a flurry of well-practiced maneuvers, the Stranger flipped the lid shut and quickly buckled up the thick leather straps, sealing the poor old man inside. Duke's screams were somewhat muffled, but still sweet music to the dark man's ears. He climbed out of the truck bed, humming happily along with Duke's tune, and slipped behind the Ford's wheel.

Without further delay, he started the pickup and

screeched out onto a gravel road that would lead him to the highway. From the highway, he'd be in Pennsylvania in no time, and from there, nothing could stop him from getting his hands on his bitter enemy.

While he drove, he killed Wilson Kemp a thousand times in his sick mind, and each death was more painful than the last. He was going to make all hell break loose when he finally held Kemp in his grasp. That entire town was going to learn what fear really was and this thought nearly brought a tear of joy to his eye.

"What a glorious morning this has turned out to be," he shouted out the window to the magic trunk behind him, as light rain began to fall from the ever-darkening morning sky. "Right, Duke, old buddy?"

Duke never answered; he'd finally stopped screaming.

The Stranger reached U.S. Highway 80, and passed a sign that said:

10 MILES TO PENNSYLVANIA BORDER

Revenge was near at hand. He slammed the pedal to the floor, gunning the engine for all it was worth. The old Ford responded with a healthy roar, rocketing the grinning Stranger into the stormy morning like a fiery red lighting bolt racing anxiously toward Armageddon.

CHAPTER TWO

THE CLOWN

Wilson Kemp's nose had fallen off again. Not a particularly good way to start his new career, certainly not like he'd hoped. This was the day he'd been nervously awaiting for almost two months. He'd marked off the days on his magnetic fridge calendar with a brand-new felt marker he'd bought just for this purpose. He'd planned, and dreamed, and hoped everything would go smoothly, that maybe today would finally be the start of something good. He knew if this afternoon went well, he'd be able to find steady work, make a little money, and maybe—just maybe—start to pick up the pieces of his shattered dreams again.

Things weren't going well.

Things had gone sour right from the start. He should have known better than to have one little sip of vodka "*to brace his nerves,*" he'd lied to himself. What a load of crap. His one little sip had led to another, then another, until in no time at all he was sloshed.

Stupid, crazy fuck.

Recovering alcoholics just never seemed to learn. To be a bit more truthful, Wilson wasn't exactly a recovering alcoholic. He was more of a full-fledged alcoholic, who happened to have a severe case of denial on his hands. Every night, he'd go to bed convinced he'd raised himself to the lofty level of a recovering alcoholic but sometime during the night, fairies or demons or who-ever the hell plotted against him always seemed to mys-teriously transform him back into a hopeless drunk again by daylight.

He'd tried countless times—hundreds—to put away the bottle, but always failed. He hardly had any confi-dence left to try. There were reasons why he was a drunk, though sometimes it was hard to remember what they were. His wife had left him three years earlier, taking his beautiful four-year-old daughter with her. He wasn't com-pletely clear anymore as to whether he'd started drinking because she'd left him, or if she had left him because he'd started drinking. Either way, it didn't really matter—his life had fallen apart without her.

He'd quickly lost his good job down at the post office. One day in a deep vodka haze, Wilson had sent every last piece of mail he could get his sweaty hands on, first-class, to the post office in Anchorage, Alaska. To this day, he still had no idea why—it had just felt like a fun thing to do at the time. Neither his boss nor the United States Postal Service had shared his sense of humor, with the former, on behalf of the latter, firing him in-stantly.

Wilson had moved around from one dead-end job to the next, hitting the bottle hard for about two years. It was only about eight months ago that he'd sobered up enough to seriously think about going back to his one great passion in life: magic.

Magic had been a part of Kemp's life for as long as he could remember. As a shy, skinny, freckle-faced kid, magic had been his only friend and only means of escape.

He'd practiced long and hard, becoming better than he had ever dreamed he could be. He wasn't a Houdini or a Copperfield, but he was damn close. He'd really made something of it too, or had been about to, but then his life had taken a downward spiral. One day, the crowds had been cheering his name, the next he was running scared, hiding in a small town that never guessed who he once was. No one, not even his ex-wife and daughter, knew what secrets lay buried in his past. He tried not to think about it; simply pushing it to the back of his mind, hoping the memories would go away.

Unfortunately, they never did.

Wilson could easily keep his past secret until the day he died, but he couldn't keep his love for magic buried forever. Which was why when he finally hit the bottom of the barrel, he thought of magic as his possible savior. He decided to revive his career. Nothing like the last time, of course, nothing even close, but something using his vast talent in magic to earn a living. Maybe, he'd thought, he could get his wife and kid back too.

So Wilson had struggled to stay out of the vodka as best he could, worked on his rusty act, and had marked off the calendar waiting for his first big gig. Finally, September the eighteenth had rolled around and he'd been too stupid to just walk out of the house and leave the damn booze behind. Now he stood, or swayed rather, in front of about fifteen nasty kids at an after-school birthday party dressed in full clown garb: white face paint with a big red smile, rainbow-colored baggy jumpsuit with a golden belt string, and matching electric blue fuzzy wig and floppy, oversize shoes.

The kids were all screaming and bawling—generally

unimpressed with the stupid magic clown named Mickey, who stumbled around and kept losing his fake red nose.

"Who wants to see a magic clown, anyway?" Wilson muttered to himself as he bent down to recover his big sponge nose again.

This was the second time it had come unstuck and fallen off. The last time, right in the middle of his vanishing-turtle trick, he'd tried to catch the falling honker as it dropped. It had been a big mistake, what with his reflexes and coordination all fouled up by the booze in his system. Not only did he drop the nose, but in the process knocked over a glass lamp, a table, and dislodged the turtle into the birthday boy's ice-cream bowl. He'd received his best applause of the performance for that little stunt but the young boy's father hadn't looked happy cleaning up the mess.

This time, Wilson's nose had dropped all the way to the floor, rolling off the dark green throw rug that had become his stage, and disappeared under a nearby love seat. He probably should have just left it there, but seeing as his entire audience was diving after it and paying no attention to him anyway, he decided he might as well join in the great nose hunt himself.

Wilson took two awkward steps before tripping over his big floppy feet. He tried to regain his balance but was unable to do so. He landed with a loud *thump*, face-down in what was left of the spaceship-shaped chocolate birthday cake. This was when all hell broke loose. The birthday boy was the first person to start screaming, but within seconds every other person in the room was screaming too. The kids were only screaming because the cake was demolished and some of them hadn't even had a piece yet, but the parents who'd gathered around to watch the nice magic show didn't give a damn about the cake.

They were screaming at Wilson.

By the time Wilson stumbled back to his feet again, vainly trying to wipe the chocolate icing out of his eyes, a group of seven angry parents had formed a circle around him. They were all yelling and jabbing his chest with pointing fingers. Wilson tried his best to calm them down, but that was impossible. Things rapidly moved from bad to worse when one of the ladies marched in close enough to smell his breath. There are people who drink vodka because they think it's one of the only drinks people can't smell on their breath, but they're wrong. Drink enough of it, and drink it day after day and the sickly sweet smell of vodka will start oozing out of your pores, as well as on your breath. Maybe not as prominently as bourbon or tequila perhaps, but it can't easily be masked. For Wilson, it was impossible.

"Oh my God!" the woman screamed. "I think he's been drinking. Smell his breath, Reggie. He smells like a distillery. No wonder he's falling all over the place . . . this guy's wasted."

Reggie, who was the birthday boy's father and six foot four to boot, thundered closer, already pissed off over having to clean up the first mess. When he smelled Wilson's breath he nearly went ballistic. With one large hand he grabbed Wilson around the throat and backed him up against the wall.

"You son of a bitch. You got nerve to come into my home all pissed up in front of my friends and all our kids. I ought to knock your stinking block off, that's what I ought to do."

"No, wait," Wilson tried to explain. "Take it easy, will you. I'll just get my things and—"

Reggie's fist cut him off midsentence and he slumped down the wall to lay prostrate on the floor. No rest for the wicked, unfortunately. The pissed-off father dragged him back to his feet and prepared to punch him again.

His wife, much to Wilson's relief, came between them—narrowly missing being whacked herself.

"Reggie, stop! He's not worth getting in trouble over. Janet already called the cops and they're on their way, so just leave him alone, okay?"

"Okay? No, it's not okay. This imbecile comes over here drunk as a skunk, ruins Timmy's birthday, smashes an expensive lamp and table, and expects to just walk? Maybe get a slap on the wrist from the cops? I don't think so. He deserves a bit more of what he's getting so move out of the way, Alice."

The argument waged on for several tense minutes, but Wilson had no intention of sticking around to see who was going to win, so at his first opportunity he ran as fast as his floppy feet would take him. He ran past Reggie and Alice, past the group of bewildered children and past the finger-jabbing group of parents to make it to the outside door. It wasn't until he hit the fourth step down on the front porch that his feet tangled up again, causing another nosedive to the ground. This time, there was no soft chocolate cake to cushion his fall, his hands and face scraping painfully along the cement walkway leading to the house. This was definitely not the way he'd hoped his day would go. Wilson wished he could just lie there and die.

What a damn day, he thought. *I get drunk and blow my first good job in months. Then I get punched out by a pissed-off macho dad who I'm sure isn't gonna pay me. What else can go wrong?*

It was then Wilson looked up into the smiling face of a Billington police officer.

"Heard you were causing trouble again, Wilson," the blond-haired policeman said. "What the heck have you been up to now?"

Wilson was on a first-name basis with most of the police in the area, seeing as most of them had scraped him out of one gutter or another during the last few years. He recognized the officer as Jacob Jackson and breathed a sigh of relief. Jacob was a whole lot nicer to him than some of the other cops in town.

"I'm not causing any trouble, Jake," Wilson slurred, staggering to his feet. "I'm just . . . ahh, I'm just—"

"You're just coming with me, clown-man," Officer Jackson said as he led Wilson toward the waiting backseat of his black-and-white.

"Yeah, okay, Jake. Whatever you say."

Jackson closed him in, went up to the house to get a few statements, and returned with something in his left hand. He climbed behind the wheel and started driving away.

"They're pretty pissed back there, Wilson. When are you ever gonna get your act together? Huh?"

Wilson put his head in his hands in a display of honest shame. "That's what I was trying to do, Jake. I guess I just fucked up again."

"Yeah, you did. Here, Reggie said to give you this."

He tossed Wilson's big red sponge nose. Wilson picked it up, and with no place else to put it, stuck it back on his scratched and bleeding face.

Officer Jackson took a peek at him in the rearview

mirror, shook his head sadly, and said, "You've been acting like a clown for years, Kemp. At least today you decided to dress the part. It's real sad, man. Pretty pathetic."

Tears ran down Wilson's made-up face. "I know, Jake. I know it is. I'm working on it."

It took another fifteen minutes for the cruiser to make it into the Billington Police Department's parking lot. Wilson's luck was looking up—his nose had stayed glued to his face for the entire trip.

CHAPTER THREE

THE PERVERT

The shades were drawn and the lights were out. A distraught man, naked as the day he'd been born, sat hunched over on a high-backed wooden desk chair with his head resting in his sweaty hands. The room was almost as bare, scantily furnished with a scarred rolltop desk and one other chair matching the one on which he sat. The walls were bare as well as the hardwood floor, save for a small pile of discarded clothing the man had recently removed.

Twilight rays still snuck their way into the shadow-filled room between the cracks in the blinds, casting a distorted silhouette of the troubled man against the far wall. He didn't know the exact time of day, but he guessed it to be around 9:15 P.M., not that it was important. All that mattered was the sun was nearly gone, only a tiny sliver hung on the horizon, and soon the sky would be dark. He hated the dark, or to be more precise, he hated himself when it was dark. When the sun abandoned this part of the world, a transformation sometimes happened to him. He changed. Nothing as drastic as sprouting hair and long, sharp teeth like the legendary werewolf; but a change nonetheless.

Ordinarily, the frightened man would have turned on

every light in the house rather than sit in the darkening gloom, but he had to keep the room dark and keep the shades drawn for fear anyone might see him change. Exposure frightened him almost as much as the metamorphosis itself. He rubbed his throbbing temples, rocking back and forth in the fading light, and waited.

The urges were strong tonight. That wasn't a good sign. Sometimes weeks would go by without them being this strong, but usually it was more likely to be just a day or two. When the urges were only whispers, he could sometimes will them away and he'd be left alone, but that wasn't going to happen tonight. Tonight, it was as if the voices had slipped into his head, conveniently sucked out his brain, and replaced it with a big bass drum that steadily pounded to the urges' beat.

"Please stop," he begged. "I don't want to go out tonight. I don't want to go back out again ever. It's wrong. Do you hear me? Wrong!"

The urges beat their drum harder and faster, heedless of his pleas. The tempo and volume spiraled ever higher, pounding and reverberating in his head like the sound of cannon fire. The pain was intolerable and getting worse, as if at any moment his skull would surely split and spatter the walls red. The urges drowned out all rational thoughts until the man knew he'd either have to obey them or go stark raving mad.

"All right . . . *All right!*" he screamed, dropping to his knees, cradling his aching head. "I'll go, I promise. Just get out of my head. Please. Give me peace and I'll do anything you want."

The pounding in his head increased momentarily, then dropped away to a distant rumble. It never fully died away, choosing rather to linger in the back of his mind, just as a warning. The heavily sweating man's relief at the receding noise was so great he temporarily lost consciousness. It was like slipping into a crystal clear pool of cool water on a scorching summer day. He slumped all the way to the floor, curled into the fetal position, and enjoyed the swim . . .

When he regained his senses, the change in him was complete. He was a different man now. This new person liked to call himself Tom, though he knew it wasn't his real name. His real identity was rendered insignificant when Tom was around. His real name was forgotten, gone with the weakling who'd earlier wanted to resist the urges. That side of him was nothing more than a pathetic fool who didn't realize how many sweet things there were in this world just waiting to be tasted. Tom wasn't scared to taste the sweeter things in life; on the contrary, he thrived on them. When the urges began to drum for Tom, they did not have to ask twice. He was off the floor, on his feet, and heading for the door in an instant. Whistling happily, he walked naked through the dark house toward the back door.

He brushed the curtain aside to peer out, checking to see if the way was clear, then backed up a few steps to open the hall closet. Inside was everything he would need for tonight's fun and games. Tom loved fun and games, but then again, most perverts did.

Yes, Tom was a pervert, and he had no qualms about admitting that to himself. His other side, the weaker part of him, might have a problem with it, but that was why Tom got to have all the fun. He never kidded himself. He believed in calling a spade a spade, so seeing as he *was* a pervert, why not call himself one?

If the truth be told, Tom was more than just your average everyday run-of-the-mill pervert, he was also a rather accomplished Peeping Tom. That's where his name had come from. Everyone knew the old story about how some poor bastard named Tom had opened the curtains at the wrong time, and mistakenly watched some stupid bitch ride by his window naked on a horse. It was a silly story, but apparently the well from which the legend of the Peeping Tom sprang.

"As far as I'm concerned," Tom whispered, "any broad who'd ride down the middle of the street naked on a freakin' horse was asking to be gawked at. She's just lucky I wasn't there."

In this modern day and time, most people referred to this indecent act as voyeurism, but Tom still preferred to describe himself in the ways of old. Remember, according to his admittedly twisted self-logic, a spade would always be a spade, and a pervert would always be a pervert, so naturally it followed a Peeping Tom would always be a Peeping Tom. In his disturbed, fragmented mind, it was simple common sense.

From separate hangers in the hall closet, Tom dressed in a pair of black Levi's jeans and an even darker black pullover sweatshirt. On another hanger, a black wool winter jacket hung, which he considered putting on but decided against. It was still a bit early in the year for that part of his disguise. On a shoe rack on the floor, a pair of black Adidas sat next to an equally black pair of Kodiak hunting boots. Tom selected the running shoes and quickly laced them up. From the wooden shelf near the top of the closet, he took down his hat and gloves. He pulled the black wool ski mask over his face first, then struggled to tug the tight leather gloves onto his sweaty hands. The only thing left on the upper shelf was a bright red high-powered flashlight.

"Everyone needs a little color in their life . . . even sicko perverts," Tom said, smiling behind his mask.

Flashlight in hand, Tom walked over to where a full-length mirror hung on the otherwise bare wall. He always paused at this mirror to admire himself before heading outside. It never failed to thrill him, seeing his powerful six-foot frame wrapped in black. His penis started to harden at the thought of what other people must think when they see him emerge out of the darkness, revealing himself to them like this. They would fear him, of course, and it was their fear that gave him power. Craving this rush of power was what drove Tom out into the night, and also caused the urges within him to beat their drums.

"Look at me. I look like something straight out of a sadomasochist's wet dream." Tom couldn't help but laugh, loving every second of this. "Let's go see what kind of fun we can find on the quiet streets of Billington tonight."

As his gloved hand grasped the back doorknob, his conscience, or maybe his real personality, broke into his dark thoughts and begged him to put away the flashlight and mask. The smile slid off Tom's face, leaving him confused, but then the urges began to pound their drums again to the hypnotic, insane beat only he could hear. He stood leaning against the wall, flickering back and forth between his dual personalities. For a few moments he didn't know what to do, but as the earth has no choice but to spin, and the waves of the ocean must obey the moon's pull, the urges in his head could not be denied.

The side of his psyche that called himself Tom snapped back in control and he quickly locked his weaker side away in the back of his mind. Back in undisputed control, with no more hesitation or doubt, Tom quietly slipped out the back door and disappeared into the chilly yet familiar embrace of the night.

CHAPTER FOUR

UNDER THE COVER OF DARKNESS

"Let me out of here," Wilson shouted at the top of his voice. "Hey, guard, can you hear me?"

He was still decked out in his magic clown getup, but had managed to wash most of the face paint off in the small, stained sink hanging precariously from the graffiti-covered wall. He'd only been awake for fifteen minutes, which had been long enough to realize where he was, register it was dark outside the bar-studded window (which meant he'd slept the rest of the afternoon away), and discover how much his body and face ached. He sure could use a shot of vodka right now.

"Come on, guys, somebody get back here," he yelled, rattling his metal drinking cup against the small holding cell's slightly rusting gray bars. Not the most original thing to do, but just like in the movies it proved to be rather effective, bringing one of the night-shift officers running. Wilson knew this cop as well.

The huge black man's uniform shirt was untucked at the waist and his sleeves rolled up to reveal melon-size biceps. He wore no badge or gun, and as he approached Wilson, his stifled yawn indicated he'd either been fast asleep or well on his way. He didn't look very happy.

"Shut up, Kemp, you damn fool. What on earth are you yelling at?"

"You've got to get me out of here. I'm starting to go nuts caged up in this damn jail. You've got your keys with you, right, Mack?" Wilson pleaded, using his hands to mimic an invisible key being twisted into an invisible lock.

Officer Byron MacKenzie, Big Mack to his friends, was in a foul mood. He'd been offered free tickets to a great jazz concert in Pittsburgh, and had been forced to pass because he hadn't been able to get anyone to change shifts. He'd been close to calling in sick and going to the show anyway, but at the last minute he canceled out and grudgingly headed to work. He'd done the right thing showing up for duty, but that didn't mean he had to pretend to be a happy camper. He was certainly in no mood to stand and argue all night with the town drunk.

"First of all, I don't think three tiny holding cells squeezed into the backroom of this building would constitute much of a jail. Second, even if you do consider this a jail, get it through your thick head real quick I'm not a guard. I'm a police officer, and a pissed off one at that. Third, things will go a lot smoother for both of us if you'd just lie down and keep quiet. You're not going anywhere, so shut the fuck up, dig?"

"Ah come on, Mack, what's the deal? I've been in here long enough to sober up. Usually, someone would have woken me up and tossed me long ago. What's happening?"

"What's happening, Kemp, is this time you're not just having a nice little snooze in the tank. This time you're being charged."

"Charged!" Wilson replied, astonished.

"Yeah, charged. You know, as in this time you fucked up royally. I heard Reggie Morris and his wife just about blew the roof off this place this afternoon after your little magic show at their place."

Wilson's memory, as always when he drank too much, wasn't all that good. He remembered his red nose kept falling off and maybe he broke a lamp. Touching his sore face, he recalled his encounter with Reggie's fist, but after that, his mind drew a blank. He had no recollection of how he'd gotten out of the Morris house, or how he'd eventually ended up in the confines of this cramped and unappealing cell.

"What are they charging me with, Mack?"

"Drunk and disorderly, malicious damage, and anything else the chief can think of. Morris really tore a chunk out of the chief's ass. He's mad as hell. You'll be awful lucky if the Morrises don't turn around and sue you on top of all this. I guess you practically wrecked their place, not to mention probably giving their kid a bad complex about birthday parties and clowns that might stay with him for freakin' life."

A vision flashed in Wilson's head of Archie, a turtle he'd recently bought, tumbling out of his pocket and landing into a big bowl of ice cream. He wasn't sure if that had really happened, so he just pushed the thought aside. Probably for the best.

"How long do I have to stay here?" he finally asked.

"Hard to say really. You might have to hang around until Monday, when the chief comes back to work."

"Monday! You've got to be kidding? Today's only . . . ahh . . . Monday's not for another . . . let's see—" He'd forgotten what day of the week today was, so he quickly changed the topic. "What about bail, Mack? Can I get out if I post bail?"

"It's about eleven o'clock on Friday night, if you'd like to know. Look Wilson, we're not playing twenty questions here; it takes a judge to set a bail amount, man, and trust me, amigo, no one is getting the judge out of bed tonight. 'Sides, even if they end up setting bail at a measly hundred bucks, I'm willing to bet my next paycheck you haven't got it, have you?"

Wilson frantically dug in the deep, baggy pockets of his rainbow-colored clown suit. There was a lump in his left-side pouch but when he pulled it out, it was only his troublesome sponge clown nose.

"Just like I thought," the burly policeman said, starting to turn and walk away.

"Wait, Mack!" Wilson yelled. "What about Susan? If you could call her, I'll bet she—"

"Forget it, already tried calling your wife. She's not around. Even if she was, you've got to stop relying on her to keep rescuing you every time you drink yourself into a jam. You've got to get your act together, man, she threw you out of the house for a reason, you know?"

"I know, but—"

"But nothing. Look, I called her and she's not home. I don't know where she is or believe me I'd try and dump you off. You're going to have to sit tight. I left a message on her machine, so she'll probably yank you out tomorrow. She'll sweet-talk somebody and you'll get out, but it's not happening tonight. No way. Now shut up and get some sleep."

Officer MacKenzie was out the door and back into

the front office before Wilson could think of anything else to say. He briefly considered trying to pick the lock on his cell, but he was *way* out of practice and had no tools with him anyway. Accepting his predicament, he set his cup back on the shelf above the sink and slouched down on the lumpy, uncomfortable bed. Something hard poked at his leg, behind his left knee, and when he reached down under the mattress he found one of the thin steel slats that crisscrossed to make the wire mesh of his bunk was loose and was sticking out a few inches. Wilson stood up and lifted the mattress to get a better look. If he wiggled the protruding slat, the entire six and a half feet of thin steel slid in and out at will. If he'd wanted to, Wilson could have slowly backed up and slid the entire slat free of the interlocking mesh pattern. Then he looked at the single wool blanket he'd been given.

With a long, thin piece of steel like this and my blanket, I could . . . I could . . .

"Oh hell, just forget it. Back in the day, maybe, but you're not the man you used to be. Never will be either, so do what Big Mack says. Shut the fuck up and get some sleep." Wilson was disgusted with himself. "Yeah, right. I've been in dreamland all day. How am I supposed to sleep through the night too?"

He couldn't come up with an answer but he pushed the steel slat back into place and lay down anyway, and tried a little soul-searching. Maybe if he thought long and hard enough, he might be able to come up with a reason why he was always such a fuckup. Half an hour later, he was still staring at the burned-out lightbulb on the ceiling, no closer to finding an answer.

"One thing's for sure. Big Mack was definitely right

about something. No matter what else happens, I really have to work on getting my act together. I can't keep screwing up like this."

A tear ran down his cheek as he lay in the dark trying to think about his wife and daughter. He loved them very much, but that wasn't his reason for crying. His tears were shed in disgust and loathing for himself. No matter how much he loved his family and tried to concentrate on them, the only thing he could think about was the bottle of vodka waiting for him on his kitchen table.

It was going to be a hell of a long night.

The Stranger pulled the pickup truck off the side of Route 62, slowing to a stop in the gravel shoulder. He was on the outskirts of the Billington town limits; so close in fact he could make out the welcome sign dead ahead. In the murky light cast by the red Ford's headlights, he could tell it was one of those monstrous billboard-type signs that marked the entrance to nearly every small town trying to look bigger and more important than they really were. He clicked on the truck's high beams to get a better look. In huge, freshly repainted foot-high golden letters, the sign said:

WELCOME TO BILLINGTON PENNSYLVANIA
We're glad you've come and hope you enjoy your stay.
Population: 21,000

It had taken the Stranger less than two hours of actual driving time to get here. If he had wanted to, he could have arrived here before noon, but he'd always been a night person and old habits died hard. He'd been anxious to get to Billington, but he'd shown caution, instinctively feeling better about entering his enemy's territory under the cover of darkness. He was a friend of the night and knew its dark cloak would shield him from anyone lying in wait, not that it was likely, since no one knew he was coming. Still, it didn't hurt to be careful.

Earlier today, after driving away from Duke's farm, he'd driven until he crossed over the Pennsylvania state line, then found a quiet side road where he could lay low. He'd slept most of the day, dreaming about revenge and gathering his strength for the battle ahead. The antique trunk had whispered to him, awakening him when it was time to go.

Now he sat, looking out all four windows of the truck, checking again to see if anyone lay in hiding along the sides of the road. No guards or sentries stood watch outside the town; no lookouts to warn Kemp. The town of Billington sat unprotected and at his mercy.

A vision began to form in his mind, surely a message from the trunk of secrets, because when he closed his eyes to concentrate there was blood everywhere. He saw himself walking through streets stained red with the life juices of his enemy, rivers of gore running in the gutters, and dead bodies of innocent people piled on the sides of the road like sacks of foul-smelling trash on garbage day. In his hands, he carried the severed head of Wilson Kemp, his ultimate prize in the coming fight. It was a wonderful revelation, a harbinger of things to come, and it pleased the Stranger immensely.

"Man, I can't wait. This is gonna be *so* much fun."

He put the Ford in gear and quietly rolled across the town line. Wilson Kemp and the Stranger were now in the same small community for the first time in years and there was no way in hell the tall dark man was going to let his enemy slip away from him.

Unknown to the 21,000 sleeping residents, death had just entered their peaceful little town, and Billington, Pennsylvania, had just been declared a war zone.

SATURDAY, SEPTEMBER 19

THE CALM BEFORE THE STORM

CHAPTER FIVE

HARDLY A LAUGHING MATTER

Although he'd thought it nearly impossible the night before, Wilson somehow managed to get a fairly decent sleep. The holding cell could never be described as anything close to comfortable: The Ritz-Carlton it certainly was not, but the small bed had been soft, the thick wool cover warm, and he'd had a dry roof overhead. All in all, not too bad a place for him to sober up. In the past, on some of his really bad drinking binges, Wilson had slept in a hell of a lot worse.

Early morning sunlight streamed in the cell window, bathing him in magnificent golden rays. He sat up on the edge of the bed, shocked to discover he felt almost human. Most mornings, his pounding head threatened to explode off his shoulders and his weary body felt as if it had been trampled by a herd of buffalo. Today, he could even open his eyes in the bright sunlight, something that ordinarily would have been agonizing. His craving for vodka had somewhat lessened overnight as well, not completely, of course, but enough that it wasn't an all-consuming passion like most mornings.

"My God," he whispered while staring down at his hands, amazed to find them barely shaking. "If I feel this good after only a day away from the bottle, what would it be like to be completely stone sober again?"

Feeling bolder than usual, he stood and walked over to the small mirror bolted by the sink on the far wall. It wasn't an actual mirror like the usual silver-backed glass; the cops weren't that stupid. They didn't want anyone breaking it and using the glass as a weapon on anyone, including themselves.

This mirror was made from a thin piece of metal, highly polished to reflect a clear, though somewhat distorted image of the unfortunates who had to use it.

Wilson gazed at his visage and was immediately disappointed. It was true he felt a whole lot better than usual, but to be honest, he sure didn't look it. His face, still smudged in streaky white and red paint, along with his greasy dark hair plastered to his sweaty head, combined to make him look positively frightful. The Joker after going ten rounds with Batman. He bent at the sink, immersing himself in a cloud of rising steam and furiously scrubbed his entire head, neck, and armpits with the soap and washcloth left at his disposal. After toweling off, he was relieved to see he looked much more presentable. Except for the scrapes on his cheek and a darkly bruised eye from yesterday afternoon's confrontation, Wilson thought he looked better now than he had in ages. The ever-present bags under his eyes seemed to be less pronounced today. The worry lines that normally cut into his forehead seemed faded and scarcely visible. It was amazing what a good night's rest could do for a person.

He should probably try it more often.

Wilson was forty-seven years old, but depending on his sobriety, he could range in appearance from a man in his midthirties all the way up to a decrepit older man in his sixties. Today, he thought he might squeak by for a man in his late thirties, which brought an approving nod and a faint, forced smile as he pondered his reflection, which soon vanished in the swirling mist engulfing the makeshift mirror. He had always thought of himself as a handsome man. Fairly handsome, anyway. With his large sparkling eyes, strong chin, and chiseled facial features, he used to think he resembled the late actor Christopher Reeve, of Superman fame, but lately, his short-cropped receding hairline had shattered that image. Maybe Kevin Costner was a closer match.

"Yeah right," Wilson chuckled to himself, thinking about the full clown suit he was still wearing. "Kevin Costner in his greatest role ever . . . starring as Bozo the drunken magic clown. That movie would really pack in the crowds."

The smile disappeared off his face as he realized the pathetic movie he'd been fantasizing about was, in reality, his own pitiful life story. Instead of sinking into a depression, Wilson forced himself to think that this time things were going to get progressively better. He'd blown his first magic clown job but there would be more. In his heart he knew he was a great magician. If he could just find the strength to stay out of the bottle for a while, who knows what good things might start happening for him?

Before anything could start happening though, he had to get his butt out of this holding cell and take care of the mess he'd made yesterday. If he apologized to the Morris family, maybe he could talk Reggie into dropping the charges against him.

A few minutes later, just as Wilson was preparing to

play the old rattle-the-drinking-cup-off-the-cell-bars game again, a policeman walked into the back room to deliver his breakfast. It was Officer Jackson, who unknown to Wilson and his alcohol-induced memory loss, was the same cop who'd picked him up yesterday from the birthday party fiasco. He was carrying a green plastic tray on which sat a big blueberry muffin and a large takeout cup of Dunkin' Donuts coffee.

"You're in luck, Wilson," the smiling officer said. "Our little fridge out front seems to have decided to stop working. I opened the door this morning to get you some of our usual chow, but the smell inside nearly floored me. We had to throw it all out, so this morning your breakfast comes catered."

Wilson walked over to the cell door and, after it was unlocked, held it open for the policeman until he'd stepped inside. The glorious aroma rising from the warm muffin and the fresh strong coffee wafted around his nostrils and activated his hunger pangs, curbing his desire to leave his overnight accommodation. A few extra minutes wouldn't hurt. Besides, he'd always been told breakfast was the most important meal of the day. This was especially true when you hadn't eaten anything the day before.

"Thanks, Jake," Wilson beamed, gratefully accepting the breakfast tray. "I'm practically starving. Wow, even fresh coffee. What's the occasion? Don't tell me your old coffeepot is broken down too?"

"Nah, it's okay. I just figured since I was already at the coffee shop to get your muffin, I may as well save you the stomachache of trying to drink our sludge. Our coffee here can sometimes be pretty nasty."

"*Sometimes?*" Wilson joked. "If you took a cup of that

black goo to a laboratory, it'd probably come back with a hazardous-waste warning label on it."

"Hah, hah, very funny. You put a clown suit on somebody and they think they're a comedian."

Jake took a seat beside Wilson and chatted with him as he ate breakfast. When he had finished, Officer Jackson accepted the tray and rose to leave.

"Say, how long do I have to wait to get out of here? They're not really going to make me stay till Monday, are they?" Wilson asked, hopeful, wiping the residue of muffin crumbs that clung to the corners of his mouth.

"Relax. When I came in this morning I talked to Big Mack. He said he tried to call your wife last night but she wasn't around. I called Susan this morning just before I brought your breakfast." He paused to pull his shirtsleeve back off his wrist so he could look at his watch. "She told me she'd already talked to the chief and she'd be here as quick as she could. Should be somewhere around ten o'clock, so you may as well sit down and take it easy. I'll be back to get you in half an hour."

It ended up being closer to an hour before Officer Jackson returned to unlock the cell door. Susan must have been delayed somewhere. Usually she was very punctual. Either that or she had just wanted him to squirm and ponder things a little longer.

"Let's move, clown-man. It's time to go," Jake said.

"Is Susan here?"

"No, Wilson, it's the bloody cavalry. Of course it's Susan. Who else would come save your raggedy ass?"

Wilson hurried to gather his things and followed Jake. They emerged into a bigger room that served as the front office and reception desk. It looked the same as any small-town police station, complete with scuffed-up tables and chairs, several desks overcrowded with stacks of loose papers, and a few telephones ringing off the hook. There were even a few tired-looking officers, lazing around with their feet up, waiting for someone other than themselves to answer the annoying phones.

Looking beyond these familiar sights, Wilson noticed his wife standing over beside the front entrance. She was reading a small, colorful poster thumbtacked to a felt bulletin board. The contents of the poster must have been very interesting because she was concentrating so hard she failed to notice his approach. Either that or she was purposely ignoring him. Not a good sign.

She looked simply magnificent; in Wilson's eyes anyway, standing with her hands on her hips, decked out in a stunning yet conservative pale blue dress. She wore low-heeled white shoes accessorized with matching white earrings, purse, and wide hair ribbon that shaped her long, curly brown hair. Her face was pretty but in a plain sort of way. She was certainly no fashion model or cover girl, but her jade-colored eyes shone brighter than the sun itself. Her body might not be shapely enough to turn the head of a Hollywood producer but she was petite and exuded a quiet confidence, moving with an athletic grace much sexier than all those busty Victoria's Secret bimbos.

As far as Wilson was concerned, there may have been more beautiful women in the world on the outside, but none could ever match the inner beauty his wife possessed in such selfless abundance. Susan was everything he'd ever wanted in a woman, and still was. His perfect ten. Even after three years of living apart he still loved her as much, if not more, than on the day he'd married her.

She'd been much younger than he was, of course. When they'd met nearly eleven years ago, Susan had just turned twenty-five. Wilson had been thirty-six. Right from the start they'd shared a special kind of love so few ever find, so age had never been a stumbling block for either of them. Within six months, Wilson had known he didn't want to live another day without her but they'd waited two full years before getting married, just to please her family. The following year their daughter, Amanda, had arrived, three weeks premature, but healthy and beautiful. With his beloved family now complete, Wilson had thought maybe he could finally put the horrors of his past behind him. He'd obviously been wrong.

When Susan finally noticed he'd walked into the room, she forgot about the poster and turned to meet him. Their eyes met and locked for a few precious seconds before she glanced away, but the eye contact had been more than enough for Wilson to see she was still in love with him. She was more than a little pissed off. That was also evident. Still, he was buoyant with the realization that after all those years, she still cared. He hated himself for the way he continually let her down. Yet, through thick and thin, she had always loved him. When others had tried to convince her he was too old for her, she had smiled and ignored them. When they said he was a loser and drank too much, she had stuck by him and tried to understand. Even when things had become intolerable, and his drinking had taken control, she was the one who'd cried for forgiveness when she threw him out. She actually believed in some way that she might have been the one who'd done something to trigger his demise.

It was simply incredulous she might harbor such a thought, but he loved her for it. He couldn't fathom why she still cared, but he thanked God she did. He just wished he could somehow find the strength to stop hurting her. He would have walked barefoot over white-hot coals rather than make this wonderful woman cry. Since the day they'd separated, he'd wanted to put things right between them but the more he tried, the more he screwed up and the more hurt he inflicted. Yesterday's stupidity was another fine example and did little to promote his cause.

"Thanks for coming, Susan," was all he could think to say as Officer Jackson returned his wallet and keys and signed his release.

"No problem," she whispered, her face cupped in her ever-so-delicate hands.

Wilson felt truly awful, thinking she was about to break into tears. He was somewhat confused when muffled laughter escaped from her concealed mouth. She tried to stop herself, but the cork was out of the bottle. She dropped her small, dainty hands and pointed her finger, trying to say something in between her uncontrolled guffaws. Finally, she turned and ran out of the open door, but not before attracting much unwanted attention around the normally quiet precinct.

Wilson couldn't help but notice the pitying glances of those nearby, as he grabbed up his belongings and dashed out in hot pursuit. What did she find so funny? Was she laughing at him? Had he read the look in her eyes wrong, and maybe she'd finally realized what a fool he really was? Had she come down here just to humiliate him in front of everyone? He couldn't blame her if she had; he certainly deserved it. Deserved or not though, it just didn't seem like something Susan would do. Wasn't her style at all.

He followed her outside and approached with his head hung low, feeling a bit hurt and disappointed. She made it all the way across the parking lot before he was able to confront her. She was leaning on the silver Honda Civic's front fender, still trying to stifle her laughter.

"Listen, Susan," Wilson pleaded. "I know what a screwup I am, and how I keep hurting you, but please don't humiliate me. I don't care if others laugh behind my back but I just can't take it when it comes from you. Besides, this is hardly a laughing matter. I've been charged this time. I could end up in jail."

Susan stood up, her jovial mood gone. An understanding smile spread across her thin face as she took a couple of steps closer until they were only a few feet apart.

"Oh Wilson," she sighed, wiping a solitary tear from the corner of her eye. "I wasn't laughing at you . . . honest. You know me better than that. I don't understand why you sometimes act the way you do, but believe me I'd never make fun of you."

Susan moved even closer, tenderly stroking his scratched cheek before pulling away. It had been like this since the breakup. She wanted to hold him, to comfort him, but she couldn't succumb to her feelings. Not yet, anyway. He had to help himself before she could allow herself to give in to her lonely, aching heart. No one ever said loving an alcoholic was easy.

Right from day one, people had been trying to tell her Wilson was no good, or that she could do much better. This was even before he'd lost his job and the drinking had gotten way out of hand. Her own mother had practically begged her to reconsider and marry some local boy—any local boy probably—one with a big reputable family who lived nearby. A big happy family was everything to Doris Summers, and the fact that Wilson had no relatives nearby and they'd seen neither hide nor hair of the family he claimed lived in rural Ohio made him a bad egg in her books. She didn't trust Wilson and probably never would. Susan didn't think like her mother though, and it never bothered her what anyone said about her man.

They hadn't been there with them on their first date, the day Wilson had taken her to Villa Roma, the fanciest and most expensive restaurant in Billington. He'd been so nervous all night, bless him, and when he'd finally worked up the nerve to reach over the table to hold her hand, he'd accidentally spilled her water glass onto the tablecloth and all over the front of her black dress. Nine times out of ten, maybe even ninety-nine times out of a hundred, something like that would have spelled disaster and ruined any chance a guy would have of continuing their relationship, but something in the pleading, honest way Wilson looked at her that night had made Susan just freeze. Instead of getting angry or storming out of the room, she just sat still for a moment, looking into Wilson's tender eyes and waited to see what would happen next. Without a word Wilson reached out, grabbed his own full water glass, and dumped it right in his own lap. Susan had burst into laughter and soon they were both smiling and killing themselves laughing as the waiter scurried around their table trying to wipe them both dry.

Probably not a textbook first date and definitely not a storybook romance, but that was just the way it was with Wilson. He was clumsy, he was a bit strange, and he was chaos on two legs, but beneath it all he was a kind, caring, wonderful man. In her heart, Susan knew he deeply loved her and even with all his faults—and he certainly had many—she would love Wilson until the day she died. Overly romantic? Perhaps. Stupid? Maybe, but that was just the way it was. She was in this for the long haul.

"Don't worry about the charges," she said. "That was why I was late. I stopped over at the Morris house and managed to smooth things out. He's going to drop the charges on Monday. The chief said he's going to let this go too, so you're off the hook."

His wife was an absolute saint. Wilson couldn't begin to tell her how grateful he was for all she'd done. She saw it in his tear-filled eyes, however, and simply returned a sympathetic nod.

"What were you laughing at, then?" he asked, breaking the silence. "What was so funny?"

"Nothing really, I just wasn't prepared to see you dressed up in your baggy clown suit, that's all. When I turned and looked at you, I sort of lost it. I'm sorry, I couldn't help myself."

Wilson could acknowledge the humor of seeing a clown being let out of the drunk tank, and smiled agreeably. "Oh, so you *were* laughing at me, huh? I suppose I did look a bit silly."

Looking serious for a moment, he looked her straight in the eye and said, "I really was trying this time. I didn't mean for things to turn out the way they did."

"I know you didn't," she replied sympathetically, although she'd heard the same line many times in the past. "And you're going to keep on trying, right?"

"Right," he answered, incredibly thankful he'd been wrong about her. It was comforting to know she hadn't given up on him. "Where were you last night, anyway?"

"Amanda and I drove up to Rochester and spent the night with my mother. She can't stand living there, but she's adamant it's her who's gonna look after Granny. We didn't get back until this morning. Why? I'm allowed to have a life of my own, aren't I? I mean, you can't expect me to sit around day after day, year after year, waiting by the phone to rescue you every time you get in trouble."

Wilson could tell she immediately regretted her harsh words but he flinched anyway, as if struck. He let the comment go. They rode in an uncomfortable silence for a few blocks, wondering what it would take to bring them together again. Neither seemed to know what to say, so they just stared straight ahead and continued on in silence.

"So how's Amanda doing?" he finally asked, unable to take the tension-filled quiet any longer.

"She's really good, but she's missed you quite a bit lately. You haven't been coming around much."

"I know. I've been pretty busy practicing my magic act. I was kind of hoping you'd bring her with you."

"Come on, Wilson . . . get real," Susan said with a touch of sarcasm. "She worships the ground you walk on. Do you really think it would be good for her to see you getting out of jail?"

"It's not jail . . . it's just . . . oh hell. No, I suppose not.

You're right, I guess I just miss her an awful lot and was hoping to see her."

"Then let's get you home. I took Amanda over to Mrs. Henderson's. She's her new babysitter. We'll get you out of that silly clown suit, and we'll go pick her up. I think Amanda will like that."

"I think I'd like that too." Wilson smiled tenderly, touching Susan's hand. This time she didn't pull away.

CHAPTER SIX

PICK A CARD ... ANY OLD CARD

"Where the hell is he?" the Stranger asked, his rough voice seething with anger, as he violently pounded the steering wheel until his hands hurt.

Most of the morning was gone, it was quarter to eleven, and he'd been looking for Kemp throughout the night. On his arrival the night before, he'd stopped at a public telephone booth on the corner of Main and Berkely. The directory listed two Kemps, one with the initial S and the other a W. The latter seemed the obvious choice, but just to be safe, he jotted both addresses and phone numbers into a small notebook he carried in one of the many pockets of his long overcoat.

His next stop had been to fill up at the twenty-four-hour Noco gas station and purchase a cheap local street map on display beside the cash register. After a quick peep at the map, he was on his way to Morgan Avenue, his adrenaline racing at the prospect of confronting the elusive Kemp. A few minutes after one o'clock, he turned onto Morgan and stopped the vehicle within sight of 256, the address listed for W. Kemp.

The house was relatively small, a one-level wooden bungalow, badly run-down and requiring extensive renovation. The house was beige with the dirt-stained windows edged with dark brown shutters. The roof was in a sad state of disrepair, its faded brown shingles buckled and worn, and the rusted rain gutters were hanging precariously, ready to fall at any moment. In short, the house looked exactly like the seedy place the Stranger had imagined Kemp would be hiding in.

Piece of shit for a piece of shit . . .

The excitement of being this close to his prey was overwhelming and almost caused the Stranger to act rashly. Thankfully, the antique trunk had spoken to him and soothed his raging desire. He'd wanted to rush into the house and slaughter Kemp without delay, but the calming voice in his head had convinced him it was wise to proceed with caution. What if he didn't have the right house? The last thing he wanted to do was to create havoc in the wrong place and perhaps alert Kemp he was here.

He'd watched the dilapidated house for well over two hours, trying unsuccessfully to detect any signs of life within. By 3:30 A.M. the street was void of movement and all the houses in this quiet neighborhood were cloaked in darkness. His frustration had grown exponentially with each passing minute until finally he couldn't contain himself. Silently, he slid out of the truck and stealthily headed for the front door. He had a gut feeling no one was home but he had no intention of waiting till daylight to find out. Ringing the doorbell was a risk, but only a small one. If Kemp answered the door—fine, he would kill him. If someone else answered, he would simply walk away, leaving them confused and probably pissed off at being woken up, but none the wiser.

As it turned out, no one answered his repeated ringing of the doorbell. Furious, the tall, dark Stranger returned to his truck to ponder his next move. Eventually, he decided to drive over and check out the second listing. It only seemed to take a few minutes as he quietly nosed the truck onto Derby Hill Road and stopped near to a one-and-a-half-story Cape Cod–style dwelling. It was white, with a predominately large sloping green roof and matching shutters that neatly ordained the windows. A small, detached single-car garage sat off to the left at the end of a recently laid blacktopped driveway. It was a far nicer home in a much nicer neighborhood, but like the first, it too was deserted.

For the remainder of the night, his frustration and anger continued to mount. He had set up a stakeout of sorts, driving back and forth between the two Kemp residences until daylight. To his dismay, no one returned to either house.

By eight o'clock, too many people were walking and driving by for the Stranger to feel comfortable; sitting parked in the open might attract unwanted attention. He decided it would be best to stay on the move, occasionally driving by each house. It was now 10:46, and he was parked inconspicuously at a nearby convenience store, incensed at not being able to find his adversary.

"Where the hell is he?" He struck the steering wheel in frustration again. "He couldn't have vanished into thin air . . . or could he?"

He stopped beating on the steering wheel long enough to ponder his dilemma. Was it possible Kemp had somehow found out he'd tracked him down and quietly left town? Had he really come this close, only to have the son of a bitch elude him once more?

A dark cloud of rage and unbearable despair filtered through his warped, demented mind. If Kemp had really left town, he might not be able to locate him again. It had taken more than a year to get this close.

Again the magic trunk soothed his feverish mind. It was telling him Kemp was still in town and unaware of his impending doom. How stupid he had been. If Kemp had left town, the antique trunk would have sensed it. Having received the good news, he felt a great sense of relief. Closing his eyes, he took a deep breath and concentrated on nothing except the smooth voice of reason now permeating his agitated mind.

The trunk of secrets explained how he was going about things the wrong way. Killing Kemp quickly would be a big mistake. Too fast and easy. The cowardly bastard deserved a hell of a lot worse fate than a quick demise. He needed to be tortured, mentally and physically, forced to learn the meaning of true fear. He shouldn't get off easy; he had earned the right to suffer.

Fortunately, the magic trunk had many suggestions as to how he could fulfill his plan of revenge, but in the meantime, driving around in a stolen pickup wasn't such a great idea. He had to find somewhere to lay low for a while, a quiet place where he could rest and plan.

"Rest and plan," the Stranger dreamily whispered as he climbed out from behind the wheel and entered the convenience store. Inside, he purchased a few bags of supplies and a newspaper in which he hoped to find the perfect hideaway.

The weekly paper, a shaggy-looking rag known as the *Billington Sentinel*, was a twenty-page hodgepodge of local news, sports, weather, and community events. On page sixteen, right beside the help-wanted ads, was a list of apartments for rent; four of those were listed as immediately available. Smiling again, the Stranger brought the old truck to life and pulled out of the parking lot, a quiet apartment now his first priority.

The first place he checked he discounted immediately without taking the time to stop. It was a basement apartment, which was fine, but the apartment upstairs looked like some type of day care center, with dozens of screaming kids continually running in and out.

The second apartment was better. It lay on a quieter street with no apparent kids around, but he decided to pass on this one too. It was one of those large three-story complexes, and kids or not, there were too many neighbors for his liking.

The dark man was once again feeling stressed out and frustrated, when driving east on Leamon Avenue he pulled to a stop in front of the third address. He instantly had a good feeling about it.

Now this place has potential.

The two-story house with an attached two-car garage was set back quite a bit from the road on a large lot filled with huge oak trees. It was an older home, spruced up with gray aluminum siding and a recently shingled roof.

The ad in the paper indicated the owner preferred a room-and-board type of arrangement, and anyone interested would have to be willing to take care of the heavy yard work as part of the deal. Probably a good indicator the owner was an older person who needed help.

Interesting.

In the ten or fifteen minutes the Stranger sat considering whether this was the right place for him, not one car passed along this unusually quiet street. Inside his mind, the magic trunk nudged him into action. It said no words but sent him a visual picture of a monstrous entity slowly nodding its deformed head, obviously well pleased. The Stranger had seen all he needed to.

"This place is perfect," he decided, getting out of the truck and heading for the front door.

He had to knock a number of times on the heavy mahogany door, each rap resounding louder than the previous before the door slowly creaked open. By then, his patience had been sorely tested, but he managed to subdue his angry scowl, promptly replacing it with another of his practiced fake smiles. The old lady stood inside the door, graciously reciprocating his smile.

"Can I help you?" she asked.

She was rather short, slightly overweight, and her badly wrinkled skin gave weight to her obvious advanced years. The Stranger guessed her age at eighty, if not older. She was wearing a full-length floral-patterned dress and white slippers. He couldn't help noticing her beautiful silver-tinted hair was pulled cruelly back in a tight bun.

The Stranger stepped closer, quite pleased. "Hello there," he purred. "I'm here to see about the room for rent. I read about it in this morning's paper." He held up the newspaper and pointed to the small ad. "I was wondering if it's still available? Hope so."

"Sure is. Come on in and I'll show you around."

The dark Stranger thanked her and pretended to listen as she led him through the house, gabbing on and on about things that didn't concern him. The only thing he cared about was the solitude and quietness her house offered. Here he could find peace and safety until he figured out how he would bring his vengeful plan to fruition.

Midway through the tour, she introduced herself as

Kathleen Pruit and said she'd been a widow for almost eight years now. The Stranger cringed briefly, expecting she'd want him to introduce himself, but she simply turned away and continued with the tour. She was boring him terribly, but through it all he feigned interest and never dropped his hollow smile.

"I'll take it," he said as they returned to the front entrance. "It's just what I'm looking for."

"Oh, that's wonderful," Kathleen said, sighing with obvious relief. "I was hoping I could get the room rented quickly. I really need the money. You do know you'll have to look after the yard work, right? You're older than I had hoped. Think you can handle it?"

"No problem there. I'm young at heart, ma'am, and I enjoy dabbling in horticulture. I'll have the yard looking like something straight out of *Better Homes and Gardens*." Always a great kidder, he reinforced his promise with a smile and a wink.

"Excellent. And the money? I'll have to ask for the first and last up front, I'm afraid."

"Got no problem with that either. Here, let me get my wallet out."

The Stranger made a show of patting his coat pockets and when he felt the moment was right, he finally exclaimed, "A-ha, found it." From an inside pocket, he withdrew an oversize deck of playing cards. He pretended to be embarrassed to see himself holding the cards instead of his wallet, and apologized immediately.

"What are those?" Kathleen asked.

"These old things? They're just a big deck of cards I sometimes use. I never told you I'm a magician, did I?"

"A magician?"

"Yeah, and a pretty good one too, if you don't mind

me saying so. Hey, seeing the cards are already out, how would you like to see a great card trick?"

The look on Kathleen Pruit's wrinkled face said she would rather see the rent money, but she went along nevertheless, not wanting to appear rude.

"Well . . . okay. If it's as good as you say."

"Sure is. One of the best." The Stranger moved closer, fanning the oversize deck in front of her face with a practiced flair.

"Let's give it a try, shall we? Go ahead and pick a card . . . any old card."

Kathleen took a moment to decide. Laughing nervously, she selected a card from the left end of the deck and held it quickly to her chest.

"Can I look at it?" she asked.

"Why, of course, but be careful not to let me see it. That would spoil all the fun."

She was smiling happily, really getting into it, but her smile froze when she looked at her card. In a quiet, surprised voice, she said, "I . . . don't understand?"

"Oh, I'm sorry," the Stranger answered. "Silly me. I forgot to tell you this isn't an ordinary set of cards. You probably were expecting to see an ace of hearts, or a seven of clubs, right?"

"Yes," she said, nodding her head in confusion. "What kind of deck is this?"

"This is a very special deck. Instead of the usual suits, this deck has pictures of objects. With these objects, not only can I guess the correct card, I can also tell you your fortune."

His explanation worked like a charm. The old woman's face lit up with a big grin. She nodded understandingly and urged him to go on.

"Let's see then." He pretended to concentrate. "The card you have chosen is . . . the dagger."

The old widow squealed in astonishment. "Why that's amazing, exactly right. Look, it's a dagger card!"

The card showed a picture of an elaborate jewel-encrusted blade sitting in the plush folds of a purple silk pillow. The background was a kaleidoscope of various shades of red.

"Thank you, thank you, thank you . . ." the tall magician said, bowing as if in front of an audience.

"What about my fortune?" she asked. "Is picking the dagger lucky?"

"Drawing that card is always considered lucky," beamed the magician. Bowing once more, he deftly withdrew a dagger with a twelve-inch blade from his right boot. "Alas, more so for me than for you I'm afraid."

He sprang out of his bow, lightning-quick. In one fluid motion he lashed out at the old woman, a deep red smile appearing across her aged neck, immediately producing two spouting geysers of thick, warm blood. With one savage stroke he'd severed her jugular vein and carotid artery. A sea of sticky redness gushed out, spraying the nearby ceiling and walls.

Kathleen tried to speak, a look of shock and confusion reflected in her frightened eyes, but no words were heard. She reached up with both hands in a vain attempt to stop the bleeding. Undaunted, the crimson fluid bubbled through the gaps in her fingers, pouring down her chest to puddle at her feet.

Grinning wickedly, the Stranger turned over the remainder of the cards, revealing the secret of his trick. Every single card in the deck had a picture of the jewel-encrusted dagger. Tossing them aside for the moment, the dark-clothed maniac moved in closer to his scarlet-soaked victim. Heedless of the sloppy gore, he shoved her hard, violently slamming her against the front door.

Reversing his grip on the blade, he viciously drove the razor-sharp dagger into the area between her eyes. The long blade sank to the hilt, piercing her brain and exiting out the back of her skull to embed itself in the thick wooden door. When the Stranger released his grip, her body remained in a standing position, firmly nailed in place. Her feet, now clear of the red-stained carpet by an inch, continued to spasm uncontrollably.

Always an affectionate man, he kissed Widow Pruit tenderly on the lips before turning away, leaving her suspended body to twitch and die on her own. He stooped down and retrieved the scattered cards, returning them to his slightly bloodied overcoat.

After exiting the house by the side-door kitchen entrance, he drove his recently acquired pickup off the street and into his new garage.

"Home sweet home," he whispered to the antique trunk as he unloaded it off the truck bed and dragged it into the coppery-tainted smell of the blood-splattered hallway.

Safely inside, he unbuckled the trunk's thick leather straps and opened the lid. He wanted to make sure the journey to Billington hadn't damaged anything. Inside, the magic trunk was empty, save for a single thin sheet of white paper. It turned out to be a note telling other prospective renters who might come calling that the vacancy had been filled and the apartment was no longer available. It was signed: Kathleen Pruit.

"Oh yeah, I'd forgotten about other renters. I'd better go hang this where it'll be seen. I'll put it on the front door; the last thing I need is a parade of nosy apartment seekers. Screw that."

In the front hall, the old woman's corpse was still fastened to the door. Her lower extremities had finally stopped their dance. The dark man couldn't fully swing open the door because her body brushed the near wall, getting in the way. Fortunately, it swung open enough that it wouldn't cause a problem. He thought he'd have to search around for a hammer and nail, but was pleased to see tools would be unnecessary. The long dagger pinning the old woman had exited out the other side of the door. The Stranger simply stuck the piece of paper onto the tip of the knife, then smiled at his handiwork for a moment before closing the front door.

Silently, he wondered if apartment hunting was always this much fun.

CHAPTER SEVEN

LOVE CAN OVERCOME ANYTHING

Susan eased the vehicle to a stop in the narrow paved driveway near the crest of Derby Hill, at about the same time the Stranger was showing old Mrs. Pruit his version of a good card trick.

Like a flash, Kemp was out of the car, unlocking the front door, and dashing upstairs for a quick shower. After a long night in the holding cell, the hot, steamy water did wonders for his aching, tired body. On another day, he might have lingered in its warm, wet embrace, but not today. Today he couldn't afford such luxury; he was in too much of a hurry. His excitement swelled at the thought of spending some much needed quality time with his daughter. He had scrubbed clean, toweled off, shaved, changed clothes (he still had a closetful here), and was ready to go by eleven fifteen.

"I'm all set, Susan," he yelled excitedly. "Let's go pick up our little pride and joy."

Susan poked her head out of the kitchen doorway and made a time-out signal with her hands. "Easy, big guy, slow down. You've been running around like someone set your feet on fire. Come have some lunch."

"Lunch? Couldn't we go pick up Amanda first, then eat something together?"

"No we can't. I called over to Mrs. Henderson's while you were in the shower. Amanda's not there right now. Edith had some housework to get finished and her husband, Earl, volunteered to take Amanda off her hands for a while. They went uptown to Harvey's for lunch and won't be back for about an hour."

"We could still have lunch together," Wilson reasoned. "I like Harvey's too. We could go uptown and meet them over there."

"No way. The Hendersons just started babysitting Amanda. No way we're gonna barge into that restaurant. Earl's trying to do something really nice and if we go charging in there, he'll think we don't trust them. Good sitters are hard to find, Wilson, so just forget it. I told Edith we'd be round at twelve thirty and not a minute sooner. Understand? You'll just have to endure the next hour with little old me. Who knows, you might even enjoy it."

And Kemp did enjoy it, every minute. It was comforting to see how easily they could fall back into familiar routines. He had helped out in the kitchen, whipping up a simple lunch of vegetable soup and ham sandwiches and big frosty mugs of ice-cold milk.

They'd laughed and giggled throughout the entire meal, each recalling happy memories of better times they'd once shared. Time passed quickly, almost too quickly, and soon it was time to go pick up their daughter. Together, they cleaned up the dishes and were on their way.

Edith and Earl Henderson lived nearby in a modest but immaculately well-kept stucco house on Milberry Lane. It took only minutes to make the short trip. Earl and Amanda must have just arrived themselves and were walking up the front steps when Susan pulled the silver Honda into the gravel driveway.

Wilson happily watched his seven-year-old daughter turn and throw her arms in the air when she recognized the car, squealing with delight as she raced across the grass to greet them.

She was a small child for her age. In almost every way she was the miniature image of her mother. Her brown hair was long and curly, stylishly pulled back with two pink butterfly berets that perfectly matched her frilly dress. Her eyes, even more striking than her mother's, were like twin electromagnets, drawing attention wherever she went. She was quite literally perfect, so beautiful he sometimes had a hard time believing she was related, much less his own flesh-and-blood daughter. She was the kind of girl destined to break many a young man's heart, and already capable of breaking his each and every time Wilson was forced to say good-bye.

"Daddy!" she shouted, leaping into his arms.

They laughed and hugged and smothered each other with kisses, neither feeling the need to say anything. For now, it was enough to hold each other close and enjoy the moment. Wilson was so happy. Tears of joy trickled down his scratched cheeks. The world was a far better place for him when his daughter was safely in his arms, as if she released him from his heavily burdened conscience. For the few brief moments they hugged, he was no longer a pathetic drunk, the laughingstock of the town, but simply her father, a man who in her big lovely eyes could do no wrong.

"I missed you, sweetie," he whispered in complete honesty, setting her gently back on the grass. "I've been pretty busy lately. Sorry I haven't been around."

"That's okay, Daddy. You're here now and you never have to go away again."

She reached up and grabbed hold of his hand as she spoke. Her tiny fingers gripped him firmly, as if hoping the force of her hold on him might somehow make her words come true. Wilson smiled, thinking how wonderful life would be if only things were that easy. Children have such a magical way of simplifying things. It's the grown-ups who screw up and complicate everything. Still, he would have given anything to make his little girl's wish come true.

"Well, I'm not sure about never having to go away, but I can promise you we're going to spend the whole day together. You, me, and Mommy. How does that sound?"

"Fantastic!" she squealed, finally releasing his hand to dash over and excitedly hug her mother.

Over Amanda's snuggling head, Susan lifted her eyes to meet Wilson's. The teary-eyed look she gave him said everything. Without a word being passed, they knew they had to keep trying to work out their problems, for their daughter's sake more than their own. Amanda was now the driving force; she was living proof their love was worth fighting for and saving. For her, they had to be willing to overcome all obstacles, to move heaven and earth if necessary.

Together, they said good-bye to the Hendersons before piling into the small Honda for the short drive home. For the remainder of the day they simply hung out around the house, relaxing, laughing, and goofing around. It was a priceless, unforgettable afternoon, just like they used to enjoy before he drank himself out the front door.

After a delicious supper of barbecued pork chops,

Wilson's favorite, the inevitable time of departure was at hand. When they'd first broken up, they'd made an agreement on visiting rights. He could stop over anytime he wanted, but it was an unwritten rule he leave no later than eight o'clock. He badly wanted to stay, but didn't bother to ask, hating it but knowing it wasn't an option. Remarkably, they accepted his leaving better than he did. The three of them, Amanda to a lesser degree, understood they'd made a few small steps in the right direction today and taking it slow was probably a good idea.

Susan drove him home, accompanied by Amanda, who hung over the front seat holding her father's hand. The dilapidated house he rented on Morgan Avenue always depressed him, but he put on a brave face as he kissed his wife and daughter good-bye. He was climbing out of the passenger side when Susan grabbed his arm and pulled him back inside the car.

"Would you maybe like to come to church tomorrow morning? Maybe Father Harris can help us build on today. What do you say?"

Wilson wasn't sure. He didn't mind going and it would certainly be great to spend more time with his family, but Father Harris worried him greatly. Patrick Harris took every opportunity to drill Kemp on the sins of alcohol. He meant well, of course, but it wasn't the kind of speech Wilson felt like listening to so early in the morning. He hesitated for a moment and thought about politely declining the offer until he noticed the hope dancing in their eyes.

"I'd love to," he replied. "What time?"

They agreed to meet on the front steps of St. Michael's at a quarter to ten the following morning. With that settled, he turned once more to leave. This time it was his daughter who caught his arm.

"Daddy?" she timidly asked. "I've been wanting to ask you something. It's been so long since you lived with us, are we ever going to be a real family again?"

Her candor temporarily stunned him. It was amazing how fast she was growing up. Instead of brushing her openness aside, he thought it over for a minute, giving it the serious consideration it deserved. Finally, he took hold of her little hand.

"Listen closely, sweetie. I know you don't quite understand the reasons why Mommy and Daddy aren't living together, but you have to realize . . . no matter what, we'll always be a real family. Nothing will *ever* change that. You and your mother will always be special to me. I'll never stop loving you. Never! Do you understand what I'm saying?"

"I think so. I love you too, Daddy."

"Why thank you. That's all I needed to hear. Although we still have some big hills to climb before we can be back together, as long as we keep loving each other, I just know we'll find a way to work things out."

"Do you really think so?" she asked, her innocent eyes widening with renewed hope.

"Why sure I do, and so should you. There's an old saying that no matter how large or overwhelming the obstacles are, never give up because love can overcome anything."

Maybe a bunch of crap and not the greatest words of wisdom ever passed along, but at least he'd tried to clear up his daughter's concern. Whether she understood or not, it seemed to please her. He kissed her again and stepped quickly from the car, not wanting Amanda to see the tears forming in his eyes. He wasn't convinced there would be a quick reconciliation and didn't want the child to see his reflection of uncertainty. Without looking back, he ran to the front door, hurriedly unlocked it, and slipped inside.

The familiar stench of alcohol immediately assaulted his nostrils as soon as he closed the door. It was barely detectable, probably most people wouldn't notice, but he did. To him, the carpets and walls smelled of vodka, as did the furniture and drapes. In fact, the odor seemed to drift toward him, almost stalking him within his own home. It was as if the entire house exuded vodka, sweating out of every tiny crack, like syrup running from a maple.

Welcome home, the ghosts of his past failures whispered. *We missed you . . .*

He ignored his conscience easily enough, but it was harder to disregard his nose. The sickly sweet odor repulsed him, causing his stomach to turn over, yet at the same time, exciting his thirsty taste buds and drawing beads of perspiration on his wrinkled brow. He followed his nose down the front hall to the cluttered kitchen, where the half-filled bottle patiently waited, still sitting on the counter where he'd left it yesterday morning.

Wilson vowed he would leave the familiar clear poison untouched, especially after the wonderful progress he and Susan had made, but once again he'd forgotten how powerful a disease alcoholism can be. Wilson soon found himself reaching for the bottle. As the liquid fire touched his eager lips, he was already loathing himself for being so weak, so stupid. Out of the corner of his eye, he noticed the front door swing open.

It was Susan.

"It's just me, Wilson. I was wondering if you needed me to iron your suit for church—"

She cut herself off midsentence, utterly shocked to see him with a bottle of booze. Her initial surprise quickly turned to anger. After all, he'd only been alone in the house for a few minutes. Didn't he have any control at all?

"Susan? What are you doing—?" Wilson started, childishly trying to hide the evidence behind his back.

"You bastard!" she cried. "Here I thought we were getting somewhere. Stupid me, I should have known better. All those sweet things you just said to Amanda about love and hope, were they *all* lies?"

"Of course not, Susan, please don't think that. Look! I'll pour it out . . . here, you can watch."

Wilson quickly moved to the sink and upended the bottle. Susan silently watched until the last drop disappeared down the drain. This small gesture was obviously hard for him to do, and it satisfied her to see it, but still, it fell short of calming her mounting rage. He'd reversed every gain they'd made, dragging them back down to where they always seemed to wallow. Before she could lose her temper, she turned and stalked to the door.

"If you know what's good for you, you'd better not show up drunk for church. And you can iron your own damn suit!" Fuming, she stormed out, slamming the door shut behind her.

Kemp walked to the kitchen window in time to see his wife back out the drive and slam the Honda into gear before speeding off. Amanda had spotted him from the front seat and managed a quick wave before they disappeared from view. In his loneliness, he found himself waving back to an empty road.

Without giving it much thought, he reached up and removed an unopened bottle from the cupboard. Unknown to his wife, every good drunk had a spare stashed in case of emergency.

Against his better judgment and obvious lack of willpower, his hands began unscrewing the cap. Why couldn't he stop? The first swallow assaulted his palate with a familiar flavor: the bitter taste of failure. He was not only failing himself, but more importantly his wife and daughter. He thought about all the things he had just said to Amanda, and how she'd looked up at him with such hope, trust, and love.

"Yeah. Love can overcome anything, sweetie . . . except for maybe your old man's stupidity."

CHAPTER EIGHT

THE DISAPPEARING MAN

He moved like a hungry black panther, silent, dangerous, and virtually invisible against the dark curtain of night. He was, as always, in total control. The night was his. He lived in a world devoid of fear, secure in the belief no one or anything could harm him. His catlike movements were lightning swift but never hurried, powerful yet lithe with elegant grace. He felt invincible, the supreme hunter, free to roam and explore at will. It was 10:35 P.M. and like the nocturnal predator he imagined, Peeping Tom was on the prowl.

The urges in his head didn't need to beat their drums too ferociously; Tom's other persona was weakening and had succumbed relatively quickly. Tom, dressed in his customary all-black apparel, had been on the prowl for thirty minutes, slinking under the blanket of night, enjoying the tremendous feeling of power and freedom that always swept over him whenever he dared venture out.

He enjoyed seeing how close he could get to his victims without being spotted. Sometimes they'd be sitting on a park bench or leaning against a tree or lamppost, and Tom would use all his considerable expertise to glide closer without ever making a sound or eye-catching movement. Usually, he could get close enough to touch, if he so chose, but rarely did he carry the game that far. Often they'd sense his presence and look round in panic. By then, he'd be gone. Slinking into the darkness to stalk his next victim.

Eventually, he found himself downtown, peeping into the main-floor bedroom of a redbrick house on Maple Drive. Inside the house, separated only by a thin pane of glass, an older woman was undressing. To Tom, she appeared to be about sixty-five but had managed to maintain her girlish figure on her aged frame. She was starting to get a little heavy, especially in the area of her hips and stomach, but when fully clothed, it probably wouldn't show too much. Her breasts, large and full, still held their shape, gamely defying gravity in a way she was obviously proud of. She stood admiring herself before a full-length mirror, teasing and stroking her erect nipples, turning this way and that, perhaps convincing herself she was still sexy, denying how much damage her increasing years had wrought.

Tom's penis began to thicken and harden inside the cramped confines of his tight black jeans. It wasn't the sight of a naked woman that excited him, she was much too old and worn out for his tastes, it was the act of watching her without her knowing it, stealing her most private moments when she thought she was alone. The intrusion into those personal minutes of unsuspecting people and watching their pathetic little lives unfold before his eyes gave him the most incredible feeling of power. Wave after wave of pure adrenaline would wash over him, caressing and tickling his nerves with mind-numbing intoxication. It delighted him, exhilarating him far more than anything he'd ever experienced from his other boring personality. This was center stage, the big thrill, a voyeur's equivalent to a junkie's heroine rush.

Once he'd been lucky enough to sneak up on Ed Bannerman, Billington's illustrious mayor, as he happily ran around his bedroom stark naked, slapping the shit out of his wife for some reason known only to the mayor himself. His blows were carefully placed so she could conceal the damage from the public's eye. Man, he gave her a real beating, but what had really interested Tom was the mayor had seemed like another person entirely while doing it. He'd changed from the businessman-of-the-year public persona he always wore, into a wild savage behind closed doors. He had been beating his chest and drooling like a madman the entire time he'd punished his wife. The session had ended with him masturbating above her trembling body, which was collapsed on the floor, then ejaculating a boatload onto her bruised and battered back. Ten seconds later, he'd returned to normal and was apologizing to his dazed wife as he helped her to her feet and into bed. The majority of this small town's population were under the impression the sun shone straight out of good old Ed's ass, that he was a God-fearing family man who had a terrific marriage. Obviously they were wrong. Only Tom and, of course, Ed's wife, knew differently.

The night after that incident, Tom had slipped an unsigned note under the mayor's door asking him if it would hurt his reelection chances if he were to expose him in the press as the cowardly, wife-beating, cock-pulling bastard he really was. He hadn't actually planned on telling anyone about the things he saw, but he greatly enjoyed watching Bannerman squirm. For a long time afterward, the mayor sported a guilty, worried appearance around town, and Tom suspected his sex life was a tad more on the tame side than it had been. To hell with him. The guy was a douche.

A flicker of movement startled Tom. The naked woman had whirled round, turning away from the dressing mirror to stare out the window. Behind the mask, Tom's lips curled into a tight grin. He was fairly sure the old lady couldn't see him, not with the bedroom lit up and the inky blackness outside. His dark clothing was also excellent camouflage.

She tried to peer out the window but could only see her own reflection. It was impossible to pierce the darkness beyond the glass with the light that shone from within. More than likely, her sudden movement had been another example of how one's sixth sense kicks in when they think they're being watched. Tom had seen examples of it time and time again. Whatever the reason, she began to edge toward the window for a closer look.

Tom's heart began to thump a little faster, his mouth went dry, and oodles of sweat began to saturate his body, dampening the inside of his tight leather gloves. His grip on the oversize flashlight tightened steadily until his knuckles turned white. It wasn't the fear of being caught; it was the excitement of the moment. Sneaking around and peeping gave him a rush, sure. It was never dull and always enjoyable, but what really got his juices flowing was the fear he instilled in his victims once they realized their homes weren't as safe as they once thought they were. Tom wanted them to see him, see him and *fear* him. The power created by that fear was what he so desperately craved, and also what the urges residing inside his head demanded. If his victims didn't eventually spot him, Tom would usually tap on the window or make some other revealing noise to get their attention.

This particular lady didn't need any encouragement on Tom's part. She had no idea what had caught her attention outside, but she seemed determined to find out. She dropped to a crouch, trying in vain to conceal her pendulous breasts with her pudgy hands. Slowly, she inched toward the window.

"Easy now, Tom . . ." he whispered, his breathing becoming rapid. "Control, Tom . . . don't blow it, hold your ground."

The naked woman dropped all show of modesty, cupping her hands around her eyes and pressing her forehead against the glass. She tried looking left and right but her eyes had not yet adjusted to the darkness.

"Control . . . control . . . control . . ." he hissed between tightly clenched teeth, his every muscle straining with delicious nervous tension. This was the moment he lived for, the moment when he felt most alive.

The woman's eyes finally began to adjust to the poor lighting condition. She looked left and right again, starting to make out images and shadows of nearby trees and bushes. She backed away for a moment as if to dismiss an uneasy feeling, but then pressed her face against the glass again and stared straight at him. Her heart was probably thumping as hard as Tom's was, pounding uncontrollably when she finally spotted him. A vague silhouette in black, a sinister shape hovering in the darkness, but certainly more than enough to convince her something was out there.

Tom waited, prolonging and relishing this sweet moment before clicking on the flashlight. Its powerful beam was aimed at his menacing black ski mask, reflecting a nightmarish appearance through the window to the woman standing so vulnerably close. Tom let the beam slide down from his face, illuminating his muscular chest and stomach, then halting at his groin. His penis was sticking out of his pants, exposed in the bright light, standing proud and hard as a fence post.

Tom waited until he saw the unmistakable look of raw fear in her widening eyes before he tucked his cock back in his pants and started running. A gut-wrenching scream cut through the still night air behind him, followed almost immediately by shouts and more lights. He didn't stick around to see if anyone was in pursuit. Most likely, they would check out the old lady before searching the area. By then it would be too late. They might call the cops but by the time they arrived and the shit hit the fan, he'd be long gone.

Since acquiring his hideout and after the murder of the previous owner, the Stranger had lain prostrate on the plastic-covered floral couch in what was now his living room. He had fallen into a deep dreamlike trance, oblivious to everything around him, except his precious antique trunk.

The magic trunk was talking to him again, soothing his feverish mind with vivid images and nasty details of Kemp's imminent slaughter. It had come up with a plan to ensure Kemp's pain and suffering would be a work of art. It lovingly stroked and caressed his psychopathic mind throughout the day until the time was right to release him from his stupor.

The magician bolted out of his semisleep, greatly surprised to realize it was dark out and he'd snoozed most of the day away. No matter, the daylight hours weren't important; he needed the rest for later. He was going on a little journey, a journey that would start phase one of the magic trunk's plan of revenge. Though he'd been dozing, he remembered every detail, especially the graphic images of Kemp's ravaged, tortured body. Gory pictures that brought a huge grin to his pallid face. He hurried into his long woolen overcoat and boots, eager to get things in motion. The sooner he implemented the plan, the sooner he would get his hands on Kemp, something he looked forward to immensely. Within minutes the Stranger was out the door, a dark farmer about to plant the first evil seeds of another man's nightmare.

It took a burst of hard running with a few evasive turns before Peeping Tom was sure he'd made a clean getaway. His erection had quickly wilted away, but the intoxicating feeling of power still coursed through his veins and would for quite some time. There was nothing quite like that king-of-the-world feeling. Nothing at all.

Tom relaxed, enjoying the moment, and leisurely turned in the general direction of home. Suddenly, the thunderous beat of the urges began to pound incessantly inside his head. For a moment, the drumming was mercilessly loud; he could only clasp his ears in a futile effort to muffle the clamor within. The pain was excruciating, actually bringing him to his knees.

"All right . . . *All right!*" he screamed. "Bloody hell, I hear you, damn it, now go away!"

But the urges didn't fade away, not until he found the strength to rise and start moving in the opposite direction, away from his house. Within a few steps, the drums ceased, allowing an inner peace that quickly soothed his frazzled nerves. He wasn't mad at the urges; after all, it had been his own fault. He shouldn't have tried going home so early. Very rarely were the urges sated after only one tiny escapade. Sometimes he would prowl for hours, hitting numerous unsuspecting victims before venturing home thoroughly exhausted but satisfied. Tonight would probably be one of those nights.

Immediately, an image of Jackie Sullivan rose in his perverted mind. He felt like testing himself tonight and she was exactly the kind of woman who made the risk of being caught worthwhile. Her fiery red hair nestled on the shoulders of an exquisite body. Her ample breasts and long, athletic legs made her very desirable, but it was her alabaster skin so smooth and delicious—like a sweet, creamy piece of white chocolate—that really turned Tom on. *Yes*, he thought. *She'll do nicely tonight. Yummy.*

Jackie was young and beautiful, an Irish-born schoolteacher who had recently moved to town. Her flawless beauty was only part of the reason he wanted to see her. Tonight, the strange urges within him craved danger; the more danger the better, and Tom knew he could find it at Jackie's. Not that the young woman posed much of a threat to Tom, but her dog sure did. It was a vicious black Lab by the name of Maxwell, who guarded her backyard as if the crown jewels and all the gold in Fort Knox were buried there. This late at night, the dog would probably be sleeping.

Tom's feet were already subconsciously moving, making up their mind before he did, running toward the west end of town, in the direction of Chestnut Avenue and Jackie's house. She went to bed late and he knew that if he hurried, and if he was lucky, she might still be up. The thrill of sneaking past that hellhound Maxwell to catch a glimpse of her was exactly the kind of challenge he loved, and exactly the kind of danger the urges within him demanded tonight.

It was nearly 11:30 P.M. by the time he slowed to a halt outside her house, which was partly hidden from the streetlight's glow by a large blue spruce. He paused to catch his breath. While he rested, he took the opportunity to scan the street and surrounding houses for signs of activity. He was pleased to find the area deserted. Good old small-town life; he could always count on the sleepyheads to be sacked out long before now, even on the weekend. *What a bunch of bores.*

Jackie Sullivan's house, like the majority of houses on this block, was a two-story older home constructed around the end of World War II, just in time for the returning fighting men and women and their soon-to-be baby-boomer generation. The dull brown-colored brick and shutters matched the equally dull brown shingled roof. The only visible splash of color came from a white trellis, which supported an ever-growing ivy plant that clung to the west side of the house and continued around the back, spreading uncontrollably like a malignant disease. Tom had always despised the sight of ivy-covered houses; they reminded him of those ridiculous Chia Pet things that used to be popular, where you added water to grow grass on an ugly ceramic sheep or whatever—but on this particular house it was a blessing. Ms. Sullivan's bedroom was on the second floor, and since there were no trees to assist his climb, the ivy-covered trellis was his only means of reaching her window. The trellis was nothing more than metal lattice work, crisscrossing to make a rather effective ladder.

It was safely bolted to the side of the house and ran right up the wall to the base of Jackie's bedroom window. Simple, really. Just a leisurely climb to paradise. Almost too easy for someone like Tom.

Until he remembered about Maxwell.

About three weeks earlier, only a few days after his weaker alter ego had been introduced to the sexy new schoolteacher for the first time, Tom had paid a visit to this same house. The backyard he'd found completely enclosed by a six-foot-high picket fence made of wood and painted off-white. He'd entered the backyard through an unlocked gate cut into the fence. The seldom-used gate had creaked slightly when opened, but not loud enough to draw attention, at least that was what he'd thought.

He listened for a minute to make sure the coast was clear before starting his move toward the ivy lattice. He hadn't gone more than three steps when a huge animal descended on him from out of nowhere. He barely managed to dive back out the gate and slam it shut in time to avoid being torn to pieces. Tom was convinced the vicious monster had actually sat back and allowed him to enter before stalking and pouncing in a deadly methodical silence.

Last time he'd been lucky as hell. If Maxwell ever got hold of him, the game would be over. The savage guard dog would tear him to shreds. Even if he did survive, he would have a hell of a time explaining to the police why he was there. When they took his black mask off and got a look at his face, the shit would really hit the fan. Tom wasn't sure which was worse. If he had to make a choice, he would probably prefer to die than be exposed. Exposure and ridicule were his greatest fear.

Coincidentally, that same fear of exposure was something the urges thrived on.

Propelled by this strange mixture of fear and excitement, Tom carefully edged along the side of the house until he came to the picket fence. By standing on his tiptoes, he could gaze over the dull wooden points and view the entire darkened yard. Maxwell was lying on his side near his doghouse. His dark coloring and the shadows made it difficult to tell if the mutt was sleeping. It could be just fooling him again, like last time. He watched the large dog for several long minutes before deciding to take a chance. It was a risk, but at this late hour it was one he felt comfortable taking.

The still-unlocked gate lay ten feet to his left but he didn't dare use it. It had to have been those creaking hinges that alerted Maxwell on his previous visit. He wasn't about to make the same mistake. This time he would climb the ivy trellis on his side of the fence. He could reach the second floor, then scuttle sideways round the corner of the house to her bedroom window. Even if Maxwell spotted him, he'd be far enough up the trellis the dog wouldn't be able to reach him. He would also have enough time to reverse his steps, drop back over the fence, and make good his escape, should the overgrown mutt decide to start barking and alert the neighborhood.

Both hands would be required to scale the wall, so he quietly set his flashlight down on the cool, damp grass and took a few deep breaths to clear his head. Quietly, he started his climb, stepping gently as if vials of nitroglycerin were strapped to his shoes.

It was taking the Stranger much longer than he'd anticipated to find what he was looking for. He'd snuck around the neighborhood, peering into windows and backyards, but nobody seemed to have what he was seeking.

"Good things come to those who wait," he chuckled to himself as he moved away from yet another unsuccessful house search.

Normally, he would have been furious by now, seething with rage at all this time-wasting, but tonight he was unusually calm. The magic trunk had eased his concerns and given him a direction and a sense of purpose. No longer was he lashing out blindly, hell-bent on revenge. Now he had a plan. It might take him a little longer, but the exquisite promise of what the future held for Wilson Kemp would be well worth the wait. Smiling happily, the tall, dark Stranger moved farther along Chestnut Avenue toward the next house.

It took an incredible amount of concentration and patience but eventually Tom found himself with his ski mask pressed to the cool glass of Jackie's window. It had taken longer than he'd imagined, but the effort was worthwhile. He'd actually made it.

A quick check over his shoulder confirmed Maxwell was still sprawled out asleep on the ground below, a comforting thought that allowed him to concentrate on the job at hand.

The moon had wrestled free of the sporadic cloud cover, illuminating the teacher's bedroom. Through the spotlessly clean windowpane, Tom could easily make out her heavenly shape lying diagonally across the double bed that occupied the far corner of the room. He'd missed her getting undressed and ready for bed, but thankfully the temperature inside must have been quite hot, forcing Jackie to kick off her sheets and give the pervert what he'd been hoping to see.

Jackie was lying on top of the bed dressed in a thin short-sleeved pink silk nightgown; her large dark nipples were hard, straining against the tight fabric, threatening to burst free at any moment. While she slept, the silk nightie had somehow managed to creep up around her slender waist, an alluring hint of white panties visible and on display for Tom below. He began to salivate with desire as he focused even lower, on the longest, most scintillating pair of legs he'd ever seen. Her beauty was truly striking. Nearly naked she looked exactly like he'd imagined. So much sweeter than the old bag he'd spied on earlier.

A magazine was curled in her hand as if she were still reading, but he knew by experience her slow and easy respiration indicated she was fast asleep. He wished he had brought his flashlight; he loved to see his victim's reaction as the blinding light jarred them awake.

Hell with the flashlight. What if I tried to open the window and have a real good look? Or a feel?

A delicious fantasy began to form in the deepest, darkest pit of his twisted mind, a fantasy that began with him towering over her slumbering body, a wet rag soaked with chloroform ready in his sweaty clenched hand. Once she was out cold, he could do anything to her he wanted.

Anything!

His cock began to harden for the second time that night, throbbing within his tight pants, demanding to be released, and just as Tom's depraved mind seriously contemplated testing the window lock and acting out his dark desires, a noise on the ground to his right broke his wicked train of thought.

His gut feeling told him it had to be the dog, awake and coming for him. The noise hadn't come from that area of the yard though, so it couldn't be. There, he heard it again, and this time he recognized the noise for what it was—the unmistakable squeaking of the gate hinges.

Tom watched nervously as a tall, dark figure walked into Jackie's backyard. His worst fears of being caught and exposed to the public began to race through his mind, causing his heart to pound. This sudden anxiety almost toppled him from his lofty perch. He was preparing to make a jump for it, but hesitated for some reason, compelled to pause and take a closer look at this intruder. The tall man was very thin, but moved with an air of heavy confidence, which made Tom believe he was stronger than he looked.

Strong and wiry . . . that's what he is. Dangerous!

The intruder was dressed in black. His full-length woolen overcoat covered most of what appeared to be a well-used pair of cowboy boots. His face was shrouded with a scraggly-looking beard, which concealed but couldn't quite cover his deathly pallid features. His eyes were the darkest Tom had ever seen, invisible really, sunk into gaunt cheeks as if they had been torn out, leaving two holes. Tom instinctively knew they weren't the eyes of a concerned neighbor or a policeman; they were the cold, vacant eyes of a criminal.

It only took Tom a few more seconds to realize this man was a burglar. He had to be. Who else would be sneaking around dressed in black at this unearthly hour? He couldn't believe this was happening. What were the chances of a burglar and a Peeping Tom hitting the same house, on the same night, at the same time? The odds must be staggering. The irony of the situation almost caused Tom to laugh out loud, but he bit his tongue and remained silent. The would-be burglar had not spotted him and Tom wasn't about to call him over for a pow-wow. There was no telling how this guy might react and violence wasn't one of Tom's best attributes. He was a lover, not a fighter.

The dark figure came to a sudden stop about ten feet inside the gate. Tom glanced back to see if Maxwell had realized he had a visitor. The alert black killing machine had more than noticed, already stealthily closing the distance on its unsuspecting prey. *Oh shit*, Tom thought. *This is going to get messy.*

Tom glanced into Jackie's window but quickly turned away. The voluptuous redhead was prime ogling meat for sure, but the real action was taking place in the back-yard battlefield below and he didn't want to miss a single moment of it.

Maxwell had managed to maneuver within striking range now and incredibly, the burglar was still unaware of the deadly shadow silently creeping toward him. The man just stood there, unmoving, apparently staring into the night sky, his hands tucked inside the pockets of his coat. Tom considered shouting out a warning but bit his tongue and watched, riveted to the scene and anticipating yet dreading what surely would happen next. If the tall man didn't turn and get out of there right now, he was a dead man.

Silently, Maxwell moved in for the kill.

The need for subterfuge gone now, a horrifying snarl shattered the stillness as the terror of Chestnut Avenue lunged forward with teeth bared. Tom briefly considered averting his eyes, but he was enjoying himself too much.

Eagerly he awaited the ensuing bloodbath, totally unprepared for the startling surprise about to transpire.

While the huge Lab was in midair, almost as if he'd known the dog had been there all along, the dark-clothed man spun around and locked his hands around Maxwell's thick, hairy neck. Even from his distant, high viewpoint, Tom could hear the neck bones snapping under the burglar's viselike grip. Within seconds, the once-vicious guard dog had ceased its whimpering, its body had gone limp, and it hung lifeless from the tall man's powerful hands.

Tom couldn't believe it. Maxwell had been a damn big dog. The strength required to crush its neck so easily would have to be incredible. He was shocked and scared by what he'd seen, but smart enough to stay quiet. This was one mean son of a bitch. He pressed against the brick wall, trying his best to disappear into the lush ivy.

Thankfully, Maxwell's killer started walking toward the rear of the yard, away from the house. The dog lay unceremoniously in a broken heap, casually discarded like some piece of trash. The killer stopped at the doghouse to retrieve two brightly colored leashes that had been hooked to a nearby fence post.

What's he going to do with dog leashes? Tom wondered, his fear and confusion growing by the minute. His curiosity piqued, he watched the mysterious visitor jam the white leash into his pocket and stroll nonchalantly back to the canine carcass. He clipped the red leash onto the unfortunate animal's collar and indifferently walked away, dragging the dead dog behind. Maxwell grotesquely bounced along, its tongue sticking out its mouth, swollen and drooling a trail of blood onto the dark green grass.

What the hell is going on? Tom asked himself up on his perch. *Why take the dead dog? Where's he going with it? Christ! Looks like he's taking the damn thing for a walk but that's insane.*

The killer stopped at the gate, cocking his head a little to the left as if he was listening to something. Tom's heart skipped a beat on seeing the man turn. His pallid face tilted slowly until he was staring directly up at Tom. Tom shrank into the ivy and the shadow of the overhanging eave. He might have been spotted but he wasn't quite sure. For one brief horrible moment, their eyes had met and locked. The temperature seemed to drop suddenly, sending a shiver down Tom's spine.

Please don't let him see me.

Tom was sure he was going to die. This unknown madman was about to walk over, haul him off the trellis, and wrap his powerful fingers around his neck, just like he'd done to Maxwell.

The killer took a step toward him before coming to an inexplicable stop. A cruel smile permeated his ghostly face followed by a hideous guttural laugh. Tom didn't share the dark man's sense of humor and was very close to a bowel movement. He'd never been this scared in his life.

For some reason known only to the sadist, he changed direction and departed through the squeaky gate, dragging the dead dog in his wake. Tom was too petrified to move. He couldn't believe the man had left. Had he really not seen him? He had to have. Didn't he? Who was he? How had he killed Maxwell so easily? And why was he taking the dead dog with him? Questions, questions, questions, but no answers. The only person with the answers had just left.

It was probably a stupid thing to do, but Tom wanted to know what was going on. He was terrified, but his curiosity was driving him crazy. He decided to creep down and quietly follow the man. Without thinking of the consequences, he quickly climbed down from the window ledge, the luscious Ms. Sullivan all but forgotten. He ran to the open gate and cautiously peered around the fence post in time to see the tip of Maxwell's limp black tail disappearing around a bush at the front of the house.

Dragging the carcass would certainly slow the lunatic down a bit, so trailing him shouldn't be too difficult. As long as he stayed out of sight, everything would be okay. Tom's bravado started to weaken when he went to retrieve his flashlight where he had left it on the grass. He was troubled to find it gone.

Or maybe not. In his desire to scale the wall, he hadn't really paid much attention to where he'd set it down. Maybe he'd placed it somewhere else? Yeah, that might be it. His frightened mind was ready to grasp at any explanation, rather than concede the killer had taken it. That would mean he had been spotted and could be walking into a trap. An image of Maxwell's unfortunate encounter began to replay in his mind.

On wobbly legs and not accustomed to feeling the effects of fear, Tom shakily moved to the front of the house. The tall man and the dog were nowhere to be found. It was impossible; he couldn't have disappeared so quickly. He didn't have enough time. Tom checked the damp ground for some evidence of direction, but found none. It was as if man and beast had simply vanished into the night air.

Fear swelled within him as he cautiously walked into

the middle of the road. He knew he shouldn't expose himself, but he was too scared to go near any of the trees and bushes that lined each side of the street. Perhaps the dog killer was lurking there, ready to pounce at any second.

His paranoia led to full-fledged panic. Soon he was running hell-bent for leather through the town streets, heading blindly for home. This wasn't supposed to happen to him. He was the Peeping Tom, the king, the powerful black panther, the man in control. He was the giver of fear, not the receiver. He was too strong and confident to fear anyone. Fear was supposed to be an attribute of his weaker personality, not him. He couldn't help it though, couldn't stop running, no matter how hard he tried.

He worried the urges in his head wouldn't let him go home again, but not once did they bang their drums, not even when he crashed through his back door and crumbled in a quivering heap on the hall floor. It was strange, but perhaps the urges also felt threatened by the evil presence he'd witnessed this night. Maybe they were just as scared of the disappearing man as he was?

SUNDAY, SEPTEMBER 20

STRAIGHT FROM THE
SKELETON'S MOUTH . . .

CHAPTER NINE

SAVIOR IN THE BOTTOM OF A BOTTLE

Wilson paced back and forth, pausing occasionally to rub the toes of his already gleaming dress shoes against the back of his pant leg. It was the appointed meeting time, but there was still no sign of his wife and daughter. He was agitated as a plump chicken being introduced to Colonel Sanders and fought the urge to turn and flee.

His nervousness had nothing to do with his wife being late. In fact, he inwardly hoped Susan might not show at all, but that was highly unlikely. He was quite sure she'd be here soon.

"But will she be able to tell I've been drinking?" he muttered under his alcohol-tinged breath.

He'd desperately tried to stay away from the booze, knowing how important this morning was, but eventually his frazzled nerves had gotten the better of him. He took some small comfort in the knowledge he wasn't drunk—nowhere near. By sheer willpower he'd found the inner strength to limit himself to a few quick shots, and as pathetic as it sounded, he actually felt quite proud.

Would Susan feel the same? Would she notice the effort he'd made? Would she give him the benefit of the doubt? Would she realize how difficult it had been for him to work up the courage to face their old friends and neighbors, or would she sniff his breath and simply pass judgment again?

The silver Honda pulled to the curb as Kemp performed one more shoe-shine on his pants before his family joined him. The tension temporarily vanished as Amanda dashed ahead of her mother and sprang into his open arms. She was cute as a button in her finest white dress, her hair tied in ponytails with bright red ribbons. Wilson hugged and kissed her, taking full advantage of the moment before reluctantly setting her down.

Two thoughts occurred to him as he straightened up to face Susan. His first was how beautiful she looked in a dazzling green dress that almost matched her eyes. He was about to compliment her when a second thought raced through his conscience.

She knows . . . my God she knows I've been drinking.

She stood there looking him over. In his mind, he had pictured her screaming at him in disgust, then storming back to the car with Amanda, leaving him standing on the sidewalk, hopelessly and deservedly alone.

Silently praying this wouldn't happen, he held his breath, worked up some courage, and asked, "Well . . . do I look okay?"

Susan took a minute. Wilson was right; she did know he'd been drinking, she just wasn't sure what to do about it. It hadn't been his breath. She saw it in his eyes. Wilson had never been able to keep a secret from her, and she'd easily spotted the guilt in his eyes the moment she stepped out of the car.

Anger started to boil within her, but then she noticed

the effort he'd put into trying to look nice for her. He was wearing a slightly baggy gray suit and red tie that she remembered buying him years ago. It fitted better back then, of course. Still, he looked very handsome. He'd also shaved and put on English Leather, her favorite cologne. She looked him over once more, then stared directly into his eyes. His puppy-dog eyes would tell her everything she needed to know.

Yes, the guilt was still noticeable, but there was also worry and hope reflecting back to her. Without Wilson saying a word, she knew he was sorry for having been so weak. He was worried about her reaction, silently hoping for the best but prepared for the worst.

Her heart, as it always did, went out to him. After all, this wasn't an easy thing for him to do and he really did put an extra effort into looking nice. She decided to give him a break and didn't make an issue out of the booze. At least he wasn't drunk.

"You look wonderful, Wilson," she said finally.

"Yes, Daddy," Amanda cut in, grabbing his hand in a show of support. "Very handsome."

Relief flooded through his veins. He relaxed, smiled, and thanked her for being so understanding. Hand in hand, they turned and headed toward the church.

"I was a little worried about this suit," Wilson admitted. "I tried to get all the wrinkles out, but you know how helpless I am . . . can't even dress myself for God's sake."

"Don't worry about it." Susan laughed. "If Amanda and I don't care, I'm sure God won't mind either."

Wilson laughed at her joke as they approached the impressive redbrick and white stone structure of St.

Michael's Catholic Church, but truth be told, it wasn't God who worried him, it was Father Patrick Harris.

That priest could single-handedly scare the devil himself, Wilson thought.

Father Harris was fifty-eight years of age and as strict a clergyman as you could find. A fiery hard-line Irishman who thought a sin against the heavenly Father was a personal attack on himself. He made no secret of his dislike for Kemp. The two had butted heads so many times in the past, Wilson's head still hurt. Relations between them had deteriorated as his drinking had gotten worse. Two weeks before Susan had thrown him out of the house, Father Harris had publicly humiliated him, banning him from church until he cleaned up his act. That was three years ago and this was his first trip back.

Father Harris was one of those priests who preferred to greet his flock at the front door. His long black robes billowed in the wind, contrasting starkly with his shock of ancestral red hair. He gestured wildly with open arms, smiling courteously and whispering with some members while silently shaking the hands of others. To say he was more than a little intimidating was like saying the Grand Canyon was an interesting little hole. Wilson tried to swallow his fear, tucking behind Susan and their daughter as they took their place in line. The procession slowly and agonizingly shuffled up the concrete steps till at last they came face-to-face with the reason for his anxiety.

Father Harris looked surprised, but still took the time to look him over. When he finally composed himself and started speaking, his tone was less severe than Wilson expected.

"So. You're back. How are you, Wilson?" he asked.

Wilson sensed nothing short of total honesty was required here and quickly replied. "Still messed up, I'm afraid, but trying my best to turn things around. May I come in, please?"

"Of course," Father Harris replied, nodding his head approvingly. "This door is always open to those in need. If you're looking for salvation, here's where you must start. I can promise you this . . . you'll never find your savior in the bottom of a bottle, son—"

"You're probably right, Father," interrupted Wilson, cutting short the priest's door sermon. "No disrespect to God, sir, or to you, but I need to work on finding myself before I think about anything else. Don't you think?"

Father Harris nodded not too sympathetically as he waved them through into the arched interior. As he walked past the priest, Wilson was startled to feel a hand on his shoulder. In a surprisingly tender, reassuring voice, Father Harris whispered, "If you ever need help finding yourself, or just feel the need to talk, I'll be here."

Wilson was genuinely touched. "Thank you, Father. I'll keep that in mind."

Their time in church seemed to pass relatively quickly, much quicker than he could recall. St. Michael's was still as Gothic and imposing as ever. Father Harris, still full of fire and brimstone, had raged about the filthy state the world was in. They still sang the same old off-tune dreary incantations that erased any interest he might have had in music. He recalled some people in the pews had cast a not-so-subtle glance his way, which he had ignored. He was enjoying this precious time with his family and nothing was going to burst his balloon. He held his wife's hand, thinking back on the good times they'd shared and hoping the future would be just as bright. Today was his best day in quite some time but, unfortunately, in less than an hour something terrible would happen that would drastically change everything.

CHAPTER TEN

A WALK IN THE PARK

Coming down the front stairs of the church, Wilson felt happy and at peace with himself. He was smart enough not to get carried away; he realized his relationship with Susan was still very much strained. It would take more than a few hours to bridge the gap, but at least they'd made progress, which gave rise to a glimmer of hope. He was confident he could rescue his marriage and realize their dreams, if he could only find a way to stay off the damn sauce.

Too daunting a task for now though. Today, he only wanted to savor the moment. He was conscious of slowing down the pace as they walked to the car, not wanting this day to end. He sensed Susan was having similar thoughts.

"Do you need to get home for anything important?" she stopped to ask.

"No. Absolutely not . . . n-not a thing," he stuttered, in his eagerness to reply. "Do you?"

She was moved by his nervous response and realized how desperately he wanted to stay with them.

"I guess I don't need to tell you how much it would mean to me if you'd stay. I'm not making a big deal out of this, Susan, I just feel we're a family today and I don't want it to end."

"I don't either, and it doesn't have to. In fact, if you're up to it, I've already made plans."

"Plans?" Wilson asked.

"We made a picnic lunch, Daddy," Amanda said, not meaning to interrupt but unable to contain her excitement.

"You did?" Wilson asked, ruffling his daughter's silky hair. He looked hopefully at Susan for confirmation, and she smiled and nodded.

"We hoped today would turn out the way it has and thought you might like to take your family for a little picnic. What do you think?"

"Yeah, Daddy . . . what do you think?" Amanda echoed, her beautiful eyes gleaming. With unabashed tears in his eyes, Wilson took them both into his arms.

It only took five minutes to drive to Riverside Park. Like the name suggested, Billington's town park ran alongside the Allegheny River, taking up the better part of twelve acres of prime real estate. It was subtly designed around the slow-moving waters, thick groves of huge oak, maple, and pine trees providing habitats for a vast array of wildlife in an effort to maintain a naturelike setting. The park was actually quite old, dating back more than one hundred years. Areas of the park had been complemented with slides, swings, seesaws, and other playthings for the kids. There were lots of picnic tables, park benches, and public washrooms dotting the landscape as well, with the focus of the park being a large wooden bandstand occupying its very center. In short, it was a beautiful, relaxing, peaceful place, ideal for lazing away the cares of the day.

They chose a semisecluded spot near the north shore to roll out their red and white checkered tablecloth. The open elevated knoll allowed a gentle east wind to carry wonderful fragrances of pine, barbecued hot dogs, and fresh cut grass. From their vantage point, they could easily see most of the park, which was attracting quite a crowd.

The food was wonderful: tuna salad sandwiches, cheese, crackers, pickles, deviled eggs, and a large thermos of pink lemonade. It was nothing fancy, but Wilson savored every bite. The company was even better; they laughed and joked until their bellies ached.

"So, Daddy," Amanda said between giggles. "I heard you know magic now."

Wilson nearly choked on his carrot cake.

"Ah . . . where did you hear that, sweetie?"

He knew she must be speaking about his magic clown act, but for a moment he thought she'd found out about his shadowy past. The last thing he wanted was his family finding out what had happened all those years ago and Amanda's offhanded remark had momentarily thrown him a curve.

"I heard some kids talking at school. Some of them saw your flyer on the telephone poles. They told me they're trying to talk their parents into hiring you for their birthday parties. Are you really a magic clown, Daddy?"

Obviously, she'd talked to these kids before the Morris house fiasco. He was glad she hadn't found out yet, and wondered if he would get a chance to redeem himself. Noticing the quick flash of anxiety crossing his face, Susan jumped in to save the day.

"You bet he is, sweetie . . . in fact, he's probably the greatest magic clown to come to these parts. Right, dear?"

If she only knew how right she was, Wilson thought as he quickly played along. "Darn right, girlie! Your old dad has lots of tricks up his sleeve."

"Oh that's super, Daddy. Show me a trick, show me a trick. Please. *Pleeeeeease!*"

Not wanting to see him embarrassed, Susan was all for changing the subject but he shrugged her off.

"I'd be happy to show our daughter a little magic, but before I can do that, she's gonna have to take that silly thing out of her ear."

"What thing?" Amanda and her mother asked in unison.

"That silly thing right there," he teased, enjoying how easily they were taking the hook.

He pointed again at Amanda's left ear then reached out, slowly turning his hand over so they could see it was empty. Momentarily pausing at her ear, he impressed his captive audience by deftly revealing a plastic saltshaker lodged in his previously empty hand. Susan and Amanda both gasped in amazement but before they could say anything, Wilson continued on, surprising himself at how he was able to fall back into the old showman routine.

"Wait a minute," he mused. "I don't think I got all of it. Just a second . . ." He again showed his sleight of hand and retrieved the matching pepper shaker. "How did those things get stuck in your ear, sweetie? It's a wonder you were able to hear anything at all."

"Oh Daddy," she squealed in delight, launching herself into his open arms. "That was terrific. How'd you do it?"

"You know magicians never reveal their secrets, kiddo. If I was to tell you, you'd tell your friends, and then everyone would be doing it and I'd be out of business."

That seemed to satisfy Amanda, squirming out of her father's arms to examine the magical shakers, but it didn't satisfy Susan. She was silently wondering how he'd done it too. That was no easy trick, and to have pulled it off twice without her seeing a thing was more than impressive, it was shocking.

"Where did you learn that?" she asked, her curiosity getting the better of her.

"Oh, it was nothing really. I just picked it up." He was trying to act casual but was wilting under his wife's determined gaze. He was hopeless at lying to her, always had been, but he gave it a try anyway.

"Really, Susan, it's no big deal. I borrowed a few magic books from the library for my clown act, and that one was fairly easy. Anyone could do it."

Susan knew he was lying; his eyes had given him away again. There might be magic books in the library that showed a few basic tricks, but she had witnessed something much more than basic. The dexterity and showmanship required to pull off a close-up stunt like that was more akin to someone who'd been practicing magic for a long time. David Copperfield could have pulled it off just as smoothly, and probably quite a few other lifelong professionals, but there was no way she was going to believe a recovering alcoholic with a kid's library book could master such skills that quickly. Something strange was going on and for the first time since meeting Wilson, she felt a little disassociated. Perhaps she didn't know him quite as well as she thought she did.

"Wilson . . . I need to know the truth now. I know you've been working hard to get your act together, but there's no way you got *that* good by reading a book. Come on, out with it. Who's been teaching you?"

A million thoughts raced through his head as he frantically tried to come up with a believable excuse. There's no way he could tell her the truth. That part of his life was locked away forever. No matter how much he loved her, he refused to give her the slightest glimpse into his murky past. He was about to tell her he was taking lessons out of town, when a high-pitched scream sounded off to their right, startling them and cutting short his response.

"What was that?" Wilson asked, grateful for the distraction giving him the opportunity to change the topic.

"I've no idea . . . but look!" Susan jumped to her feet, excitedly pointing toward the bandstand. "Why are those people running?"

Sure enough, Wilson saw literally dozens of people converging on the wooden bandstand, pointing, shouting, and pushing one another in a frenzy to get a better glimpse. Whatever was garnering such sudden attention was hidden from their view. The elaborate cedar-shingled roof draping the large circular platform concealed the mysterious spectacle. If they wanted to find out what was going on, they'd have to run down and join the crowd.

"Let's go," Wilson and Susan shouted simultaneously, temporarily leaving their possessions to dash headlong down the slope toward the gathering throng below.

Wilson arrived well ahead of his wife, who'd been forced to slow down considerably to keep pace with Amanda. Not waiting for them to catch up, he elbowed, pushed, and squirmed his way through the thickening crowd until he stood a few feet from the cause of all this turmoil.

Until now, he'd been so preoccupied with getting to the scene, he hadn't thought much about what he might find once he got there. It was just as well; nothing in his wildest imagination could have prepared him for such a ghastly sight.

On the bandstand's stage lay three bodies. One had obviously been human, and the other two appeared to be dogs, one larger than the other. *Bodies* wasn't really a good word, since nothing was left except bare skeletons, most of their white bones held together with the darkening remnants of spongy muscles, leathery tendons, and some other foul-smelling, stringy tissue. Other bones lay piled in heaps around them, having fallen off or been torn away from the three ghastly stripped bodies. It was an incredibly bizarre scene that left everyone stunned and somewhat horrified.

There was a distinct absence of blood, flesh, and organs; hell, not even a fly. The remains were nearly picked clean, the bones glistening as if bleached, or perhaps even licked.

What the hell? Wilson thought, truly shocked at what he was seeing.

The condition of the clean bones added to the strangeness of this gruesome scene, and whoever deposited these skeletons hadn't simply dumped them but had taken the time to set them up as if on display.

The human skeleton was lying on its left side; the clenched fingers of its right hand held the thick leather straps of two dog leashes. The red one led down to the larger dog, and the white was firmly wrapped around the tiny neck of the smaller. To anyone looking, it almost appeared as if someone had been taking their dogs for a relaxing walk, when suddenly everything about them, save for their bones, had instantly evaporated.

Wilson finally tore his eyes away to look for his family. The pushing and shouting was quickly developing into an ugly scene. Things were starting to get out of hand as the onlookers crowded closer. He was worried his wife and daughter might be caught up in the crowd but, thankfully, Susan had anticipated the chaos and kept herself and Amanda well back. He managed to make eye contact and signal her to keep Amanda away from the bandstand. Once he was sure they were safe, he turned his attention back to the macabre scene.

Who could have done something like this? And why?

The milling, frightened crowd, searching for a rational explanation for this gruesome display of evil, was tossing around these questions and many more. Some tried to dismiss what they were seeing, to convince themselves and others that the skeletons weren't real and all this was simply a tasteless hoax. Wilson and most of the others knew better. This madness was no hoax.

It was cold-blooded murder.

CHAPTER ELEVEN

INTERESTING

He was far enough away to avoid unwanted attention, but close enough to revel in the ensuing panic. Hidden within the dense foliage of a towering maple tree, the Stranger watched as three police cruisers were summoned to the macabre calling card he'd left for Wilson Kemp. Lurking around in daylight was something he usually avoided, but today was an exception. The magic trunk's plan had swung into action and he didn't want to miss Kemp's reaction.

The skeletons had been discovered about twenty minutes ago, yet the real surprise was still hidden. With the arrival of the local law enforcement, it would only be a matter of time. The thought of how Kemp might react had the tall Stranger tingling with excitement.

Somehow the trunk of secrets had known Kemp would be coming to the park today and the evil magician had long ago learned to trust and obey its directives. After killing the black dog last night, he'd dragged the huge animal back to his hideaway and deposited its stiffening corpse into the deceptive emptiness of the trunk. When the savage ripping, chewing, and slurping had ceased, a contented whisper inside his head told him it was time to take action. It was news that brought a sadistic grin to the Stranger's thin, pallid face.

Following instructions, the scruffy-faced man with no name had dragged his beloved magical trunk out of the house and onto the back of the red pickup. In that last blissful hour before dawn, he'd driven the rusty Ford directly to Riverside Park. Taking full advantage of the early morning solitude, he'd driven off the road onto the dew-covered grass and backed the truck up to the wooden steps of the circular bandstand.

The stooped skeleton of the old farmer, Duke Winslow, laid waiting at the bottom of the trunk but there had been no sign of the two dogs. Not worried in the least, the Stranger had lifted the surprisingly heavy skeleton out of the trunk and gently set it down on the truck's bed. By the time he'd returned to the trunk, the freshly polished bones of the large black dog lay waiting. Setting these bones down beside the old man's, he returned once more to the trunk for the smaller mutt. From the way its tiny neck was snapped, he easily identified it as the scraggly Benji he'd killed by the campfire early Friday morning. It seemed ages ago since he'd sat in the woods planning revenge, still unaware how close he was to actually achieving it.

After removing all three sets of polished bones, it had only taken a few minutes up and down the stairs to artfully arrange his ghastly masterpiece. The skeletons had hung together surprisingly well, considering their condition. Many of the bones had fallen to the ground and the bottom half of Maxwell's spine had snapped clean off above its hips but the Stranger had pieced the skeletons back together as best he could and was pleased with his efforts. He took a few satisfying minutes to savor his display, then another few seconds to plant his surprise for Kemp, but then he knew it was time to leave. He hid the truck nearby and climbed the maple that would offer him a perfect vantage spot but at the same time, screen his presence.

The Stranger settled in and waited.

Impossible as it seemed high up in the tree, but far too exhausted to fight it, the tall man drifted off to sleep. When the Stranger dreamed, it was always about violence and pain, suffering and death, and this dream was no different. Today, he was bombarded with gruesome images of a man covered in blood and missing nearly all of his skin. He was a mess of veins and muscles and open, weeping sores. It was a familiar dream about a real man the Stranger had once known years earlier. In the dream, the flayed man was screaming in agony but still stood up and twirled around to let the Stranger see him better, even though every movement caused great torment and made his raw wounds bleed anew.

The skinless man was another magician—no, wait; he'd only wanted to be a magician—but at the moment the Stranger couldn't recall what the man's name was. Theodore something-or-other. Didn't matter; the Stranger had only ever called him by the name *Peeler*, and he'd been out of his mind long before they'd met. This deranged man had lost much of his skin in a horrible accident and the pain and suffering of countless failed skin grafts and the torture of endless rehab had driven him completely bonkers. He'd somehow come to the irrational conclusion his only salvation might be if he could peel off the rest of his damaged skin, freeing his mind and soul to travel away from his hideous body, which had become his excruciating prison. Yeah, Peeler had been a pretty fucked-up guy, but that hadn't stopped the Stranger from being his friend.

Or from supplying him with razor blades . . .

With a contented smile on his face, the Stranger slept on, happy to replay memories of the good old days. He would have loved to sleep longer, to watch crazy Peeler tear more strips of skin off his arms with his bloody teeth, but eventually people started drifting into the park and the trunk of secrets whispered in his head that it was time to open his eyes. His memories of Peeler instantly forgotten and refreshed from his short nap, he watched the people of Billington coming and going, his powerful body tensed and ready for what was soon to come.

It had frustrated him how long it had taken for someone to notice his handiwork. Hardly anyone had entered the park before nine, and the majority of those first people had been walkers and joggers, far too intent on their own activities. It wasn't until the churches started spewing out their faithful that the park started to really come to life. Hundreds of people soon converged on the picturesque riverside setting. He was glad he'd taken the extra effort to conceal himself high in the maple's thick branches, unconsciously holding on to its solid limbs tighter than necessary, relishing its cold, lonely embrace. He was a hunter, a solitary man, and crowds always disturbed him. Fortunately, the magic trunk whispered reassuringly, always there to soothe and calm his paranoid fears.

The Stranger hadn't even known his quarry was in the park until after the skeletons had been found. Only after the first scream and the initial chaos had died down did he catch sight of Kemp running among the gathering crowd. A strange chill ran down the dark man's spine, a cold shock unlike anything he'd felt since beginning the long hunt. An excited chill brought on by seeing his long-lost enemy would have been normal, almost expected. The strange part of it all, however, was an amazing revelation that almost took his breath away.

His dark thoughts should have been centered on Kemp, and on the brutal revenge plan that constantly preoccupied him.

But they weren't.

He should have been happily thinking about all the fear, confusion, and panic unfolding before him.

But he wasn't.

He should have at least been planning a quiet way of slipping away after the discovery of his little surprise.

But he couldn't.

He couldn't do any of these things because one icy thought swirled through the pathways of his sick, degenerating mind. A secret he had just learned.

"Kemp has a wife and daughter," he whispered, astonished. "My God! The bastard has a family!"

Interesting. Very interesting.

CHAPTER TWELVE

MESSAGE FROM THE HEATSEEKER

Six burly policemen continually urged the gathering throng of onlookers to move back from the scene. At first they tried politely interjecting, but the pushing and shoving continued. Angry glares and veiled threats failed to hold the ring at bay; within minutes of pushing them back, they'd creep in to where they'd stood before. Eventually they gave up trying and allowed the crowd to just mill around.

Wilson recognized most of the cops, although this was the first time he'd seen them in an official capacity outside the drunk tank or issuing the occasional speeding ticket. They seemed to be more enthusiastic and on the ball today than when Wilson usually saw them. Officer Jackson stood next to his partner, Byron "Big Mack" MacKenzie, and rubbing the baby stubble on his chin to their immediate left stood Sandy Carson, Billington's newest and youngest recruit. Carson was a tall, awkward-looking kid trying to put on the tight-lipped, weathered scowl of an experienced veteran. His uniform, seemingly designed for someone much larger, hung loose on his not-so-copious frame, giving him a somewhat clownish appearance. A boy playing dress-up cops and robbers.

The other officers looked familiar but, for the moment, Wilson couldn't recall their names.

When all the pushing had started Wilson almost left but was reluctant to give up the excellent front view to this rather odd spectacle. Like everyone else, he was partly fascinated, partly repulsed by this macabre scene and found it awfully hard to look away. He did take the time, however, to make sure his wife and daughter were out of harm's way before taking the liberty of watching Billington's finest in action. They too looked bewildered, not quite knowing what to do next.

After giving up on the crowd-control idea, they looked just as confused as everyone else. Was this a murder scene or a joke? Were these skeletons for real or simply impressive fakes? They sure smelled real, that was for sure. It wasn't an overpowering stench, perhaps because there was so little meat and tissue left on the bones, but there was still a definite odor of rot and decay lingering in the air. It was the smell of death.

None of the officers had ever been confronted with such a situation before. Wilson figured if they wanted answers, rather than chaos, they'd better start asking questions or taking some sort of progressive action in a hurry.

Acting on his own initiative, young Officer Carson began telling the crowd not to worry, the mobile crime lab would soon be on its way and the matter would soon be resolved. This raised many an eyebrow among not only the onlookers, but also his uniformed buddies who'd never heard of such a van. Most people present were smart enough to know a small town like Billington didn't have the resources to afford such luxury, but

Carson annoyingly kept repeating his ridiculous message until finally Big Mack couldn't take it anymore and not so quietly told the inexperienced youngster to shut the fuck up.

It took the law a few minutes to recover from their embarrassment and resume their former position of uniformed observers. They still weren't accomplishing much, but at least Mack's outburst had quieted the crowd down enough to let them all think.

It ended up being a twelve-year-old boy who spotted it first. He had red spiked hair, round chubby cheeks, and a nasty purple shiner shadowing his left eye. He wormed his way under a few people's legs and walked right up to the male skeleton and said, "Hey, guys . . . what's that thing sticking out of its mouth?"

The curious crowd, policemen included, temporarily went silent as all eyes followed the small, pudgy finger pointing toward the largest of the three skeletons. Within seconds they all saw it too and once again tongues were wagging.

If this had been a large city, such as New York or Washington, things would have been handled much differently. The crowd would have been moved back clear of the crime scene and the area sealed off with ribbons of fancy yellow tape. Wilson wondered why the local fuzz hadn't thought about doing just that.

Maybe they don't watch enough TV, he thought. *The CSI guys would have had this scene under control ages ago.*

In a properly cordoned-off crime scene, no one would have been allowed inside, never mind touch or possibly destroy vital evidence. Sadly, this wasn't one of those big cities, and none of these procedures were followed.

Small-time cops or not, they should have had the good

sense to leave the bony remains alone, but they too were just as excited to find out what was inside the human skeleton's gaping mouth. Sandy Carson, still smarting over his earlier chastisement, had moved away to avoid the crowd and consequently was the closest to the bones. Without a thought toward preserving evidence, he bent down and removed a small scroll from the grinning skull.

It looked like an unfiltered cigarette, but after unrolling it, everyone could see it was a piece of white writing paper containing a scribbled note. Even to the untrained eye, for anyone standing close enough, it was easy to tell the crimson words had been written in blood.

"What's it say?" echoed the crowd in almost perfect synchronization.

Obviously, the police would never answer that question and divulge such vital evidence, or would they?

Quickly recovering from his recent embarrassment concerning the nonexistent crime lab, Officer Carson was enjoying the sudden attention. Unable to control himself, and before Big Mack could get near him, his mouth got in the way of common sense again.

"It doesn't make much sense to me," he started, then raised his voice so everyone in the area could easily hear him. "It says . . . *'This is a message from the Heatseeker. What I've done here is nothing compared to what I'll do to you when I get my hands around your treacherous throat. You know who you are. There is nowhere left to hide!'"*

"What on earth does it mean?" Officer Jackson asked to no one in particular. "Sounds like a freakin' nutcase to me," he added, laughing nervously.

No one else was laughing. Mayhem had broken loose. People were yelling and screaming, and looking at the skeletons again as if seeing them in a whole new way.

There was little doubt they were real now. The message confirmed this was no hoax. This was serious—deadly serious.

Billington had a madman on the loose. People were trying to come up with reasonable explanations for the unfolding chaos, but none of them could. No one, not even the veteran police officers, had any idea what was going on. Every man, woman, and child in the park was clueless.

Except for one of them.

Wilson Kemp stood among the rabble as if in a trance, the color slowly draining from his usually flushed face. A knot of burning fear was growing in the pit of his stomach, swelling by the second like a rampant malignant tumor.

It can't be, Wilson thought, denying the horrifying thoughts now threatening to engulf him. *It simply can't be! I must not have heard right. Yeah, that's it.*

He was standing in close proximity to Officer Carson when he heard the officer reread the same macabre message. Without warning his vision blurred, cold beads of sweat oozed from his pores, and he felt light-headed and giddy. His legs began to buckle but, fortunately, the tightly packed crowd prevented his collapse.

Wilson knew he had to get away from here but wasn't sure if he possessed the strength to walk. It was only when someone excitedly asked him who he thought this Heatseeker might be that his feet started to move. Hot bile rose in his throat just thinking about that name. No one could possibly know who the Heatseeker was, but he certainly did. The Heatseeker was the . . .

"No!" he yelled, quickly and effectively derailing that train of thought.

This can't be him, he silently prayed. *It's impossible. Something strange is going on here, but not that. Anything but that! It must be some kind of strange coincidence, that's all.* He tried not to torment himself or jump to conclusions but his mind would not let go.

His dark thoughts nibbled, scratched, and clawed their way deeper into the haunted space of his subconscious mind, where all bad memories of his hidden past were locked away. Years of agonizing memories began to boil to the surface, erupting out of his tortured soul to fill his entire being with hot molten fear.

He fought his way through the mob and down the bandstand stairs before staggering across the open ground to where his family anxiously waited. He tried to hide his mounting fear, tried to harness the overload of emotions swirling unchecked inside his head, but Susan sensed something was wrong.

"Wilson . . . your face? It's so pale. What's the matter? You look like you've seen a ghost. What happened?"

"Nothing," he lied. "It's all just so creepy. I guess I'm spooked a little."

Susan thought to question him further but Amanda began to cry and ran to her father, burying her face in his pant leg, her muffled cries still very much audible.

"What's happening, Daddy? Why is everybody yelling?"

"It's nothing to worry about, honey. Trust me, everything is going to be okay."

While he lovingly stroked the back of his daughter's head, trying his best to reassure her, Wilson quietly whispered to Susan, "Maybe you'd better get her home. I think she's had enough for one day."

"I think we all have. Can I give you a lift?"

"No, I don't need it. It's only a few blocks and I could use the walk to clear my head."

Wilson walked them to the car, putting on a brave front, and breathed a sigh of relief as Susan backed out of the parking lot and waved good-bye as she sped away. Wilson could only return an acknowledging nod. He wanted to blow Amanda a kiss, but couldn't risk taking his shaking hands out of his pant pockets. No sense in upsetting them any more than they already were.

He left the park the moment their car was out of sight, trying to convince himself he was leaving because of the noisy crowd, but deep down he knew it was because of the bloody note found inside the skeleton's mouth.

And because he needed a drink.

Several, actually, or as much booze as it took to extinguish the red-hot fear smoldering within his trembling body. He walked quickly, willing himself to think of only the vodka bottle waiting at home, but the incident in the park made it difficult to concentrate on anything else.

"Stop it," he scolded himself, a series of black memories already filtering across the movie screen of his mind. "I'm wrong. That's all there is to it. I have to be, right? Because if I'm not . . . God help us all."

Wrapped up in his troubled thoughts and his urgent desire to get home to his bottle of liquid poison as soon as possible, Wilson was completely unaware that less than a block away a slow-moving red pickup truck was inching along the road behind him.

CHAPTER THIRTEEN

TEMPTATION

The settling sun nose-dived below the western horizon a little faster than usual, or at least seemed to for many of Billington's frightened citizens. Word that a killer was in their midst raced through the small community, spreading fear and uncertainty.

Within hours, the rumors had effectively shut down the town. Everything closed early, some through fear and others due to a lack of business. A few local churches even canceled their evening activities, suggesting perhaps their fear was greater than their faith. By ten o'clock, the streets were strangely quiet; only the occasional wailing of a police siren broke the stillness and gave rise to some optimism that perhaps the cops might get lucky and nail this madman before he struck again.

The disturbed man who liked to call himself Peeping Tom quickly stepped back from the window as another cruiser silently glided past the house. The room was in darkness and he could not be seen from the outside; moving away from the window was a reaction brought on by habit and his desire not to be seen.

He was completely naked, heedless of the cooling temperature. He paced back and forth, pausing now and then to glance at his black prowling outfit, which lay draped over a high-backed wooden chair. He wasn't thinking about the warmth it would afford him, but of the extreme power he felt tapped into when he put it on.

The urges had returned, steadily beating their drums inside his head, insisting he go out on the prowl again. His weaker side was reluctant to obey and continued to resist. He was quite confused by his indecisiveness; the queer sensation now flowing through him was an entirely new experience. The temptation to go on the prowl was definitely there; he felt its allure each time he glanced at his evening clothes. The only thing holding him back was the weakening resistance of his alter ego and fear; an emotion he had never felt before.

He'd been part of the crowd in the park that afternoon. He'd seen the skeletons and heard the killer's strange message. In all probability, he was the only one who recognized the two distinctive dog leashes. He could still vividly recall the events of last night and the sudden disappearance of the scruffy-faced dog strangler.

"I know who dumped those skeletons at the bandstand. I don't know his name, but I'll never forget that face. I can't believe it. I know who the killer is."

A mixed chill of excitement and fear galloped up his spine, saturating his perverted mind with sensations far more intense than he'd felt previously. *Who was the disappearing man, and what did he want? Why had he left such a ghastly display in the park? Who was the Heatseeker? And what was that cryptic message all about?*

"What the hell is happening around here?" Tom asked himself, returning again to gaze out the darkened window. He figured there were probably a lot of people asking that same question tonight. Only a few knew the answer.

Outside, nothing moved. It was almost as if he were alone in the world for the very first time.

MONDAY, SEPTEMBER 21

THINGS CAN ONLY GET WORSE

CHAPTER FOURTEEN

THE STAIRWAY TO HELL

"Ready or not . . . here I come."

Wilson's playful shout rang out louder than expected, reverberating along the narrow hallway. He was positive Amanda had heard him but he hesitated coming after her too quickly. She loved to play hide-and-seek and he knew how disappointed she would be if he came looking before she'd found the perfect hiding spot. Before beginning the hunt, he called out once more, counted slowly to ten just to give her some extra time.

Amanda loved this silly cat-and-mouse game and had always taken it seriously. She tried with all her heart to find a good hiding spot but, in truth, she wasn't very good at it and invariably Wilson had been able to track her down in a relatively short time. Sometimes he'd prolong the search by looking in places other than where she was, just so she could enjoy thinking she had outsmarted him. Today would probably be like any other day, but if it made her happy, he was glad to go through the motions.

It only took five minutes for Wilson to change his mind. He had started out searching effortlessly as always; looking in ridiculous places such as the refrigerator and the bathroom towel hamper before turning his eye to the more obvious areas. He checked all her usual hiding spots, under the beds, behind the hallway's free-standing mirror, the bathtub where she sometimes lay down with a towel over her. Now and again, she'd curl round the base of a brass lamp in the corner of the living room impersonating a ball, or simply sprawled under the dining room table pretending to be asleep. She wasn't in any of these places.

A few more minutes of fruitless searching had Wilson thinking maybe she'd left the house. He didn't think she would do such a thing, but he checked outside anyway. Wilson dashed to the rear of the house; from his bedroom window he was able to check the small backyard. Amanda was nowhere in sight; his curiosity changed to puzzlement and then fear.

"Where can she be?" he wondered aloud. "I've checked the whole house. Everywhere!"

A rattling noise from behind startled him away from the window. It ceased before he could turn about but he'd heard enough to zero in on the bedroom closet. It was one of those large double closets with bifold doors fixed on a sliding metal track. Wilson had already looked inside; twice, in fact, and distinctly remembered leaving the doors ajar. The sturdy oak doors were now shut tight. Obviously someone had closed them, causing the rattling noise. It didn't take a rocket scientist to figure out who.

"Now I've got you. Ready or not, here I come."

Wilson hurriedly crossed the room, laughing loudly, feeling like a fool for allowing himself to worry needlessly. He was quite positive she hadn't been in the closet when he checked it before. Where else could she hide?

His curiosity piqued, he took hold of each knob and threw open the closet doors.

"Ah-hahhh!" he cried, trying his best to surprise her, but again it was he who was caught off guard.

The closet was empty.

Not completely empty. Some of his clothes were still hanging there: a few shirts, sweaters, and pants either on hangers or scattered haphazardly on the floor, a selection of shoes, the odd glove or two, and a tangled knot of colorful neckties. Besides clothes, two unopened vodka bottles sat collecting dust on the top shelf. There were also a cluttered box of mementos wrapped inside a pillowcase and a few stringy cobwebs here and there, but otherwise the closet was bare. Where was his daughter?

"Amanda?" Wilson called out, speaking loudly but not quite scared enough to yell yet.

Frustration and anxiety began to overpower him when suddenly he heard Amanda laugh. She was trying hard to contain it but without success. Once she started giggling there was no stopping her. Great bursts of laughter seemed to be coming from beneath his feet and, amazingly, a few shoes started to shake before a two-foot section of the floor opened up as if on hinges. Beaming with joy, Amanda was holding the trapdoor open with one hand and pointing victoriously at her stunned father with the other.

"I got you, Daddy. I finally got you! After all these years, I finally found a place to hide where you couldn't find me."

"You sure did, sweetie," Wilson responded. "If you hadn't laughed, I'd never have found you."

He'd lived in this old house for three years, since

Susan had been forced to throw him out. In all that time, he'd been using the closet without the slightest inkling of a secret trapdoor. The landlord had certainly never mentioned it and in all probability didn't even know it was there. No wonder he'd had such a hard time finding Amanda.

"When did you find this hiding place, sweetie? You've never hid in there before."

"I just found it today. I was gonna hide in the back of the closet behind your pants but I tripped on something. I looked and found this little brass ring. I gave it a good yank and the floor lifted up. It's real dark and spooky down here but I heard you shout you were coming so I climbed down anyway. Neat hiding spot, huh?"

"Yeah . . . great, honey. You really fooled me this time. I don't know why I've never noticed that brass ring before. It's probably not the best place to play though. Probably filled with spiders and things, isn't it? Climb out of there and let me take a look, okay?"

"Sure, Daddy. Ready or not . . . here I come."

Amanda took two steps up and was almost clear of the hole when the huge grin on her face fell away, suddenly replaced by fear and shock. Her widening eyes appealed to him for help, the message loud and clear and delivered faster than she could have screamed the words. Wilson couldn't fathom what the problem was and could only look on uncomprehendingly until she finally did find her voice and let out a long, hideous scream.

What's wrong? Why's she so frightened? These questions flashed through Wilson's mind before he looked down at her feet and understood what had happened.

Someone had grabbed hold of her ankles.

It seemed impossible, ludicrous in fact, but someone was hiding in the hole with her. Inside the trapdoor, visibility was poor but he was able to see two huge, grimy, long-fingered hands firmly locked on Amanda's ankles. For a moment Wilson was unable to move, unable to help, he was so shocked and perplexed by the absurdity of the situation.

With a savage yank, the monstrous hands of the unseen predator effortlessly dragged his terrified child down into the dark void, pulling Amanda quickly out of sight. Wilson reached out despairingly but was too late, almost jamming his fingers as the trapdoor slammed shut.

"This can't be happening," screamed Wilson, his panic-stricken voice resounding in the emptiness around him. A painful scream from below was more than enough to convince him the danger was very real.

He dropped to his knees and frantically began searching for the small brass ring concealed in the carpet. Although he'd gone years without knowing it was there, today his trembling fingers found it almost immediately. He pulled sharply on the ring and for a brief tortuous moment he was sure it was locked, but it thankfully released and the small section of flooring lifted up.

Below his closet floor was much more than a tiny secret cubbyhole, there was a full staircase leading down into darkness. *Where does this go?* Wilson thought, his head spinning. *There's no basement in this house. Not that I know of, anyway.*

Without delaying a moment to consider his own personal safety, he charged down the secret staircase into the silent darkness below. Come hell or high water, he was determined to save his daughter.

* * *

Outside Kemp's run-down bungalow, nothing moved. A cool breeze rustled the treetops, interrupting the peaceful stillness on Morgan Street. The loud rumbling sound of a powerful engine sparking to life disturbed it even more. Ever so slowly, the old red pickup nosed toward the dilapidated dwelling. Inside the cab, a man shrouded in shadow began to squeeze the steering wheel tighter and tighter, tension building within him with every revolution of the tires.

"Are you sure this is a good idea?" the dark man asked for the third time.

Yes . . . trust me, the magic trunk replied, a silky whisper deep inside his mind.

It was the same response he'd been given each time he'd asked and although the words were spoken with confidence, the Stranger wasn't fully convinced. He wanted to leave the truck at the end of the block, where he'd been sitting since following Kemp home from the park. He could have walked down the street and surprised him. Starting up the old truck at this time of the morning on such a quiet street was sure to draw unwanted attention. He was only going to get one chance at this. What if Kemp was expecting him? He'd surely be able to hear him coming and the element of surprise would be lost. What was the trunk of secrets thinking?

Relax, my friend, the mysterious voice soothed, picking up on the Stranger's doubt. *I promise you things are under control. Kemp is in a deep sleep and won't hear your approach. He is having a sweet little dream about his lovely daughter. They were playing hide-and-seek and having so much fun it was making me sick, so I . . . how shall I put it . . . decided to join in. They're not having quite as much fun anymore!*

The power in the magic trunk never ceased to amaze the evil magician. As he turned into Kemp's driveway and killed the engine he wondered how the trunk could not only know about Kemp's dream but somehow influence and control it too? Not trusting himself to speak, he asked in his mind, *Are you sure he won't wake up?*

He was staggered to find out the keeper of the trunk had already read his mind.

Of course I'm sure, the trunk spat back, a hint of annoyance in its tone. *Kemp will do what I tell him to do. Right now, his sweet little dream is snowballing into a full-fledged nightmare he'd gladly wake up from, but he'll sleep till I wake him. I won't do that until you're ready. Now go . . . it's time.*

A wicked grin stretched across the thin man's pallid face, distorting his usually calm, controlled features. He bent slightly and removed a long-bladed dagger from the inside of his right boot. It wasn't nearly as beautiful as the jewel-encrusted work of art he'd used on his landlady; this one had a dull gray blade with a worn leather hilt, but it was sharp enough to cut through a steel nail and it felt real good in his big sweaty hand. He was sure it would do nicely.

"Yes . . . I agree. It's definitely time," he hissed between clenched teeth. Stepping from the truck, he headed for Kemp's front door. "Sweet dreams, you slimy bastard. Sweet dreams!"

Unaware he was merely a pawn in a twisted dream that had once been one of his most precious memories, Wilson continued down the staircase, following the pitiful cries of his frightened daughter. His little girl's cries for help seemed to grow fainter in the impenetrable darkness, urging Wilson to move faster to try and keep pace. He stumbled constantly, continually scraping and bumping his arms, knees, and forehead on the rough stone walls until he realized the design of his surroundings. It was a spiral staircase, like something out of a medieval castle: made of stone or rock, precariously steep, and tightly curving in on itself to Kemp's right. Once he had the layout visualized, he made much faster progress with far fewer bumps and bruises.

He never once stopped to wonder why such a staircase existed under his rented house or how impossibly long and deep into the ground it seemed to go. As with most dreams, none of that crossed his mind. For the moment, all he could think about was Amanda. He had to save her. Simply had to. If anything happened to her, he'd never forgive himself.

Amanda's shrieks were less frequent now, yet Wilson could take some comfort in the knowledge he seemed to be closing the distance between them. *Hold on, sweetie,* he silently prayed, not wanting to give his position away, yet hoping that telepathically she could hear his plea and know he was on his way to rescue her.

One more curve to the right and Wilson nearly scorched himself running into a flaming torch mounted at head level on the rock wall. Luck was with him; he avoided the flames but had to momentarily pause to recover from the blinding light assaulting his dilated eyes. When he'd adjusted to the changing light, he noticed the torch was barely hanging on an old rusted metal bracket. He easily pulled the two-foot-long torch out of its holder and was soon back in pursuit. The light was a welcome relief, sure, but if the situation warranted it, he might be able to use the torch as a weapon as well.

Around the next bend, Wilson pulled to a sudden stop, the breath sucked out of his lungs. Two steps down, one of the stairs had a small splash of blood streaked across it.

Amanda's blood, he thought. *Hurry, Wilson . . . hurry!*

He was about to jump over the stained step and continue on, but at the last minute he spotted something else on the stair—something tubelike and thin—sitting in the pool of blood. At a quick glance he thought it might be a plump worm sitting in his path, lying still, its flesh splashed red from the sticky mess it rested in, but Wilson knew better.

Oh my God! Her finger! The bastard's cut off my angel's finger!

Sure enough, one of Amanda's digits lay on the step, severed below the second knuckle. Wilson gently picked it up and held it in his shaking hands, gently, as tenderly as he remembered holding Amanda herself as a newborn baby. Tears of sorrow, frustration, and rage spilled down his cheeks, and he might have stayed there lost in despair but Amanda screamed again farther down the stairs, bringing Wilson's confused mind back into focus.

"I'm coming, Amanda," he screamed, not giving a damn if his adversary heard him now or not. "Daddy's coming!"

Wilson tore off down the stairs, hell-bent on getting his hands on the madman who had disfigured and tortured his sweet, innocent child, but had hardly made it ten stairs when once again a splash of crimson brought him to a stop.

Another puddle of blood.

Another severed finger.

"You bastard!" Wilson screamed, stooping to pick up another piece of his daughter. "Leave her alone! Please!"

Farther down, he found another of Amanda's digits, and then another. And then another. Every ten to fifteen stairs his eyes would spot a small circle of blood and his heart would break again as he stopped to collect more bits of his pretty little girl's hands. Why he stopped to collect them he didn't know. There was no way to put them back on, even if he did manage to rescue her. Deep down he knew it was a futile effort but he just couldn't leave them behind. He couldn't leave his angel alone on the steps, even if it was slowing him down and jeopardizing her life further.

Maybe the doctors can stitch . . . he thought, but stopped, not even able to convince himself. Best to just keep moving and not to think about the growing weight in his pocket anymore. Thinking would cripple him and ensure his daughter's grisly death. Right now, all he could do was put his head down and pursue this madman. Get his hands on him and make him pay for what he'd done.

The chase didn't last long. A few more curving steps and suddenly the staircase opened up into a small dirt-floor corridor. The hallway was completely bare, straight ahead, a sturdy wooden door its only exit. He couldn't help but notice the sign secured to the oak panel. Its large scrawled red letters were an open invitation he'd rather not accept.

It simply said: **WELCOME TO HELL.**

With no other options open to him, Wilson pushed his way through the heavy oak door and found himself standing in a large circular chamber with a high domed roof, the meager light reflecting from the torch barely revealing its apex. This immense room had been formed out of solid rock and its entire area painted in red, perhaps by the hand of Satan himself.

In front of Wilson, just off to his immediate left, a skinless man was shackled to the wall with heavy silver chains. He was nothing more than greasy muscles, raw flesh, exposed bones, and a grinning bloody skull with oversize bulging eyeballs that followed Wilson's every move. This grotesque man stood ramrod straight, clearly standing at attention like some bloodied soldier or sentinel and playing his weird part in this, licked his exposed teeth, clicked his heels together, and raised a bony hand to his forehead to salute a silent greeting. With a theatrical sweep of his skinless hand, the man stepped out of Wilson's way and bid him enter farther into the cavern.

The sentinel was hideous and frightening to look at, but what waited for Wilson beyond the skinless man scared him much worse. On the far side of the room, partially hidden in shadow, a monstrous man stood facing him. In one hand he held Amanda, and in the other a rather menacing stainless-steel meat cleaver, its razor edge stained red with his daughter's blood.

At least she's still alive, Wilson thought.

When Amanda saw her father she struggled to pull free of her captor, but to no avail. She cried for help, reaching out to Wilson with bloody stumps, which were all that remained of her once-delicate hands. Wilson tried not to look at her injuries because he knew it would be the end of him. Instead, he concentrated on the man-beast holding on to her.

This grotesque figure had to be at least seven feet tall

and easily 300 pounds. He was dressed in an old-fashioned magician's costume: polished black dress shoes, shiny black tuxedo with a silk bow tie, an extra tall black top hat, and a red silk floor-length cape. His mis-shapen face was hidden in the shadow created by the large brim of his top hat, but Wilson could clearly see a mouthful of frightfully long, jagged teeth.

"Who are you?" Wilson managed to ask. "Why are you doing this?"

"It's not what I want, little man," the deformed giant answered, his voice thundering across the room. "It's what the Heatseeker demands."

Against the wall, the skinless man began to rattle his chains and laugh. It was a high-pitched hysterical giggle that sent a chill down Wilson's back. He stopped abruptly though, when Wilson turned to look at him and sulked back against the stone wall wetly licking his teeth again, but thankfully remaining quiet.

"The Heatseeker?" Wilson asked, turning his attention back to the monster magician who'd spoken. He knew full well whom the cloaked figure was referred to but felt compelled to ask anyway. "What does he want?"

"Want? I thought you already knew. He wants your life . . . your eternal pain . . . your soul!"

The huge assailant had said all he intended to and surprisingly released his hold on Amanda, allowing her to take a tentative step toward her father. A brief spark of hope surged through Wilson before he realized the awful truth. He started to run toward his daughter, although he knew it was too late, and watched helplessly as the monstrous figure raised the deadly meat cleaver and, without hesitation, viciously sliced Amanda's head from her shoulders.

* * *

"NOOOOOO!" Wilson screamed himself awake. A cry so raw and anguished, it physically hurt his throat.

"NOOOOOO!" he screamed once more, ignoring the pain, still not realizing he was back in his stuffy bedroom and not in the bowels of the earth trying to pluck his daughter from the jaws of hell.

When the reality of him being awake finally dawned, he couldn't stop shaking. He lay curled into a ball, crying uncontrollably, still picturing himself trying to carry his daughter's bloody fingers. Never had he experienced a dream such as that—NEVER. Hopefully, he never would again. It had been so horrible; so damn real.

It took another minute and a few slugs of vodka to calm his shattered nerves. He eventually lay back down to try and relax, but was terrified he might fall back asleep. There was no way he wanted to sleep and risk returning to his recent nightmare again, so he climbed unsteadily to his feet and paced around his bedroom floor trying to make some sense of things. He wasn't quite sure what to do next when the front doorbell rang. It took him by surprise, the loud buzzing nearly stopping his heart. He glanced at the bedside clock and saw it was 3:30 A.M. Who could be coming to see him at this time of the bloody morning? Maybe if he just ignored it, they'd simply go away. It rang a second time though, and a third; the incessant ringing forced him to abandon his bedroom and go answer the door.

His legs wobbled like jelly as he headed down the hallway, his hands also shaking badly. Was this fear a lingering consequence of his terrible nightmare or did it have something to do with this early morning visitor?

Maybe it was a lack of proper sleep or perhaps vodka withdrawal. Most likely, it was a combination of all those things.

The doorbell rang again. Wilson uttered a half-hearted, "I'm coming, damn it . . . hold your horses," but doubted the caller had heard. A fiberglass hockey stick that had never been used was the closest thing to a weapon Wilson could find on short notice, so before answering the door, Wilson paused to grab it. He had no reason to believe he would have to defend himself, it could be his wife at the door for all he knew, but it felt good to have something in his trembling hands, just in case.

The front door was at the end of the hallway and could be reached in seconds, but every step he took seemed to take longer than the one before. Fear has a way of doing that, numbing the senses and slowing one's ability to function.

"What if it's *him?*" Wilson asked himself.

"It's not," he countered. "It can't be. Impossible!"

"What about the skeletons in the park, and the message stuffed in the skeleton's mouth?"

Good question. Wilson didn't have a snappy answer to negate that one. What if the Heatseeker really has found him? What if he's standing at the door?

Wilson slowly shuffled his way closer, his tightening fingers picking up slivers from the fiberglass stick. Ten feet away now, the doorbell continued its monotonous ring. His life had come down to this pivotal moment. For the last twenty years, he'd been living a lie, hiding from the horrors of his youth. If the Heatseeker really was here, there was nothing left to do but open the door. He'd been a coward for too long, and now he had nowhere left to run. The time had come to stand and fight. Offering one last silent prayer, he threw caution to the wind and yanked open the door.

To his utter amazement, no one was there. No one stood on the front porch, the driveway, or out on the street. Everything was quiet and desolate. Could he have possibly imagined it? Maybe the nightmare had affected him more than he'd realized?

Maybe I'm just going bonkers?

It was then he noticed the long-bladed dagger stuck deep into the wood close to the now-silent doorbell. Fear squeezed the air from his lungs and chilled the blood pumping through his heart. He definitely hadn't imagined the doorbell ringing; ample proof was right here in front of him. Someone had stood with this deadly weapon, prepared to carry out some foul deed had he answered the door.

With a bit of levering, he managed to remove the dagger and noticed a small card had been pinned to the doorjamb. The light had long burned out on the porch, so Wilson brought the offensive weapon and the attached item inside to examine them. When he did, he wished he hadn't. The long blade was frightening for sure, but it was the little card that grabbed his attention and caused his heart to start thumping crazily inside his chest.

It was an adult admission ticket to a magic show. A magic show that had taken place many years ago. A magic show that had changed Wilson Kemp's life forever. Holding the small, faded ticket in his badly quivering hand, he read and then reread the familiar words:

NAGS HEAD NORTH - BALTIMORE, MARYLAND
FIRE AND ICE
THE GREATEST SHOW ON EARTH
GENERAL ADMISSION: $10.00
MARCH 10, 1988

March 10, 1988. That date had transformed his whole life. In one night, he'd gone from stratospheric success with the world at his feet to a life of alcoholism, fear, and lies. The weight of secret memories and unpaid burdens brought him to his knees.

Only one person knew who he was. Only one person could have such a ticket stub in their possession. Only one person could make Wilson feel the unimaginable terror he was feeling right now. He could deny it all he wanted but, in truth, his worst fears were coming true. The Heatseeker had found him.

Although he realized the futility of it all, Wilson locked every window and door in the house. If the Heatseeker were in fact here in Billington, a few cheap pieces of wood and glass sure weren't going to stop him.

Nothing would.

Head spinning, Wilson returned to his bedroom and climbed back into bed with a bottle of vodka. He had no idea how any of this could be happening or how he'd been tracked down. More terrifying yet, was what might lie ahead for him and his family.

Susan! he thought, but his wife's image was quickly replaced by a vision from his recent nightmare, of his daughter reaching out to him with bloody, fingerless hands, asking for help and how he'd been unable to save her. *Amanda! Oh my God! What am I going to do?*

Wilson didn't have an answer and the pressure to do

something—anything—was too much for him. He wasn't strong enough to deal with this. Wasn't strong enough to deal with normal life, never mind this insanity.

Time was of the essence; there would be no need for a glass tonight. Wilson quickly downed the entire bottle before lapsing into a pitiful yet welcome drunken stupor.

CHAPTER FIFTEEN

· WE'VE ONLY JUST BEGUN

"I could have taken him out right then and there," the Stranger said, his voice quiet but filled with venomous rage. "Just wait for the door to open and WHAM . . . drive my knife right through his fucking heart!"

He took out his frustration on the pickup's steering wheel, lashing out and pounding it so hard the truck's horn stuck on, blaring continually as he sped across town, heading home. Being on the razor-thin edge of madness at the moment, he barely heard it, but the irritating noise eventually broke through the dark, angry clouds swirling in his head and he pulled over to unplug the horn beneath the hood. The last thing he wanted to do was to draw unwanted attention to himself. Taking a deep breath, he tried to calm down and regain his composure. When he felt capable of driving again, he fired up the old Ford and resumed his journey home. He was still furious, of course, but back in control for now.

"It's a bad idea letting him know we're here. Why do I play with him? Why? All I want to do is rip his throat out and be done with it!"

You already know the answer to that one, my friend, the trunk of secrets spoke. It talked in a calm, quiet, logical voice that abated the tall Stranger's anger, soothing his madness and bringing his potentially volcanic rage back down to a manageable simmer once again. *Killing Kemp will be sweet, but ultimately unsatisfying. If you simply let blind rage get the upper hand, we'll miss out on all the sweet suffering to come.*

We have a plan, you and I. A plan we are committed to, which is already reaping rewards. Kemp is already terrified and we've only just begun. Before we're finished with him, he'll be begging you to kill him to end his misery. Only then, once we've pushed him beyond his wildest nightmares, will he have suffered enough to be granted death. Trust me, when the time comes . . . and it will come soon, Kemp's screams of agony will more than make up for these delays.

The words were music to the tall magician's ears and they calmed him down sufficiently that he had no further problems on his drive home. A small, satisfied smile crept across his face as the trunk began showing him image after sickening image of Wilson Kemp's eventual slaughter. It was brutal and bloody, just the way the Stranger liked it. Chances were things wouldn't play out exactly like his visions, but he could always hope. He was just pulling into the driveway of his hideout when a troubling thought occurred to him.

"What if Kemp saw me, or saw the truck pulling away? If he knows our vehicle, he might try to find us. I know he's a drunk and a coward, but if he knows what kind of danger he's in—"

Relax, my friend . . . he knows nothing. He's already crawled back inside his bottle, I'm sure, so there's nothing to worry about. Everything is under control.

"Perfect," the Stranger said, easing the truck to a stop beside the side entrance to the two-story house. He had to learn to trust the trunk more; it had never been wrong before.

He carefully unloaded the trunk, one corner at a time, and moved it as gently as he could inside the house again. Placing it reverently in the center of the living room, he hoped he didn't have to move it anymore. Experience had taught him he needed to be in close proximity of the trunk of secrets for it to be able to communicate with him, but it was just too damn hard carting it around with him. Potentially dangerous too, now that Kemp was aware of their presence. The tall man shuddered at the thought of Kemp getting his hands on the power within the trunk. No, he could never allow that to happen. Safer to just leave it here in the borrowed house and do what was required on his own from here on out.

"Well . . . what's next in our grand master plan?" he asked, trying hard not to sound as impatient as he felt.

Have a look for yourself, was the trunk's reply.

Like an excited schoolboy, the Stranger was on his knees undoing the thick leather straps as quickly as he could, lifting the trunk's heavy lid. Inside, the trunk was empty again, save for a small 5"×8" picture of a little girl in pigtails with beautiful jade-colored eyes. The sight of her took the dark man's breath away, his heart already pounding inside his chest with excitement and anticipation.

"Kemp's daughter?" he whispered. "Yes . . . oh hell yes!"

He was starting to like this plan more and more.

CHAPTER SIXTEEN

KING OF THE CASTLE

Last night had been an abomination, a terrible blow to Peeping Tom's delusional, inflated ego. It would not be repeated. Even now, in the wee hours of the morning, he could hardly believe he'd been too scared to venture out into the night, choosing instead to cower inside his home like some frightened puppy. Puppy ... *bah*! He was the black panther, the hunter, the fearless predator. He owned the night here, and it was he who spread fear in this town. He couldn't let anyone challenge his supremacy here in Billington.

This crazy killer roaming the streets was admirable, even if for nothing more than his sheer audacity, but he was nothing to be afraid of. Avoided, for sure, but feared—never. The police would catch this madman soon and lock him away for a couple hundred years or so, and that would be the end of it. Billington would once again be his own.

In the meantime, nothing was going to keep him from prowling the streets, doing what he loved doing most. There were far too many succulent young bodies and depraved men and woman out there doing nasty things for his eyes only for him to shut himself inside. The extrawary citizens along with the increased police presence in the streets were all the more of a challenge for his considerable skills. When it came to nocturnal fun and games, police and sadistic killers included, Tom was still the king of the castle. No question about it—at least not in his warped mind.

Tom had stayed awake all night long, pacing the house, frequently watching the flow of police cars racing by his front window. The urges in his head had beat their drums for hours, demanding he go outside, but Tom had ignored them. He'd never disobeyed them before but his fear had trapped him inside his house, in a cage of his own making. In the early morning he considered making his move, thought about heading out to get some action, but it was already too late. The sky was getting lighter, the sun rising in the east and forcing him to let his frail alter ego have control of his body again.

It made him sick to think he'd acted like him last night: weak, cowardly, pathetic. Tom vowed it would never happen again. Afraid or not, madman on the loose or not, tonight he was suiting up in all his darkened glory and was heading out to regain his hold on this town.

CHAPTER SEVENTEEN

MISSING THE BUS

The telephone sat on the nightstand beside Wilson's bed, and when it rang near his ear it sounded like a thunderclap inside his aching head, a nuclear explosion startling him out of his drunken sleep and nearly causing him heart failure.

Wilson leaped out of bed, adrenaline pumping, head thumping, legs all rubbery, heart doing cartwheels, having no idea what was happening; only that something had scared the hell out of him and he was getting ready to run. It was a classic fight-or-flight nervous response to fear and it made him feel cowardly and foolish when the noise came again and he realized it was only the phone.

Idiot! he thought, trying to laugh it off as he reached for the receiver, but he pulled his hand back at the last moment, finally remembering what had scared him so much last night. *The dream . . . the staircase . . . Amanda.* It all came back to him in an instant, even the magic show ticket pinned by his front door.

The telephone rang again.

What if it's him?

That was crazy. If the Heatseeker was coming to kill him, Wilson highly doubted he'd call to say hi first. Still, it took him another two rings before he could bring himself to pick up the phone. He put the receiver to his ear carefully, like it might bite him.

"Ah . . . Hello?"

"Oh, you're home, Wilson? I was just about to hang up."

Wilson had been prepared for the worst, expecting it even, but was relieved to hear his wife's cheery voice on the line. "I'm here, Susan. Where else would I be? I just woke up and I'm feeling a little—"

"Just woke up?" Susan interrupted. "Christ, Wilson, it's nearly three o'clock in the afternoon."

Wilson didn't know what to say to that. "Really? I . . . I didn't think it was that late. I was just—"

"Save it, Wilson. I probably don't want to know, okay? I need a favor today. You up for it?"

"Sure. Anything, Susan. What's up?"

"I'm stuck at the mall and running late. Any chance you can pop over and meet Amanda when she gets off the school bus today? I'll be on my way soon, but I'm not going to get there on time. Just be there when she gets off the bus and walk her home. I'll get there as soon as I can."

"No problem. What time?"

"Soon. Let's see . . . she usually gets on the bus by three and it's not far. She's one of the first stops. About quarter after, I guess. Gives you about twenty minutes."

"Lots of time. I'll grab her and see you at the house. Take your time." As an afterthought, Wilson added, "You can always count on me, honey." He meant it as a bit of a light-hearted joke, but there was nothing but silence on the other end of the line.

"Just be there on time, okay?" Susan said.

"Absolutely." Wilson hung up and went to get dressed.

* * *

Amanda Kemp wasn't a huge fan of being in the second grade at Howard Avenue Public School, wasn't a huge fan of school at all, in fact, but she loved her teacher this year, Mrs. Czepek, and liked getting to hang out with her friends too. It was just the math and science and endless sitting around in her uncomfortable seat she disliked so much. She wasn't the kind of kid who liked sitting still. Besides, Amanda planned on being a rich-and-famous doctor when she grew up, and she doubted she'd need to know anything about math or science for that.

After the bell rang, Amanda knew she was supposed to head straight to the bus loop out in front of the school, beside the teachers' parking lot, where she would wait in line to get on board bus number seventeen headed downtown, in the direction of Riverside Park. Her mother had worried herself sick thinking she'd never remember the right bus number but it was no big deal really. Besides, there were only four yellow and black buses that ever showed up in the loop and hers was always parked at the back of the line. Anyone could remember that. What did her mother think . . . she was in kindergarten? *Geesh!*

Today though, she'd stopped in the hall for a minute to talk with her friend Emily Parker, who was telling her about how her parents had taken her to Disney World over the summer holidays and how fabulous it had been. Amanda had never been to Disney World, never really been anywhere because her mother didn't have much money for trips like that. Someday they'd go; her dad too, all of them together as a family, but for now Amanda was captivated just listening to Emily tell her what Cinderella's Castle had been like. Losing all track of time, she was still standing there gabbing when she noticed through one of the classroom windows that the buses were starting to pull away.

"Oh no!" Amanda shouted, waving to her friend as she ran for the door. "I'll miss my bus. See ya."

Outside, Amanda sprinted for the corner of the school but she wasn't the fastest runner and was weighed down by her full backpack. By the time she made it to the front of the school, the last bus—*her bus*—was slipping out onto Howard Avenue and rumbling off down the road. Amanda yelled and waved her hands in the air but it was no use; bus number seventeen had left without her.

"Ah . . . damn!" she said. It was a bad word; a big person's word, and she knew she wasn't supposed to say it but she was frustrated and didn't know what to do now. She'd never missed her bus before; not once in the two years she'd been taking it, since starting grade one when her mother had to begin a new job and could no longer drive her. "Maybe I'd better go back in and tell Mrs. Czepek? She'll know what to do."

Thinking about her teacher made her think of the staff parking lot next to the bus loop. School was over for the day, so there was every chance she might be already at her car getting ready to leave. Amanda had no idea what kind of car her teacher drove but there was only one way to find out. The last thing she wanted to do was stand around and let Mrs. Czepek drive away too. She could end up here at the school all alone for the night maybe, and the thought of that got her legs moving, a shiver of fear tickling the back of her small neck.

Before she'd walked five steps, a car pulled up beside

her on the bus loop. No, wait; it was a truck. A red pickup with a loud engine that sounded like it had seen better days. The driver shut off the motor and reached across the seat to swing open the passenger door.

"Hi, Amanda," the driver said, smiling at her in a friendly way. "You probably don't remember me, but I'm an old pal of your dad's. I was just on my way over to see him actually, when I spotted you standing here all alone. Everything okay?"

Amanda wasn't sure if she should speak to this man or not. Her parents and teachers had taught her to run away from strangers, and this guy certainly looked strange dressed all in black. Still, he'd known her name and said he was friends with her father. That had to make him all right, didn't it?

"I kind of missed my bus."

The Stranger put on his *oh shucks* grin, and layered on the charm. "Kind of? Ha! I did that a million times when I was a kid. It's no big deal. Hop in and I'll give you a lift home."

Amanda still wasn't sure what to do but what other choice did she have? Her ride home was long gone. She took one last look around to see if she could spot Mrs. Czepek but she was nowhere in sight.

"You said you knew my dad?" she asked, seeking reassurance but already moving toward the open door.

"Of course, sweetie. He and I were great friends once upon a time. Real chums! Climb on in here. I'll take good care of you . . . promise."

Satisfied, and filled with the boundless trust in adults of an innocent seven-year-old, Amanda Kemp climbed into the cab beside the dark-clothed man, and closed the door.

CHAPTER EIGHTEEN

BLOATED, DISEASE-RIDDEN ANTS

Wilson made it to the bus stop in record time. As soon as he hung up the phone with Susan, he'd done the mad dash into the bathroom, brushed his teeth while taking a leak, grabbed a fresh T-shirt, and was out the door hitting the streets running in minutes. He'd made it with lots of time to spare. Well, a minute or two to spare, anyway. Just enough time to try and catch his breath.

Woefully out of shape as he was, the run had done Wilson some good. After yesterday's craziness in the park and then last night's horrible dream, he needed to clear his head and get his mind off the Heatseeker and all the bad memories associated with that name. Tonight he'd force himself to sit down and make a plan of action about what he intended to do about this madman in town, but for today it had to wait. Susan needed his help and damned if he was going to let her and Amanda down. He'd done enough of that already to last a lifetime.

It would have been much easier for Wilson and Susan if Amanda's bus picked her up and dropped her off right out front of her house, but unfortunately that wasn't the case. She and all the other schoolkids on Derby Hill Road had to walk to the bottom of the street where it crossed Lincoln Avenue. It was only two city blocks and hardly more than a stone's throw away, but Amanda was still far too small to make the journey herself twice a day. She had a few older friends from the neighborhood who walked with her most of the time, but Susan wasn't ready to trust her on her own yet. Maybe she was being overly protective, but for now that was the way it was.

While Wilson waited, he tried to ignore some of the looks he was getting from the other parents standing at the bus stop, but it wasn't easy to do. Some would glare at him with disgusted scowls, while others just laughed, jeering at him with big dumb grins plastered on their faces. People loved to kick someone when they were down and although Wilson was used to it by now, it still made his blood boil sometimes. Who the hell were they to judge him? He was only here to pick up his little girl. What the hell was it to them? Like they'd never done anything wrong or stupid in their lives, right? Sure enough, one of the men had to open his trap.

"Wilson, my man," a fat man in a checkered golf shirt said. Wilson thought his name might have been Ralph, but couldn't remember. Didn't matter. "Heard you got yourself a magic act together?"

"Ah . . . yeah. I'm working on one. Just trying to make a living, ya know?"

"Sure, Wilson. I hear you. I bet you'll be great!" Fat Ralph, or whoever the hell he was, barely finished his sentence before bursting into laughter. Within seconds, some of the other parents were snickering too.

Ignoring them all, Wilson moved back away from the curb to wait under the shade of a huge maple tree and hummed an off-key rendition of ELO's "Don't Bring Me Down," a band and song Susan and he had loved back in the day.

They can only bother you if you let them, he thought. Good advice, but it still pissed him off. He was sick of being the town bum. Sick and fucking tired of people laughing at him. *Then do something about it, man. Clean up your act and no one will have anything to bug you about.*

Thankfully the big yellow bus came rolling into view along Lincoln, saving Wilson any further humiliation. The group of parents could pick up their rotten little brats and go home, leaving Wilson alone with his daughter. Susan and Amanda were the only things that mattered to him anyway. The rest of this town could go jump in the Allegheny River for all he cared.

The school bus pulled to a stop and the group of screaming kids started bursting out onto the side of the road like they were on fire, finally released from school for another day and chaotically thrilled about it. One by one the children's parents met or waved them over and everyone started scurrying home up Derby Hill. When the horde of kids ended and Amanda wasn't one of them, Wilson figured she was still sitting on the bus. She wasn't good with directions and maybe wasn't 100% sure which stop was hers.

"Amanda?" Wilson called out, walking along the bus, peeking through the line of windows to see if he could spot her but he couldn't. The bus driver started to close the door, getting ready to pull away, so Wilson screamed at him to wait a minute. Luckily the driver heard him and opened the door back up.

"What's the matter?" the driver asked. Turned out it was a woman, not a man like Wilson had presumed. She was a thin older lady with thick glasses hanging off her nose. Wilson had never met her before but she seemed friendly enough. She reminded Wilson of one of his old Sunday schoolteachers. "Missing someone?"

"Yes. My daughter. Amanda Kemp. Pretty little dark-haired girl; usually in ponytails. She's in grade two. I'm supposed to pick her up."

"Hmmm . . . think I know who you mean. She never got on here today. Maybe her mom picked her up?"

"No. Susan just called and asked me to come get her. Amanda's supposed to be on here."

"Oh Jesus. No idea where she is. She must still be back at school. You best go back and check. I'll put in a call for you but get your butt over there and get her."

"No, don't bother calling. I'm sure it's just a screwup. She's probably standing at the school waiting for me. I'll go get her. Thanks."

"Okay then. Sorry about that. We keep telling the kids they gotta be out at the bus on time. I can't wait all day, mister. Have a schedule to keep, you know?"

The driver swung the door closed and pulled the bus off the shoulder of the road and continued down Lincoln Avenue, leaving Wilson alone with a knot of fear starting to grow inside his belly. He wasn't quite ready to push the panic button yet, but he was damn close. Had Amanda simply missed the bus? Or had something happened to her? A series of images from last night's dream flashed across his mind, of him stopping on every tenth or fifteenth stair to pick up another of his daughter's severed fingers, and Wilson stubbornly refusing to leave any of them behind.

Mother of God!

Wilson started to run.

Please let her be okay . . . Please let her be okay . . .

Wilson repeated this prayer over and over as he ran

back along Lincoln Avenue and raced toward the school. He ran as fast as his weakening body would allow him to move; and then he ran faster. He'd never forgive himself if anything bad happened to Amanda. If there was a madman loose in Billington with revenge in his heart, then let him come take it out on Wilson. In his heart, he'd always expected this to happen eventually, and truth be told, thought he might even deserve it. Not sweet little Amanda though. She'd never harmed a soul.

Five minutes into his run, Wilson knew he was taking too damn long and finally came to his senses. He was considering trying to hitchhike but lucked out when a white and blue city taxi rolled by with no passenger in the backseat and loud reggae music blaring out the open windows. It was nearly a miracle finding a cab in this town. They didn't just cruise the streets like they might in a big city. This guy must have been out on a call and was on his way back to the depot or home. Wilson frantically flagged down the driver, and climbed in the cab's front seat.

Wilson immediately reached out and shut off the irritatingly noisy music and said, "Get me to Howard Avenue Public School, right now. Fast as you can!"

The driver, a young black man with a shaved head and a bushy goatee, seemed about to turn his reggae music back on, or at least tell his passenger to get in the backseat, but must have seen the desperation in Wilson's face because he just shrugged, said, "No worries, dude," and floored it. The young man weaved in and out of traffic like a drunken NASCAR driver, but that was perfectly fine with Wilson. The faster the better as far as he was concerned.

They made it to Amanda's school in less than ten minutes, but the ball of anxiety in Wilson's belly was growing larger by the second. His daughter wasn't there. They raced past the main building, swung around in the bus loop, and even drove onto the grass to get a quick peek at the school playground but Amanda wasn't anywhere.

"Wait here. Please, don't move," Wilson said, and jumped out of the cab without paying, and headed for the front door. He checked Mrs. Czepek's room first, but the lights were out and it was locked up tight. Mr. Dunham, the school principal, was in his office but he hadn't seen Amanda since lunch that day. He offered to help Wilson search the school and suggested calling the police if they couldn't find her, but again Wilson refused. He'd find her himself. The last people he wanted involved here were the cops. A lot of those guys hated him. He took one more tour of the halls and gymnasium but by this time was convinced he wasn't going to find her here at school. In the end, he returned to the taxi and climbed back inside.

"Take me to 549 Derby Hill Road, okay?"

"Sure. Have you lost someone?" the cabbie asked.

All Wilson could do was nod as the driver gunned the taxi back onto the road. He didn't trust himself to speak right now because he was on the verge of throwing up. It was definitely time to panic now; and he was. The pressure inside Wilson was building, the anxiety churning in his stomach, growing larger still and taking on a life of its own. It felt like he had a bellyful of bloated, disease-ridden ants crawling around inside him, biting him, and eating their way to the outside world through the walls of his stomach.

He's got her. I know he does. The Heatseeker has Amanda and I'll never see her again!

It was a terrible thought, but Wilson couldn't help but think it. Where else could his daughter be? He and Susan were Amanda's entire world. There was no one else who might have picked her up or invited her home with them—certainly not without consulting with Susan first.

The taxi skidded to a stop out front of Wilson's old house just as Susan was pulling into the driveway, arriving home from her trip to the mall. Wilson numbly thanked the driver for his efforts, paid him, and stepped out of the cab just as Susan was wrestling with the trunk of her Honda, several big white shopping bags in her hands getting in her way. She managed to slam the trunk shut and turned to face Wilson with a huge smile on her pretty face. In an instant, she knew something was wrong though, and dropped her grin.

"What's the matter, Wilson?" she asked, meeting him halfway across the front yard. "Why did you need a taxi? And where's Amanda? Don't tell me you forgot about her! Damn it, Wilson, I told you—"

"I didn't forget, Susan. She wasn't on the bus. Listen, honey . . . I think something bad—"

"What do you mean she wasn't on the bus? Oh my God! Where the hell is she?"

Wilson wasn't sure what to say. He couldn't very well tell her the truth, could he? Then again, how could he keep it from her? Their only child might be in mortal danger right now and all his secrets wouldn't do him much good if something terrible happened to Amanda. Best to spill the beans now and hope Susan, who was ten times smarter than Wilson on his best day, could think of something they could do to find her. Just as he was about to open his mouth, a cheery voice spoke off to his left.

"I'm right here, Mom. What took you guys so long?"

Both Wilson and Susan snapped their heads toward the house and there was Amanda on the porch leaning halfway out the front door. She was smiling and looked absolutely fine, other than pretending to be a little miffed at the moment.

"I've been here alone for ten or fifteen minutes now and I'm *starving* already. Can someone make me a snack?" That said, Amanda pulled her head back inside and the door clanked shut behind her, leaving her parents staring at the front door with their mouths hanging open.

"How did she get home?" Susan asked.

"I don't know," Wilson answered, confused as well, but more relieved than Susan would ever know. And to think he had almost told her everything about his past. "She wasn't on her bus. I took the cab to check her school but she wasn't there either. Nobody had seen her."

"Then how did she get here?"

"Don't have a clue, Susan. Let's bloody well find out though. Come on."

Wilson took a few of Susan's shopping bags to lighten her load, and together they raced into the house to confront their daughter. They found her sacked out on the living room floor in front of the television, a purple throw pillow under her head. She was watching an old Bugs Bunny cartoon and didn't look like she had a care in the world.

"Honey?" Susan began. "Daddy says you missed your bus today. That true?"

Without looking away from the show, Amanda said, "Yep. Sorry. Emily Parker was telling me about Cinderella's Castle and the bus kind of pulled away without me."

Susan and Wilson exchanged puzzled glances.

"Who brought you home then, sweetie? Your teacher?" Wilson asked. "I was worried sick about you."

"Why? I was fine. And no, it wasn't Mrs. Czepek."

Needing his daughter's full attention, Wilson walked over and shut off the television. "Who brought you home, Amanda? Mommy and I need to know."

"Your friend did, actually. I liked him. He was very nice. Funny too."

"Which friend?" Wilson and Susan both spoke at the same time, both knowing Wilson didn't really have any friends here in town.

"I don't know. He never said his name. He drives a big red pickup truck. He said you and him were friends a long time ago."

"What did he look like?" Wilson asked, the ants in his stomach biting and ripping his insides apart again.

"Tall guy. Kinda skinny with dark hair."

For Wilson it was as if the temperature in the room had cooled twenty degrees instantly. Susan asked him if he knew who Amanda was talking about, and he managed to convince her that he didn't, but it was a lie. He knew exactly who had picked up his daughter and driven her home.

An old friend, he thought, a shiver running down his back as a thousand bad memories fought for pecking order inside his mind. Susan would have noticed the look on his face eventually, and called his bluff, but Amanda had more to say.

"Oh, I almost forgot. He gave me something to give to you, Dad. Said it was important. I put it into my backpack . . . just a sec." Amanda tore off into the kitchen to retrieve her book bag, and came back into the living room with a white letter-size envelope in her hand. "Here, Daddy."

Wilson took the letter with a shaking hand. The envelope was sealed and had his name written on the front. With no other option, he tore it open and read the short one-line message typed on the center of the page. In bold capital letters, the message said:

SOON, THE ICEMAN WILL DIE!

Wilson froze for a moment, unable to move or think. If he'd had his wits about him, he'd have crumpled up the paper, ripped it to shreds, and destroyed it before anyone else could read it, but he didn't. Susan grabbed the sheet out of his hand and stared in puzzled shock at the cryptic message in front of her. Unlike Wilson, she had no idea what it meant or why it had been delivered to her estranged husband through their daughter.

"What the heck is this?" she asked Wilson, but he wasn't in any condition to answer her. His only thought was to get out of this house and get as far away from here as he could before it was too late. He couldn't stay with his wife and daughter another second—he'd already jeopardized them enough just by knowing him.

"Wilson?" Susan asked, shaking his arm. "What's the matter? You look like you've seen a damn ghost again."

"I . . . I gotta go, Susan. Right now." Wilson ran for the front door, knowing his fear was contagious and he was scaring his wife and daughter but he couldn't help himself. He needed to get home. He needed to find a place to hide.

He needed a drink.

Halfway out the door, Susan caught his arm, begging him not to run off. "Don't leave, Wilson. Please. You're scaring me. Tell me what's going on? Who sent this letter? I know you know him. Tell me, damn it!"

Wilson shrugged her off and was down the stairs heading for the sidewalk but his wife's sobs stopped him. He hated the way he was treating her right now and wished there was some way to keep all this grief away from her and Amanda. Neither of them deserved the black cloud that was descending on them, but there was nothing Wilson could do to stop it. He turned back to face Susan, but could only shrug his shoulders in defeat. No words came to him that could soothe her or make her understand. The truth would only make things worse.

"Who's the Iceman, Wilson?" Susan pleaded.

More afraid for his family's lives than he was for himself, Wilson finally admitted to a part of his past that he hadn't shared with anyone in over twenty years.

"I am, Susan. I'm the Iceman. You and Amanda have to stay away from me."

TUESDAY, SEPTEMBER 22

A PAST FILLED WITH STRANGE MAGIC

CHAPTER NINETEEN

LAST DAY

Wilson was spiraling down a cold, dark staircase collecting his daughter's bloody fingers again, when an incessant shrill thankfully brought him out of a deep, alcohol-induced slumber. He had no idea how long the phone had been ringing, but he was damn happy the person on the other end was persistent enough to hang on long enough to drag him out of his nightmare. The last thing Wilson had wanted to do was follow that dream staircase to the bottom and see Amanda decapitated again. His nerves were already shot without having to experience that again.

Sitting up and reaching for the phone, Wilson's eyes burned like they'd been dipped in lighter fluid, and his aching head felt like it just might explode if he was forced to endure one more loud noise this morning. He lifted the receiver off the cradle before it could send another needle of agony into his brain, but hesitated putting the phone to his ear. He felt nauseated all of a sudden and had no desire to talk to anyone today. He knew it was probably Susan on the phone and, to be honest, didn't want to have to lie to her about what had happened last night or why he'd raced home and drank himself into a deep sleep. Still, he'd already picked up the phone. It was a bit late to hang up now.

"Hello?" Wilson finally said.

It wasn't Susan.

"Morning, asshole!" the Stranger said. "Thought you could hide from me forever, did you?"

"Who's this?" Wilson said, simply to stall for time. Obviously he knew who was on the other end of the line; he just didn't know what to do about it yet. "Take your crank calls and go bother someone who cares. I'm hanging up now."

"You do . . . and I'll go slit your pretty little wife's throat. I'm parked on Derby Hill Road already, in fact."

Wilson badly wanted to slam down the phone and yank the cord out of the wall, but he knew there was no way he could do that. His old friend would keep his word and Wilson wouldn't be able to save Susan in time. "You can't be here," he said, fear constricting his throat down to a whisper. "It's . . . it's impossible."

"Is it now? You mean you *hoped* it was, but you were wrong, old friend. It's taken me forever to find you but I did. Now you're going to pay the price!"

"What do you want from me?"

"Everything!" the Stranger hissed. "More than I can ever take, but I'll start with your miserable life. Then maybe I'll move on to your wife and kid."

"You leave them out of it, you bastard. They've got nothing to do with this. They don't even know you exist. I've told them nothing about . . . about us. This is between you and me, and no one else."

"Is it? You sure about that? Maybe. I haven't decided yet. Either way, it won't matter to you. I'm coming for you, shithead. Today! I wanted to scare you first but I'm tired of fucking around. I waited too long to get my fingers around your lying, treacherous throat. Today is your last day alive. I'll be there to see you . . . soon!"

"Wait! I never lied to you. Not once. What happened to you was your own damn fault. You can't blame me for—"

But the line had gone dead, the silence on the other end of the line heavy, suffocating, crippling, a grand piano dropped onto his head from a thousand feet. Wilson couldn't take the receiver away from his ear, hoping his enemy would come back on the line and threaten him some more. Maybe Wilson could talk some sense into him. Maybe he could . . .

Today is your last day alive!

The phone dropped from his hand to the floor, and Wilson raced to the bathroom to be violently sick. He buried his head in the porcelain bowl for a long time, his hands shaking, barely able to keep his aching head up out of the foul water as his stomach heaved again and again.

CHAPTER TWENTY

DARK SECRETS

Wilson was still curled in a ball on the bathroom floor, halfway between sleep and death, when the front doorbell rang forty-five minutes later. Although his head felt like it were filled with concrete and his legs barely seemed to have the strength to support him, he somehow made it to his feet. He had no choice. The hair on the back of his neck was standing straight up and he felt like he either had to get up and be ready to fight, or close his eyes and wait to die. Coward or not, that was something he wasn't ready to do. Wilson wasn't worried about himself, but his family needed him to be strong and do the right thing for once in his life. If that meant taking on a madman, so be it.

But first, Wilson needed a weapon.

Back in his bedroom, Wilson went directly to his closet and quickly found the aluminum softball bat he stored in there. He and Susan had tried joining a mixed league several years ago, before Wilson's drinking had gotten out of control, but they'd never really fit in with the other couples and had only lasted about half a season. The bat had been stuffed in this closet ever since Wilson had moved out and rented this dump. He'd nearly thrown it away on half a dozen occasions but today he was damn glad he'd kept it.

In his hands, the heavy aluminum club felt pretty good and he took a few tentative practice swings to get a feel for it. He'd prefer to defend himself with a shotgun or maybe a Dirty Harry .44 Magnum, but he'd never been a big believer in firearms and had never bothered getting one. The bat would have to do.

The doorbell rang again.

I'm coming . . . you son of a bitch, Wilson thought, creeping as quietly as he could to a spot just on the edge of the front hallway. From there, Wilson could peek around the corner and see the door rattling quietly in its frame. The Heatseeker was trying to get inside. From his vantage point, Wilson could see the dead bolt wasn't even latched. In his rush to start drinking last night, he'd completely forgotten to lock the door. Inevitably, the second his eyes fell on it, the doorknob slowly began to turn.

Wilson pulled back into the hallway and waited until the Heatseeker was inside the house and quietly closing the door. Steeling his nerves, Wilson raised the baseball bat and lunged around the corner, ready to bash in his enemy's skull with one smooth strike.

"Motherfucker!" he screamed.

Susan was standing in front of him, shock and terror in her eyes, and she threw her arms up in front of her face to protect herself. "Wilson, don't! It's me!"

Wilson stopped his swing—but only barely. Staring down at his wife and contemplating what he'd almost done, he tossed the bat to the floor, dropping it like it were something slimy and alive. "I'm sorry, Susan. Bloody hell! I . . . I thought you were someone else. You know I'd never hurt you. Shouldn't you be at work or something?"

"Christ Almighty, Wilson." Some of the fire was back in Susan's eyes. "I'm going into work late. After last night, I wanted to see how you were doing, but apparently you've lost your freakin' mind. Whose head were you planning on busting open?"

Wilson had no answer for her. He felt like such a failure. Such a fool. "I can't tell you, honey. I can't." Tears welled in his eyes and he turned away from her so she couldn't see his shame. "You have to stay away from me, Susan. For your own good. Take Amanda and get as far away from Billington as you can."

"What are you talking about? Why? You're not making any sense."

"None of this makes any sense, damn it! You have to trust me though. Get out before it's too late."

"I'm not going anywhere, Wilson. Forget it. Tell me what's going on and I'll help you."

"You can't. Not with this."

"Try me. There's been too many lies lately. Too many secrets. I'm not leaving here until you tell me the truth. I'm your wife, for God's sake!"

"I can't tell you, Susan. You'd never believe me. It's total fucking madness and . . ." Wilson's voice dropped to a whisper, fresh tears pouring down his cheeks. ". . . and you'd never forgive me if you knew the truth."

Wilson broke down then, dropping to his knees in the hall, weeping into his hands. He didn't want her to see him like this, a drunken wreck, but he couldn't help it. Part of him hoped she would be disgusted by his weakness and walk out on him—but she didn't. Susan held him close and stroked the back of his head as she held him against her stomach. For a few blissful moments, time stood still, but then she broke their embrace and helped Wilson to his feet.

"Come on," she said. "Let's get you to the couch."

"Okay," Wilson said, allowing himself to be led into the living room and over to the ratty old couch he'd picked up at a nearby yard sale. "Man, I don't think I've ever needed a drink so badly in my whole life."

"And I'll get you one . . . of coffee. Couple of cups, by the look of those red eyes and the smell of your breath. And then we're getting to the bottom of this."

She was out into the kitchen before Wilson could object. Ten minutes later she was back with a large steaming mug of strong java, with cream and two sugars, just the way she knew he liked it. She let him drink the entire cup in silence, then refilled him another, not bothering him until she saw him relax a little and his hands had stopped shaking. That was when she pounced.

"Okay, Wilson. Listen close. I love you. I've loved you since the minute I laid eyes on you, I think. We've been through a lot of crap together. Some great times, sure, but a lot of nasty days too. Agreed?"

"Of course. And I love you too but—"

"But nothing. I've been beside you through thick and thin and now you have the nerve to try and shut me out. That's not fair. You tell me to take Amanda and run away? To where? Our entire life is here with you. We're a family, damn it, and families stick together. I'm not going anywhere, Wilson. Not until you tell me the truth."

Wilson put down his coffee and closed his eyes for a

moment. How could he possibly tell her the things she wanted to know? She'd hate him forever. Wouldn't she? Or was he underestimating her love again?

"I've been hiding things from you about my past. Dark, dark secrets, worse than you can possibly imagine, Susan. You prepared for that?"

"Anything, Wilson . . . as long as it's the truth."

Where can I even start? he thought.

"Okay. First things first. Everything you think you know about me is a lie."

CHAPTER TWENTY-ONE

THE GREATEST SHOW ON EARTH

"My name isn't Wilson Kemp."

"It's not?" Susan asked, already stunned. She wasn't sure what her husband might have to tell her but she wasn't expecting this. "I think I better take a seat for this."

"Good idea," Wilson said. "My real name is . . . or I should say *was*, Brendan Wilson. You thought I grew up in Ohio, but I really grew up in upstate New York, in a little place called North Tonawanda. It's near Niagara Falls. Everyone used to call me Wilson anyway, using my last name, so when I went into hiding I figured I'd use that as my first. I was used to hearing it and I wouldn't get caught staring into space forgetting my new name when someone was trying to talk to me. Kemp was the last name of a friend I'd had in junior high. I was trying to keep things as simple as possible."

"When you went into *hiding*?" Susan asked. "Jesus! Why did you have to hide? Did you rob a bank or something?"

"Do you want to hear this or not? Let me get it out before I change my mind, okay?"

"Okay. Sorry. I'll shut up and listen."

"Thanks. No, I didn't rob a bank. It was nothing like

that. But let me start from the beginning. I think you'll understand it better. Maybe.

"I was a bit of a loner as a kid. No brothers or sisters. Just me and my parents, and they seemed to have more important things on the go than worrying about me. I don't remember having too many friends, and we never took a family vacation. Not that I remember, anyway. Basically I was on my own. I did decently in school, okay grades, and it wasn't like people didn't like me. I wasn't bullied any more than any other skinny little kid, so school wasn't really the problem. It was after school ended and I had to spend hours alone waiting for my parents to get home from work and then waiting for bedtime.

"I started getting in trouble. Nothing major. I'd steal a candy bar at the convenience store, or pull out the carnations in our neighbor's flower garden. You know . . . stupid shit. I think I was trying to get my parents' attention, even if it meant negative attention. And trust me, my dad could dole out the negative love in bunches. I used to get the belt a lot.

"When I got a little older, maybe eleven or twelve, I broke into a car and tried to hot-wire it. I had no idea what I was doing and all I did was rip all the wiring to hell and cause a lot of damage. My dad had to pay five hundred dollars to get the guy's car fixed. One thing led to another and pretty soon my dad started locking me in the house after supper, to keep me out of trouble. He was convinced I was a bad apple and was destined for a jail cell but he was wrong. I wasn't a bad kid . . . I was lonely. I just needed attention. A friend, or a grown-up to spend time with me. Hard to have that though, when you're locked in your room every night."

"That's terrible, Wilson," Susan said. "I'm so sorry."

"Don't be. It was the best thing my parents ever did for me. Seriously. It directly led me to the one great love of my life . . . other than you and Amanda, of course. *Magic*. It started simple enough, with me just picking up a silly card-trick book while at school. I brought it home just to have something to kill some time with after supper in my room. I devoured it though, and every other book on magic and magicians I could get my hands on. I loved magic. Became obsessed with it, and before long I was putting on little magic shows at recess and trying to impress the girls with the things I could do.

"Eventually things like card tricks and making things appear or disappear out of a hat bored me. I was damn good at them, but what really excited me was escape tricks. In truth, I probably only wanted to figure out a way to get out of my locked bedroom. If I could become a great escape artist, my dad could never lock me up ever again. It was the perfect thing for me and although I was still young, I knew I'd found my calling in life. Handcuffs, ropes, straitjackets, boxes, safes . . . anything that could draw a crowd; I wanted a part of it. Houdini was a god to me. Blackstone too. I studied all the greats, and maybe it was arrogance, but I thought I could be just as good. All I needed was time . . . and a good mentor.

"I dropped out of school and ran away from home when I was sixteen. All I took with me was a small suitcase filled with T-shirts and jeans, and a couple of my favorite magic books. For money, I'd saved up nearly two hundred dollars doing odd jobs in the neighborhood and a paper route after school. I was smart enough to realize that wasn't a whole lot of money and it wouldn't last me long, so I didn't run too far. I ended up thumbing my way to Jamestown, New York, knocking on the door of Lucius Barber, a retired magician I used to see all the time at the state fair and on the local cable network. He was a hero of mine, sort of, a local guy who'd made it big, touring his act as far as New York City, performing live on TV and at Radio City Music Hall. His illusions weren't spectacular, but his escapes definitely were. In my corner of the world, Lucius was as good as it got, and I desperately wanted him to take me into his confidence and teach me everything he knew.

"I'm not sure how old Lucius was at the time, midthirties, I'd say; still fairly young. He hadn't been a working escape artist in several years though, and with his dark bushy beard and his large beer belly hanging over his belt, I hardly recognized him when he answered the door. Not wanting to waste his time, or my own, I told him straight out what I wanted. He had his doubts, of course, but once I'd performed my act for him, simplistic and raw as it was, he saw potential in me, and probably more importantly, my passion for learning magic. We talked for hours about the history of magic and again I impressed him with my knowledge of our profession's early greats; legends like Joseph Pinetti, Alexander Herrmann, and Horace Goldin. By the end of the first day, he'd agreed to take me in and put me to work.

"I hadn't know it then, but I wasn't his only student. The following morning I was introduced to another teenage boy named Douglas Williams. Doug was a year older than me and a hell of a lot better than I was. His sleight-of-hand tricks and one-on-one illusions were damn near brilliant. I'd never seen anyone that good and that fast up close before, and he was only seventeen at the time.

"Together we trained hard, and Lucius brought out the strengths in both of us. Doug stayed with his incredible talent for illusions, while I concentrated on becoming the escape artist I'd always dreamed of. Month after month we trained, year after year, both of us obsessed with our growing skills. We did dozens of small shows, performing at private parties, malls, outdoor carnivals, or wherever Lucius could get us booked. It was terrifying going onstage but we were good and were meant to be there.

"The happiest day of my life was the day Lucius handed me his entire collection of handwritten journals he'd spent a lifetime collecting and writing. Inside them were the really special illusions and escapes, the ones only masters of the art would even try attempting. That was the day I knew I had arrived as a magician."

"That's incredible, Wilson," Susan said. "Why would you hide all this from me?"

"I'm getting to that. Be patient a bit longer."

"Okay. Let me just refill our coffees." Susan ran into the kitchen and was back on the couch in less than a minute. Wilson had a drink from his mug and carried on.

"Back then, the popular magicians were guys like Doug Henning, and The Amazing Randi. David Copperfield was starting to make a name for himself too. Lucius was always looking for an angle for us, a way to get our foot in the door, and it was him who suggested we team up to give the crowds something they'd never seen before. Sure, there was Siegfried and Roy in Vegas, but what Lucius was planning was miles away from their family-friendly show.

"He suggested we go a darker route than most magicians had ever tried. Back in the seventies and early eighties, musicians like Alice Cooper, Kiss, and Mötley Crüe had taken the world by storm with their theatrical live shows, mysterious face makeup, and incredible pyrotechnics . . . so why couldn't we? No one said magic had to be boring, or that we had to dress up in black tuxedos and top hats. No, we were going to do it our way, with a show so dark and edgy we'd scare the crowd as much as thrill them.

"We worked on the show together, tried a million different things, but in the end we agreed on something called Fire and Ice. The deal was we'd wear masks to conceal our identities. You know those theatrical yin-and-yang masks? They're opposites of each other, representing comedy and tragedy? We used them but had them custom-made slightly skewed, a bit cruel and sinister. To the crowds, we would almost appear to be the same magician, and in our press releases we played that up even more, explaining how we were one magical entity, but polar opposites of each other, two halves of one bastardized soul . . . one the master illusionist, the other the master escape artist. Him, the Heatseeker . . . and me, the Iceman."

A chill ran down Wilson's back and he shuddered just saying those names out loud again. Susan noticed but remained silent, swallowing down her own taste of fear.

"The fans couldn't get enough of us, Susan, but more importantly, neither could the critics. We'd turned a magic show into a rock concert, and they loved us for it. I was twenty-one when we did our first full-blown gig, and we kicked ass, Susan. It was SHOWTIME and man did we deliver. Ha! We used to say that all the time. It's SHOWTIME, baby! I'd forgotten all about that. Anyway, we closed the night with my version of Houdini's

Metamorphosis, where I amped up the illusion by not only changing places with my assistant in a heartbeat, but did it chained up within a glass water-filled box. The reviews were off the charts, we had a full tour booked, and we were finally on our way. We'd punched our ticket to fame and fortune and it was only a matter of time until we started reaping the rewards."

"Oh come on, Wilson," Susan interrupted. "You guys couldn't have been *that* famous. I've never heard of either of you and you're obviously not rich and famous, so maybe you're exaggerating things a little, huh?"

Her skepticism didn't bother Wilson at all. In fact, he'd been expecting it. "Actually, no . . . and I can prove it. Just a sec—" He left Susan in the living room and went to his bedroom, to a box he kept hidden on the top shelf of his closet, wrapped in an old pillowcase. Taking the box down, he carried it to the bed and carefully opened the lid.

Inside, the first thing his eyes landed on was a small glass jug—Teflon-coated on the inside, it contained every magician's friend, Aqua Regia—a mixture of nitric and hydrochloric acids, one of the most corrosive liquids on earth, and a lot of magicians the world over—the serious ones—often kept some handy because it could eat through steel chains, metal locks, and damn near anything else it touched. In the James Bond film *Octopussy*, Bond is provided a fountain pen containing a mixture of this nasty acid, which he uses to cut his way through metal prison bars. Magicians used it the same way. In a tough bind, when an escape had gone really bad, potentially deadly, this clear liquid could be a lifesaver. Wilson set it carefully to the side. After all these years it might not be as corrosive, but then again, it might be even worse—what did he know? Best to be careful with it anyway.

Besides the acid, there were several mementos from Wilson's glory days as an escape artist; things like a pair of platinum handcuffs given to him by the chief of police in New York City, a first-place ribbon and medallion he'd won at the Erie County Fair talent show when he was nineteen, Lucius Barber's collection of magic journals, and the two other things he'd come in to get: a scrapbook of pictures and press clippings from back in their brief heyday, and one of the multicolored masks he'd worn during his final tour all those years ago. Wilson removed those two things, being careful not to smash the acid, put the box back onto his top shelf, and returned to the living room.

"Here, have a look at these." Wilson handed the items to Susan, who took them with trepidation. Just the sight of the white leather mask with a gold, red, and green distorted sad face printed on it was almost enough to make her believe everything her husband had said. Why else would he have kept this creepy thing?

Inside the scrapbook, she flipped through page after page of news clippings and press releases from all over New York State and the East Coast. There were pictures of Wilson and his one-time partner dressed in their ghoulish stage personas, their hands raised in triumph at the end of one performance or another. Mixed throughout were brightly colored ticket stubs and other promotional material like stickers and buttons; all of which prominently displayed the Fire and Ice logo.

"It's true," Susan said, closing the book and setting it to the side. "All of it, right?"

"Every word," Wilson said, taking a seat.

"Well, that explains how you pulled that great trick in the park the other day, but it still makes no sense. If you two were partners and on the verge of stardom, why did you have to change your name and go into hiding? More importantly, why is this bastard here in Billington all these years later, threatening to kill you?"

Wilson considered his answer carefully before saying, "The question isn't as much *why*, Susan. It's *how*. You see, there's something else you don't know. Douglas Williams, my partner, died twenty-two years ago in 1988. I'm being hunted by a dead man."

"But . . . that's insane, Wilson. Obviously you're wrong."

"No way. I wish I was, but I'm not. The Heatseeker died a long time ago."

Susan had no idea how to respond. She didn't like talking about any of this craziness but she felt compelled to ask, "How can you be sure?"

"Easy," Wilson said, taking his wife's hand in his own. "I was the one who killed him."

CHAPTER TWENTY-TWO

DIGGING UP CORPSES

"Don't stare at me like that, Susan," Wilson said, shocked at the look on his wife's face. "I didn't actually murder him, for God's sake! It was an accident . . . but I was the one who got blamed for it."

"What happened?" Susan asked, relieved to hear her husband wasn't a killer like she'd started to think.

"Well, our ride to stardom took a lot longer than we thought. We were still making headway and starting to make excellent cash but we couldn't seem to get on television like we needed to get national exposure. We were huge along the Eastern seaboard and in our home state of New York, but man it was hard breaking ground anywhere else.

"On top of that, Doug was starting to get pissed off I was getting the lion's share of the interviews, publicity, and applause. He was a brilliant illusionist, but people seemed to want more and more escape tricks, where the thrills and potential for blood and excitement were better. It was completely unfair; Doug was a far better magician than me, but there was nothing I could do about it and to tell you the truth, my ego was growing along with my bank account and I loved it. There's nothing like the roar of crowd inside a packed house when you've defied death for another day, and everyone there is wondering how the hell you did it. The adulation from the fans and press was intoxicating . . . addictive even.

"I barely noticed Doug was sliding into depression, and I might not have cared even if I did. I was young, and far too busy having a good time living the dream, you know? He started drinking a lot more and it messed with his illusions. Slowed down his mind, and hands.

"I can still remember the first few nights the crowds started booing him, unimpressed by a drunk in a creepy mask who messed up most of his tricks. I tried to talk to him, get him to lay off the booze, but he wouldn't listen. He started screaming at me all the time, nonsense stuff, or saying I was jealous of him and trying to steal all his fans. It wasn't true, I still considered him my best friend, but the bridge between us was burned, the gap in our relationship widening by the day.

"Even with our act spiraling out of control, I had no idea how bad things had actually gotten for Doug. In my heart I'd always assumed he'd get past it, sober up, and we'd carry on as always. Wasn't going to happen though. Doug lost his mind. It's the only explanation I have; the only way I can understand what he eventually did."

"What happened, Wilson?" Susan asked. "Did he try to hurt you?"

"No. Sometimes I wish he had though. It was the spring of 1988, March tenth to be exact, and we were on tour in Baltimore, Maryland. The Inner Harbor wasn't as touristy as it is now, but we still used to pack in the crowds there. Locals, mostly, but I think people came from as far away as Washington, D.C., too.

"Before the show, Doug came into my dressing room with two mugs of coffee and said he wanted to talk. I took it as a good sign he was drinking coffee, not whiskey, but it was all a sham. He'd drugged my coffee and laughed as I slipped off my chair and slumped to the concrete floor. When I woke up, I was alone, my mask was missing, and I could hear the crowds cheering wildly out in the concert hall. Part of me knew what he'd done but my groggy brain was trying to deny it, hoping Doug wasn't that stupid. I knew he wanted the cheers I'd been getting, but it wasn't until I heard Alice Cooper's 'Welcome to My Nightmare,' the theme music for the new escape I'd been working on, that I realized just how far off the deep end Doug had slid.

"The escape was called the Devil's Drill Bit, and it was the most dangerous escape trick I'd ever attempted and even I hadn't performed it live yet. In the trick, I would be chained and handcuffed to a thick wooden table while a huge six-inch-diameter spiral drill bit pushed steadily closer to me, aimed directly at my exposed chest if I couldn't get out of the chains in time. The drill was real too. Nothing fake about it. Solid steel and sharp as a razor. Once activated, I'd have about fifty seconds to get off that table. If everything went well, I'd slip off the table just as the spinning bit chewed into the wooden table and drilled a massive hole clear through it. If I didn't get clear of the chains, well . . ."

"Oh my God, Wilson!" Susan gasped. "Your partner was going to try it himself?"

"Yes. And Doug was a brilliant illusionist, no question, but he wasn't an escape artist. He could slip a knot or get out of some simple rope and chain tricks, but he wasn't trained to do the things I could do. He couldn't get out of the handcuffs, and I knew as soon as I heard the music he was in huge trouble.

"I raced toward the stage, hoping I could stop things in time, but the loud buzz of the drill bit whirling to life told me I was going to be too late. When I got there Doug was still trapped in the chains, the handcuffs still around his wrists and ankles, and the drill bit was less than a foot away from bare skin. The secret to handcuffs is you have to be double-jointed, or be able to dislocate the lower joint at the base of your thumbs, or depending on where you're cuffed, your ankles so you can slip them free. Houdini was a master at it, and I could do it too. He used to escape from straitjackets by dislocating both his shoulders. It hurt a bit popping the bones back in place, but it allowed a magician to do what seemed like the impossible. It was the only way off that table and Doug couldn't do it. He was trapped, as the drill kept getting closer and closer."

"What about your stage crew? Couldn't they shut down the drill? Pull the plug or something?"

"No, they all thought it was me. Doug was wearing my mask, and everyone thought I was just hamming it up for the crowd, waiting until the last few seconds before making my escape. The audience was eating it up too, cheering exactly like Doug had always wanted. Over the howl of the drill I could hear him laughing, clearly out of his mind and enjoying the roar of his fans right up until the drill bit dug into his chest and chewed his heart out in front of two thousand shocked people."

Wilson was about to say more but decided to leave it

at that. Susan didn't need to know how the geyser of blood had sprayed everywhere, the high RPM of the drill spewing bones, skin, and other chunks of gore across the stage and more than twenty rows out into the crowd.

"Couldn't you have helped him?" Susan asked quietly. "You knew he was in trouble. Surely you could have shut off the drill. Couldn't you?"

It was a question that had haunted Wilson every day of his life since then, a question he'd asked himself a million times as he'd lain awake in bed shaking from yet another nightmare reenactment. Vodka had been the only way to shut down those dreams, to push back those awful memories at least temporarily. No amount of booze had allowed Wilson to forget though, or to forgive himself.

"I couldn't, Susan. I don't know why. I was terrified, I guess, and I just . . . froze. No other word for it. I just stood there and watched that drill shred him apart, but I couldn't make my feet move onstage to help. You have no idea how many nights I lay awake wondering how my life might have turned out differently if only I'd done something . . . *anything* to try and help. Even if I'd failed and he'd still died, at least I could have lived with the fact I'd given him a chance. But I didn't. I stood offstage and did nothing. I've never forgiven myself, and neither did anyone else."

Susan took her husband's hand. It was sweaty, but cold as ice. "That's crazy talk, honey. No one could blame you. Doug lost his mind. He drugged you and tried an escape he wasn't trained to do. How can that be your fault?"

"I said and thought the same thing, Susan. Doug basically committed suicide, but some of the crowd had spotted me offstage and blamed me for not helping him. Right or wrong, our fans were fanatical and Doug had more of a following than he thought. People started screaming at me and pointing fingers and soon it was bedlam in there. Everything was covered in blood and people were crying and working themselves into a frenzy. They were heartbroken, shocked, and angry, and there was no one else to blame really. I barely made it out of that building alive. Wouldn't have, probably, if not for the police and emergency crews that showed up on the scene."

"But that's crazy, Wilson. There's no way any of it was your fault."

"Wasn't it? You sure about that? I could have saved him, Susan. Could have saved him easily . . . but I didn't. I let my best friend die, and I've been on the run, paying the price ever since. Now it seems he's come back from the dead to get his revenge. Part of me thinks I might even deserve it."

"Don't talk like that," Susan said, lifting Wilson's chin to look him in the eye. "You're a good man, and a good father, and we're not giving up. No way! We just have to find out who this clown is. Obviously it can't be your partner. The dead stay dead, Wilson. End of story."

"That's not what Harry Houdini believed. He always said if there was a way back from the grave, he'd find it and return some day."

"Well, last I checked, Harry's still dead too, so what's that tell you?"

"It tells me the Heatseeker found a way back before Harry did. I've talked to him, Susan, on the phone. It was him. For sure. Somehow he came back. I don't know how, but it's true."

"Jesus, Wilson!" Susan shouted, standing up to pace the room. "Stop it. That's insane and you damn well know it. It's impossible!"

"I understand that . . . honest I do, but there are things you don't understand. Doug was into the occult. Hell, both of us were, but he was into it *deep*! Meditation, Ouija boards, séances, self-hypnosis, lucid dreaming, mind reading, telekinesis . . . you name it; he was involved. Both of us believed in the power of the human mind, in a great untapped resource within all of us, just waiting for someone to swing open the right door within our subconscious and walk on in. I think Doug found it.

"There were things he could do, Susan . . . some illusions he pulled off that just weren't possible. Disappearances, mind-reading abilities, levitations. Things he wouldn't tell me about, things I just couldn't explain. You know that new magician people are raving about lately . . . Criss Angel? He's really good, but there's something about him that just isn't right, if you know what I mean. He's tapped into some power outside of this world. Can do things no one should be able to. Doug was like him, but even better. He terrified me sometimes, especially the more he started drinking. With magic . . . nothing's impossible, Susan. Nothing! He believed that, and so do I. He's alive, I know he is, and he's out there somewhere coming for me."

"Stop it, Wilson. You're scaring me now."

"We've got a lot to be scared about. I know you don't believe me, but you have to trust me and there's only one way I can think of to prove to you I'm right."

"How?"

"I know where he was buried. It's in Jamestown, New York, near where we trained at Lucius Barber's house.

Less than three hours from here. I never went to the funeral, but I know where he is. It's time I went back. If he's there, you win, and I'll call the cops or do whatever you want about this guy who's threatening me. Deal?"

"Okay. And what if he's *not* there?"

Wilson had no answer.

CHAPTER TWENTY-THREE

NIGHT FALLS FASTER

It ended up being after lunch, 2:10 P.M. by the dashboard clock, before Susan backed the Honda out of the driveway and she and Wilson began their trip to the Jamestown cemetery. They'd taken Amanda out of school early and left her over with the Hendersons, although she'd kicked up a hell of a fuss, wanting to come along on what she thought was to be a fun family outing. If only she knew the truth.

"Did you bring a shovel?" Susan asked.

"I brought a few tools, but no shovel. We won't need one where he's buried."

Susan had no idea what that meant but decided to let it go. "Are you sure about this?" she asked, still not convinced they weren't about to make a big mistake. Not only was this idea slightly crazy, but also potentially illegal if they were caught tampering with a grave site.

"Yes. I need to know, Susan. This is driving me nuts and I have to know what we're up against . . . man or monster."

"Monster? Come on, Wilson. Surely you don't believe—"

"If the Heatseeker has returned from the dead, what

else would you call him? I have to know for sure. We have to know. Right?"

Susan didn't answer. She didn't have it in her to argue with her husband but there was no way she was buying into his theory about who was threatening him. No way. Someone was out there, and from everything Susan had seen and heard, they were highly unstable and dangerous, but whoever it was, he was a man. Maybe a jealous ex-friend or a deranged fan, but there was no way the Heatseeker was Wilson's old partner, Douglas Williams. This was the real world and no matter how much Wilson had convinced himself he knew the truth, Susan wasn't going to accept it. She'd only agreed to come to help Wilson accept the truth and to keep him from getting in trouble. After that, they could start figuring out what to do about their *real* problem.

They rode most of the way in an awkward silence, something quite unusual for them but perhaps for the best. The tension was thick between them today; the stakes higher than they'd ever known and neither really knew how to deal with it. Wilson badly wanted a drink, of course, but pushed that thought as far away as his stressed mind would allow.

There are more important things in the world than alcohol, right? Right?

Jamestown wasn't far away, distancewise, but Highway 62 North onto 17 West, the route they traveled to get there, took forever to drive, the traffic crazy and the roads twisting and turning more like a roller-coaster ride than a proper highway. Still, they made decent time, uncertainty and fear urging Susan to drive faster than normal, pulling into the city limits bang on five o'clock.

Jamestown was an old industrial city that had a small-town feel to it. It had once been tagged with the lofty title "Furniture Capital of the World," but those thriving days were long gone, leaving behind a quaint, family-oriented community that was neither fast paced nor particularly boring. It walked a fine line between past charms and modern conveniences and would likely be described as "just right" by most of the 35,000 people who lived there.

Unfortunately, Wilson didn't share their enthusiasm. It had been twenty-two years since he'd last been in this city, but there were no warm feelings about returning, no nostalgic thoughts about better days gone by. No, all Wilson wanted to do was confirm his worst fears, convince Susan he hadn't gone completely loony, then get the hell out of this shithole as fast as they could. The sooner the better as far as he was concerned. In, out, gone.

"Where we going?" Susan asked.

"Lake View Cemetery . . . it's easy to find. Just head for the high ground. Take a right on Main Street. Should be a couple lights up."

Susan followed Main Street north, heading uphill until Wilson directed her to hang a right on Buffalo Street, then a quick left onto Lake View. The cemetery sat on one of the highest spots in town, and it was easy to see why it had been given its name. Looking directly west, the dark blue waters of Chautaugua Lake filled their vision, looking stunning under a late-afternoon sun that was slowly diving into the deep end of the lake and setting the cloud-covered horizon ablaze. Susan parked the car in the empty gravel lot and shut off the engine, but they hesitated getting out. Both knew there was no turning back now, but were stalling the inevitable.

"Ready?" Wilson asked, touching his wife's hand. He noticed his hand was trembling far more than hers.

"Sure. Let's do it."

Wilson leaned over and kissed her on the cheek, then got out to meet her at the front of the car.

Lake View Cemetery wasn't huge, by city standards, but it sure wasn't small either. Hundreds of rows of headstones spread out around them to the north and west, a seemingly unending pattern of marble, stone, and brass dominoes just waiting for the first gentle push to begin the chain reaction of destruction that would topple the lot. Finding one specific grave in this endless field wasn't going to be easy.

"This will take forever, Wilson. There must be ten thousand graves here. Maybe more."

"True, but you're forgetting something. Doug was pretty famous. Not everywhere, but here in Jamestown he was. If you go down to city hall, you'll find a picture of him on their wall of fame. This cemetery has a special section reserved for town founders, public officials, and other influential people who're buried here. We'll find Doug's grave . . ." Wilson paused to look around, then pointed to where a dozen aboveground concrete mausoleum-type crypts were grouped together. "Over there! Let's go."

The Stranger parked his borrowed truck several houses down the street from Susan's place on Derby Hill, pausing to wipe his sweaty forehead with the tail of his untucked shirt before climbing from behind the wheel. He wasn't feverish with sickness; no, it was the sweat of pleasures promised running down his cheeks, of soon-to-be-realized dreams, of unbearable anticipation. The waiting game was nearly over now and his excitement was building by the minute, making the tall man want to jump out of his skin and scream at the top of his lungs. He wouldn't do that, of course. He would stay in command of his dark desires, in control for as long as he needed to.

He'd taken a hot shower and was dressed much more appropriately today, having found half a closetful of men's clothes in the house he'd taken over. The clothes might have been Kathleen Pruit's dead husband's or perhaps just a former renter's leftovers; who knew, but they fit his tall, lanky body fairly well all things considered, and faded blue jeans and a beige button-down shirt wouldn't get nearly as much attention as his black leather outfit did.

Stepping away from the pickup, the Stranger began calmly walking toward the front of Susan Kemp's home, the madness and rage within him contained, but just barely. He forced a smile on his pallid face as he passed a neighbor outside watering her front flowers in what looked like her best Sunday dress. The young woman nodded and smiled back, then pretended to go about her business but the magician could see she was still watching him closely out the corner of her eye.

Seeing that Susan's car wasn't home put a dent in the Stranger's plans and he almost decided to call it off and return to his truck but he was sick and tired of playing this game of cat and mouse. The trunk of secrets might be enjoying the fear they were stirring up in this little community, but he just wanted to get his hands on the ultimate prize. Today was the day he'd been dreaming of for a long time, and nothing, not even a nosy neighbor, was going to deny him what he was owed. Seeing as he was already here, he may as well check to see if anyone was home. Maybe he'd get lucky. After all, it wasn't Susan he was here to see. It wasn't Wilson either.

The tall magician rang the bell three times, his anger building to volcanic proportion when no one came to the door. *Damn it!* They'd slipped by him again. He was close to putting his fist through the front screen when a woman's voice spoke from behind him.

"Excuse me," she said. Not surprisingly, it was the well-dressed nosy neighbor who'd been watering her flowers. "Are you looking for Susan?"

The Stranger cranked up his fake smile and turned on the charm. "Why, yes. I'm an old friend of Susan's husband and I'm new in town. My, you look awfully pretty today. Love that dress."

The neighbor took the bait, grinning sheepishly. "What, this old thing? Thank you. Didn't I see you dropping off Susan's little girl the other day? Not that I make a habit of spying, mind you, but I just happened to look out when you pulled up to let Amanda out."

Sure you don't, you gossiping bitch, the Stranger thought. *I'll bet there isn't a thing happens on this street you don't know about.* "That was me, all right. Like I said, I'm an old family friend. Say . . . you wouldn't happen to know where they are, would you? It's kind of important I find them."

"Actually, I'm not sure where Susan went. She and Wilson took off together a few hours ago, but I did hear her saying they had to pick up Amanda at school and drop her off at the babysitter's, so maybe the Hendersons can tell you where they went."

"The Hendersons?"

"Yes. Edith and Earl. Really nice older couple. It was me who introduced Susan to them, actually. They live over on Milberry Lane, about three blocks that way. Can't miss their place; it's the big stucco house on the corner."

"Why, thank you, ma'am," the Stranger said, the smile on his face genuine now. "You've been a huge help. More than you'll ever know."

"No problem. Make sure you say hi to Edith for me."

"Oh, I will. You can count on it."

Although it was still early, only 5:30 P.M., the sunlight was starting to fade as Wilson took Susan by the hand and led her toward the mausoleums. Wilson's grandmother on his mother's side, Annie Wilkins, bless her miserable old soul, had lived to be ninety years old, spending seventy of them living next door to the graveyard in North Tonawanda they eventually buried her in. She used to tell Wilson when he was a kid that night always falls faster in a cemetery, so he'd better keep his eyes on the sky and his wits about him or he'd end up lost in the dark with a bunch of dead people. Annie was crazy as a bedbug by then, of course, and Wilson had tried his best to ignore everything she said, but looking at the rapidly darkening sky tonight he thought maybe the old bird wasn't far off the mark with that one.

Murky clouds the purple-black color of fresh bruises were settling in over Jamestown for the night, threatening rain soon. Wilson hoped they'd hold off until they'd at least had a chance to check out what they needed to. The wind was picking up a little too, a chill in the air just enough to remind everyone that summertime was officially over.

Together they walked, slogging through deep emerald green grass badly in need of cutting, stirring up the late-season mosquitoes into a feeding frenzy around their feet. There were also freshly fallen leaves underfoot that cracked with the sound of pulverized bones, but none of these things bothered Susan and Wilson. Not the clouds, or the wind, or the bugs, or the leaves—they had their minds on the task at hand, both silently wondering what they might find in the next few minutes.

But first they had to find the Heatseeker's grave.

As it turned out, the small mausoleums containing the remains of Jamestown's elite unexpectedly held more than one body. They were bigger than they'd first appeared from the parking lot too, each memorial the size of a large backyard shed and holding upward of a dozen people, all interred within their own concrete slots in the walls. On the outside four walls were the brass or matching concrete doors identifying the person inside. These small doors were sealed shut once the caskets had been slipped into their final resting place and that was how they were intended to stay. Susan and Wilson decided to split up and walk around each building, checking all the nameplates individually. Wilson spotted the one they were looking for long before he was close enough to actually read the name on the door.

"There it is, Susan. Over there, bottom row."

"How do you . . ." she started to say, but then saw what Wilson had already spotted. Fear closed off her throat and wouldn't let her finish her sentence.

On the bottom row of the next mausoleum to their left, one of the nameplates said:

GONE BUT NOT FORGOTTEN:
DOUGLAS ADAM WILLIAMS
1962–1988

The door was slightly but noticeably crooked, the seal around it broken at some point in the past. When Wilson and Susan walked nearer, they could see someone had shabbily repaired the damage, and tried to reseal the crypt, but even to their untrained eye, it was obvious the mortar used around the door was different than all the other doors, a different shade of gray and much fresher, and the person who had applied it had no idea what they were doing.

"Someone opened this wall up, Wilson," Susan said, her voice quiet but still loud in the silent graveyard.

"Yeah. Definitely. They weren't careful about it either. Smashed the crap out of it and half-assed fixed it later. I'm gonna need my tools."

"What? Why? You're not going to do what I think you are I hope?"

"You have a better idea? We have to know if he's still in there, Susan. There's no other way to know the truth. Stay here. I'll be right back."

"Wilson you can't . . . wait!" Susan tried, but before she could argue, Wilson was running back up the hill toward the parking lot and digging around in the Honda's small trunk. He returned a few minutes later, out of breath and white as a ghost, with a crowbar and a mini sledgehammer.

"Don't do this, Wilson," Susan pleaded, her hope that this trip would put an end to her husband's fears all but gone now. "You'll end up in jail, for God's sake!"

"I have to know the truth, damn it! We need to know, so stand back. This won't take long."

Wilson moved in close and it only took three smacks of the sledge for the steel bar to work its way deeper into a crack in the seal. The ringing noise was loud, but not as bad as he'd expected. He set the hammer aside and, using all his weight as leverage, pulled down on the crowbar. The crack along the top edge of the door split farther. Wilson worked the bar loose and repeated the same steps on both sides of the door as well, and the fourth time he threw his weight against the bar, the seal broke and the small door snapped open. Instead of falling to the ground as Wilson had thought it might, the door lay down flat on hinges set into the bottom edge.

"Hurry, Wilson," Susan said. "We gotta get out of here before someone shows up."

"I know . . . I know," Wilson said, crouching down low to the ground to try to look inside the chamber. There was a faint unpleasant smell inside the shaft, but it was more of a musty, stale smell than anything rotting or decayed. "Hmmm . . . well there's his coffin. Pretty tight fit. Might be hard to get it out."

"Get it out? What? The coffin? No way. He's obviously still there, Wilson. Haven't you seen enough?"

"Not yet." Wilson reached inside and gave the handle a yank, just to test it out, and was surprised when the casket moved about an inch. Obviously there were rollers either on the coffin, or inside the concrete slot. "Wait, it's moving! Just give me a sec."

With a mighty pull, Wilson rolled the casket halfway out if its concrete enclosure, making sure he stopped its progress before it reached the tipping point. The last thing he wanted was for the entire box to dump out onto the grass and burst open at their feet. Just to be sure, he pushed the coffin back in a few inches, not needing it exposed that far anyway, because this particular casket had a duel-hinged lid with a section that lifted to reveal just the head and torso of the person within.

Wilson wasn't exactly sure how to open a sealed coffin, having no idea how the morticians went about locking them in the first place, but it only took him a glance to see that it wouldn't matter.

Doug Williams's casket wasn't locked.

Not anymore, anyway. Once it surely must have been, but there were deep scratches and part of a broken brass latch hanging on the side of the coffin from where someone had repeatedly hammered their way inside. Whoever had broken into the crypt chamber hadn't been satisfied just getting inside, they'd apparently went all the way and broke into the locked coffin as well.

Was someone else here before us? Wilson wondered. *Something very weird is going on here.*

"Stand back," Wilson told Susan. "Whatever's left inside here . . . you don't need to see it." Susan couldn't agree more, and stepped back out of the way.

Wilson took a deep breath, steeling himself for what he might find. Part of his mind was envisioning seeing the skeletal skull of his old friend grinning up at him, a few straggly clumps of hair clinging to Doug's head as dozens of scavenger bugs crawled in and out of his mouth and open nasal cavity. The other part of him was convinced the casket would be empty, nothing to see but silk sheets with the dirty, greasy stains showing where a man's body had once been laid to rest. Wilson wasn't sure which he was hoping for more.

The top half of the lid lifted easily, silently gliding on unseen hinges as quietly as the day it had first been closed over twenty years ago. Looking inside, Wilson was relieved and terrified at the same time. Relieved, because now he finally knew he wasn't going crazy. Terrified, because the inside of the coffin was empty.

The Heatseeker was gone.

CHAPTER TWENTY-FOUR

PICK A CARD ... (REDUX)

Edith Henderson was just about to cut the first slice of one of her famous homemade cinnamon-apple pies, fresh out of the oven, when the front doorbell rang. She and Amanda had been baking all afternoon, having a grand time together, but they were both covered in flour and not exactly as presentable for guests as she would have liked.

"Oh dear," Edith said. "Who on earth could that be? And just look at me. I'm a fright. Could you go see who it is, honey, while I wash my hands?"

"Sure, Mrs. H," Amanda said, content to just wipe her equally messy hands on the front of her pink T-shirt as she headed for the door.

She could never understand why grown-ups always worried so much about how they looked. Amanda liked to look nice too, but heck, it was only a little bit of flour and she thought Mrs. H looked just fine for an older gal. Still, she didn't mind helping out and she'd been having a lot of fun today helping Mrs. Henderson out in the kitchen. Her mother rarely had time to bake anything anymore; she worked too much, so it was cool getting a chance to get her hands into a gooey bowl of batter and help roll the pie crust. By the wonderfully yummy smell of cinnamon and baked apples wafting through the house, she was also really looking forward to helping eat their hard work too.

Amanda noticed that Earl Henderson, Edith's husband, was fast asleep on the couch as she walked past the living room, his snores so loud she was surprised they'd been able to hear the doorbell even ring. *Old people sure sleep a lot too,* she thought. *I hope I never get old. Doesn't seem like much fun at all.*

When she opened the heavy wooden door a little, just enough to get a peek, Amanda recognized the dark-haired visitor on the other side of the screen door as her dad's old friend. The guy who'd given her the ride home from school yesterday. Her mother had been mad at her for some reason, telling her she should never talk to strangers, much less get in a car with them, but Amanda didn't understand what the big deal was. First off, it had been a truck, not a car, and he wasn't a stranger—not really—he was one of Dad's old friends. Didn't that make things all right? Amanda couldn't remember his name, or even if he'd ever told her what it was, but she'd never forget how funny he was, or his pale, skinny face. He was the type of guy who looked hungry all the time, like he needed to eat a few bacon cheeseburgers, or better yet, a few slices of Mrs. H's apple pie.

The tall man smiled down at her, gave a quick little military salute, and said, "Hi, toots. Long time no see."

Amanda giggled. Now this older guy she kind of liked. He was always smiling and trying to make her laugh. "Hello yourself. What are you doing here?"

The man was about to answer when Mrs. Henderson came to the door behind Amanda. She'd washed her hands and face and removed her flour-covered apron, getting as presentable as she could in a hurry. "Who's there, sweetie?" she asked, opening the front door a little farther to see for herself.

"I don't know," Amanda said. "He's a friend of Dad's. That's all I know. Maybe he can come in and have some pie with us. He's awfully skinny. You hungry, mister?"

"Why, yes, as a matter of fact I am." The Stranger made a move to open the screen door, presumably intending to walk inside, but the screen was locked.

"Just a second," Edith said to the man outside, giving him a rather stern look, then turned to bend over beside Amanda. "Can you go wake up Earl, honey? Tell him his pie is ready. Thanks." When Amanda ran off into the living room, Edith addressed the odd-looking man outside again. He had one of those lean, muscular bodies and gaunt faces that made it nearly impossible to guess his age. He could be anywhere from late forties into his sixties and there was just something sinister about his overly friendly smile that set off her alarm bells. "No offense, sir, but I'd prefer if you stayed where you are. I've never met you before and I'm not in the habit of letting strangers into my home. What is it you want, anyway, Mr. . . . ?"

"Mr. Black, ma'am, and I totally understand," the dark magician said, his face never betraying the rage burning inside of him. He so badly wanted to kick in this flimsy screen door and beat this old bitch's face against the newel post behind her. He wanted to watch her teeth splinter onto the rug, the bones of her face snap into dozens of sharp fragments, and smell her soggy gray brain as her skull finally caved in, spraying buckets of blood against the stairs and hallway wall. Instead of doing that, he calmly said, "Sorry for being so presumptuous,

I'm a friend of the family you see, and darling little Amanda invited me in—"

"Well, Amanda is a bit too sweet for her own good. You still haven't told me what you want?"

"Of course. I'm trying to find Wilson. Susan's neighbor suggested I try here. I missed him the other day when I drove Amanda home from school and I'm looking forward to catching up on old times. Been a long time. Call it a reunion of sorts."

"Well, he's not here. Susan and him had some important business in Jamestown this afternoon. Earl and I are just looking after Amanda."

The mention of Jamestown certainly caught the Stranger by surprise. Stopped him cold, in fact, his practiced smile slipping for a moment. *Why would they go there?* Recovering quickly, he said, "Oh . . . okay. Did they say when they'd be coming back?"

"They weren't sure, but said they wouldn't be late. Probably by eight or nine o'clock, but that's a guess."

"No worries. Thanks. Ahh . . . any chance I can come in and wait for them. I don't really have anywhere else to—"

"No," Edith quickly interrupted. Her alarm bells didn't ring often, but when they did she was smart enough to listen. Something wasn't right about this man. "I don't think that's a good idea. I'll tell him you stopped by and you can check with him later tonight at his place."

Edith started to close the door, but the Stranger said, "Wait . . . wait! I think you've got me all wrong, ma'am. I'm a friend of Wilson's. We were both magicians back in the day. Good ones too. Here . . . let me show you a card trick. It's a beauty!" The Stranger produced his special oversize deck seemingly out of thin air and fanned out the cards in front of Edith's face. "Pick a card, ma'am . . . any old card. I'm not here to cause any trouble."

"Glad to hear that, Mr. Black, but I'm not interested in your silly card tricks. I've already told you Wilson isn't here, so I'd appreciate it if you left now. Either that, or I'll have Earl call the cops. Understand?"

"Perfectly," the Stranger said, but the smile was sliding from his face, the pin holding his insanity in check slowly working itself loose somewhere deep within him. He was so tired of playing games with people, so fucking weary of trying to appear calm and happy when every fiber of his body wanted nothing more than to beat, crush, and destroy everything in sight.

The smug look of superiority on this old bag's face was the final straw, the meltdown to end all meltdowns building to the point where there was no turning back, even if he'd wanted to. "Edith, you old cunt . . ." he shouted, giving in to the rage entirely. In one smooth motion he returned the cards to his pocket with one hand and produced a large serrated dagger with the other. He showed the hunting knife to the shocked woman, then pressed his face tight against the locked screen door. Whispering now, he said, *"It's SHOWTIME, baby!"*

Susan saw the blank look on Wilson's face and came over to look inside the casket for herself. She prepared herself to see a ghastly skeleton decomposing toward dust, but wasn't expecting to see only rumpled silk sheets. "It's empty," she said, stating the obvious because she couldn't think of anything else to say.

"I warned you, didn't I?"

"But where did it go? Who took him?"

"What makes you so sure someone took him? Take a look at the inside of the coffin . . . it's all ripped to shreds. Maybe he clawed his way out himself?"

"What? I know this is crazy shit, Wilson, but don't go off the deep end on me. That's not possible and I can prove it. Look at how tight that casket fits into the concrete slot. There's no way of opening the lid once its slid into place inside there. No way to get to the sealed door to claw out of anything. Right?"

"Wrong, actually. You're not going to like this but I know this coffin. I've laid in it before—one just like it anyway. It was part of our show. Look . . . it has brass lettering on the end here. F. A. I. it says. That stands for—"

"Fire and Ice?" Susan guessed.

"Exactly. When we did outdoor shows I used to do an escape where I was buried alive in concrete, or sometimes just plain old dirt or mud. They chained and locked me inside the coffin, lowered me into the ground, then filled up the hole. With all that weight on the coffin lid, there's no way for anyone to open the lid and get out, which is why we had these ones designed with a secret door on the end. Watch this . . ."

Wilson reached inside the coffin beneath the torn silk pillow and found what he was looking for. "If I hit this release button, it should . . ." The end of the coffin nearest Susan fell over, allowing her to see all the way to the feet end of the box. "There. See?"

"So they buried your partner inside one of your props? Big deal. A coffin is a coffin. Probably saved a lot of money. What you keep forgetting is Doug's dead. You can't push secret buttons and smash open concrete vaults when you're dead, Wilson. You can't just get up and walk away after laying in a bloody box for decades either. For Christ's sake, get a grip, will you? Some maniac has dug your partner's bones up, sure, that's obvious, and it might be the same lunatic that's threatening you back home but it's not Doug Williams. It's just *NOT*!"

"I know how silly it sounds. Trust me, I do. But you've got to believe me. I wasn't sure myself until I saw our show initials on here. Now I'm positive I'm right. Hell, I spoke to him on the phone, Susan. It was *him*! I'd know Doug's voice anywhere. Here . . . look at the silk sheets. They're all ripped up . . . clawed to shreds from the *inside*, damn it! How do you explain that?"

Susan couldn't, or didn't want to. She'd had enough and wanted no more of this conversation. "Can we put this coffin back in its hole and go home now? Please? Before the police show up to drag us to jail?"

Wilson recognized that harsh tone of voice and knew when he was beaten. It was the same voice she used to chastise him about drinking. "Sure, Susan. Whatever you want." Sulking slightly, he stuffed the vacant coffin back inside the concrete chamber and closed the hinged door as best he could. It didn't look pretty and someone would notice it easy enough if they bothered to look, but they'd be long gone by then. Wilson hoped so, anyway.

Carrying his tools, Wilson followed his wife to her car, put the hammer and crowbar in the trunk, and climbed into the passenger seat. Susan was already on the phone when he sat down. "Just checking in with Edith and Earl," she whispered, the phone pressed to her ear, ringing in the background.

"Good idea. Let them know we'll be home in a couple hours. What time is it, anyway? Maybe we can stop for a coffee?" Wilson felt Susan go rigid beside him, her knuckles cracking from holding the cell so tightly. When he glanced up, he was taken aback at how pale and frightened Susan looked. "What's the matter?"

"There's no answer. Ten rings now. Eleven. Why wouldn't they answer? Edith told me they were just going to stay home and do some baking."

"I . . . I don't know," Wilson said, a cold sweat taking over his body as a very bad thought started to form in his head. "Maybe Earl took them out for supper?"

Both Wilson and Susan looked outside and down the hill toward the group of concrete mausoleums, where one of the vaults held one less famous tenant than the cemetery officials believed.

"Oh shit!" Wilson said. "Start the car, Susan, and get us home as fast as you can."

The Stranger was back to smiling as he slammed his mighty black boot into the locked screen door frame, ripping the flimsy barrier off its hinges and sending wood shrapnel everywhere. The scream that came out of Edith Henderson's throat, raw and piercing enough to shatter glass, greatly improved his foul mood.

Mrs. Henderson tried to make a run for the second floor, dashing as fast as her old legs could carry her up the staircase. She wasn't nearly fast enough though—the Stranger catching her a third of the way upstairs, cleanly severing the old dame's Achilles tendon just above her left heel with a wicked swipe of his dagger. With his weight holding her down, he sliced the right tendon too.

Ha! That'll slow the bitch down.

"How do you like me now, Edith?" the Stranger

asked as Mrs. Henderson cried out in excruciating pain. He slapped her on the ass as hard as he could, enjoying every second of this. "Not so fucking smug now, are you?"

"Drop the knife and hold it right there, freako!" Earl Henderson shouted from behind the Stranger, standing at the bottom of the stairs. His voice was a bit shaky with fear, but the hand in which he held the .38 caliber trained between the Stranger's shoulder blades was steady as a rock. In fact, he'd have fired by now, with no hesitation, if he wasn't so worried about hitting Edith. He'd been in the army for sixteen years, a hunter all his life, and had been target and skeet shooting for the last thirty years down at the local gun club in town. Earl was a good shot and knew he wouldn't miss from this range, but he was concerned the bullets would pass through the tall man and hit his wife behind him. As soon as Amanda had woken him up off the couch and he'd heard his wife arguing with someone outside, he'd headed immediately to his office on the main floor to his gun cabinet where he kept his Smith & Wesson military-issue handgun, just in case. Turned out his instincts had been right. "One wrong move, fella, and I'll put a half dozen bullets in your skull."

Doubtful, pops, but I admire the effort.

"Okay . . . okay. Relax. I give up," the Stranger lied, turning quickly to face Earl, and with a lightning-quick flick of his wrist hurled the blood-smeared blade all in one motion.

The dagger flew true and deadly, catching Earl in the left eye and sinking at least six inches into his brain. Earl was dead before the blade stopped moving, the knife switching off his life as fast as flicking a light switch, but his finger didn't know it yet, spasming and firing the .38 Special twice before his body collapsed backward into the front hallway. The bullets both went high, burying into the plaster walls at the top of the stairs, but the last one came so close the Stranger felt it part through his hair, nearly finding its mark.

The Stranger casually walked down the stairs and tugged his dagger free from Earl's skull. His eyeball came with it, split down the middle and running onto the Stranger's hand like an undercooked boiled egg. The dark magician wiped the blood and gore onto his pant leg and was about to go search for the little girl when a ceramic vase hit him in the side of the head, causing him to see tiny dots of light in his vision, nearly bringing him to his knees. Something else banged painfully against his shoulder and he looked down to see a hardcover book lying at his feet.

"What the fuck!" he said, looking up, surprised to see that the old woman, despite her injuries, had somehow managed to climb to the top landing and was throwing everything within reach down on him. She was loading up to throw a cordless telephone at him next, which he easily ducked now that he was onto her.

"Some people just don't know when to quit," he said, climbing the stairs to take care of the problem.

Edith screamed and tried to stand up but there was no way she was walking anywhere. Knowing she was about to die, as a last-ditch effort she launched her considerable bulk off the top stair and tried to take the Stranger out too as he made his way toward her.

Surprised for sure, but not unprepared for her trying to defend herself, the Stranger tensed for the inevitable collision and turned to push Edith's bulk to the left as they hit. She managed to scratch the side of his face on the way past, drawing blood, but he shoved her body off course just enough to drive her out over the open wooden railing. Edith's body landed on the banister but flipped out into open air, about to plunge headfirst toward the hardwood floor below. The powerful magician caught her before she fell though, grabbing her by her already grievously injured ankles. With incredible strength and effort, he managed to hold her suspended upside down like that, enjoying the way she shrieked as the severed tendons and muscles in her heels snapped further, blood pouring out her wounds now, gravity causing it to stream down her legs and rain down all around her.

The Stranger's one hand was slipping, so he let go of her left ankle and held on to her right with both hands, putting more pressure on her damaged foot, digging and twisting his fingers into the massive tear and ripping the meaty gash open even further. He worked his hand in right down to the bone and swung Edith's flailing body hard against the railing. With a satisfying *snap* sound, her bones shattered, leaving the Stranger holding only a bloody foot as her body plummeted to the unforgiving floor below. She screamed the whole way down and it made the Stranger feel wonderful to hear the solid *thud* her head made when she hit bottom.

"Serves you right, ya stupid whore!" he shouted down at her still form. "Just couldn't leave well enough alone, could ya?"

He tossed Edith's severed foot down the stairs as he descended, the grisly trophy bouncing off the wall and coming to rest on her husband's big fat belly. The Stranger stepped over Earl without a thought, but he paused at Edith's tortured body to give it one last good kick—she'd pissed him off that much. *Fuck you*, he thought, and went in search of Wilson's precious little daughter.

CHAPTER TWENTY-FIVE

SHE'S DEAD

Susan drove like a woman possessed, which was exactly what she'd become—possessed by a bone-chilling fear her baby girl was in big trouble and in dire need of help. Wilson wasn't much help, slumped over in his seat, white as a beluga whale, and looking like he might vomit at any moment. He'd convinced himself his version of things was the truth and their family was being pursued by a man who'd denied death and somehow returned from the grave. Susan didn't care if this maniac had risen from hell, came from outer space, or was just a screwball who lived down the street, her only concern was to get back to Billington to help Amanda before it was too late.

Too late for what? she wondered, but couldn't bring herself to follow that train of thought any further. She put her right foot down to the mat, pushing the small Honda to the limits with no regard for her own safety or those on the road with her. If they knew what was good for them, they'd get the hell out of her way.

The clock on the dashboard continued to flash, the minutes ticking away far too quickly, precious time draining away that they'd never get back. With every passing second, a little bit of hope drained with it.

* * *

Amanda Kemp squeezed her eyes shut as tight as she could, hugged her legs in close to her chest, and tried her best to disappear. She'd wiggled into a small compartment under the kitchen island counter, where Mrs. H stored all of her pots and pans. Normally there would be no room under there, but since they'd been baking all afternoon, most of the big pans were either in the oven, the sink, or waiting to be loaded into the dishwasher. Tears spilled freely down her flour-covered cheeks, but she refused to wipe them away. She tried to remain calm, to stay statue still, but it was hard when she was so frightened.

Please don't let him find me. Make him go away. Please don't let him find me. Make him go away . . .

Amanda had played hide-and-seek with her dad for years now, always enjoying herself, but even at the tender age of seven she was wise enough to understand the rules had now changed and she was no longer playing for fun. There would be no "do-overs," no second chances this time. If the bad man she'd thought was her father's friend caught her, she was in big trouble.

Luckily, she hadn't seen what the Stranger had done to the Hendersons out in the other room, but she'd heard Edith screaming in pain and had squealed herself when Earl's gun had started firing. Instinctively knowing something had gone horribly wrong, Amanda had immediately tried to get out of the house, but the back door was locked and she couldn't figure out how to work the dead bolt. That was when she'd decided to find a place to hide and had wiggled under the island countertop as quickly and silently as she could. Now all she could do was sit and wait. If she was lucky, maybe one of the neighbors had heard the gunshots and called the police. Maybe the tall man had gotten scared and ran away, or maybe Earl had managed to shoot him, or maybe Mrs. H had . . .

The Stranger walked into the kitchen, his black boots loud on the wooden floor, silencing her thoughts. Amanda listened intently as the footsteps walked around the island and checked the back door, then doubled back to stand by the kitchen closet. She heard the pantry door open and then close and the kitchen was suddenly so quiet she thought the bad man must have walked into the closet and was searching in there. Part of her wanted to run, to use this opportunity to dash for the front door and get outside. She was small but she sure could run. If she got a head start on him, this old guy would never . . .

Footsteps moving away from the pantry again. Moving toward the island again. Toward her. Amanda held her breath, desperately willing the bad man to go away and leave her alone. When the noise stopped again, the only sound she could hear was of her own racing heart thumping inside her tiny chest and although it was the last thing she really wanted to do, she opened her eyes to have a look around. Bad idea. The tall man was crouched down beside her, smiling at her as he licked blood from his gore-covered fingers.

"Hiya, pretty girl," the Stranger said.

Amanda screamed then, louder than she probably ever had in her entire life, but it didn't do her any good. The bad man seemed to like it, in fact. Liked it a lot.

When Susan and Wilson made it back to Billington, a hair-raising, tire-screeching, nail-biting trip covered in an amazingly short two hours and twenty minutes, they went directly to the Hendersons' house on Milberry Lane. The two-story house sat dark and quiet, far too closely resembling the dead place they'd just come from for comfort. It was approaching 8:30 P.M. and full dark now, so they failed to see the smashed screen door until Susan had parked the car and they were hurrying up the front walk.

"Oh my God . . . look!" Susan said when she saw the screen.

"What? Oh . . ." Wilson gasped, taking off at a run for the steps, his anxiety levels rising by the second and hitting a fever pitch by the time he reached the front door and found it unlocked. Wasting no time, Wilson flung open the door and shouted, "Edith? Earl? Amanda? Anybody home?"

Wilson's hand found the light switch and when he threw on the power, the scene in front of him was like something out of a slaughterhouse, only there were no animals anywhere in sight. Unfortunately, Edith and Earl Henderson were, their bloody corpses waiting just inside the door. Earl was lying just off to the right at the foot of the stairs, his body unharmed and looking like he might have just been asleep if it weren't for the gaping bloody hole where his left eye had once been. It took Wilson a moment to realize Earl had a severed foot lying on his belly, twin broken leg bones sticking sharply up a few inches out of the deep red flesh above the ankle.

Edith was in far worse condition, of course, her right leg ending in a ragged stump, her entire lower body painted in dark blood, and her forehead dented in from where she'd crashed to the unforgiving hardwood floor. Her eyes were still wide-open, looking shocked that she was actually dead. She was though, and it was obvious to Wilson she'd died a ghastly, agonizing death, so he warned Susan to not look at her.

"Stay out of here, Susan. Let me do this."

Susan was having none of that though, and pushed past Wilson into the house. She screamed when she saw how the sweet old lady and her husband had been violently tortured, but pushed past her fears and moved farther into the house, intent on finding her daughter but dreading they were already too late. *She's probably dead. Tortured just like Edith and Earl. No no no! Stop it!* She scolded herself. *No one would ever do that to her. She's only a little girl.* She skirted around Edith's abused body and moved off deeper into the house, praying she were right.

It wasn't until after she was gone from sight, moving through the dining room and headed for the kitchen, Wilson first began to wonder if the Hendersons' killer was still here. Was the Heatseeker still inside the house? Was he hiding somewhere close, listening and waiting for them to walk into his trap?

Oh shit! "Susan! Get your ass back here."

There was no reply. Wilson was about to chase into the kitchen after her, but out of the corner of his eye he spotted something black and shiny in Earl Henderson's hand. Almost unbelievably, he had a gun clutched tightly in his right hand. Wilson didn't know much about firearms, almost nothing really, but this was one of the most beautiful things he'd ever seen in his life. He grabbed it like a drowning man would a lifesaving ring tossed to him in a cold, stormy sea, having to pry the older man's fingers away from the handle to get it. Feeling much more confident now, he wondered where to start searching first. Upstairs maybe? No, ground floor first. Make sure it was clear.

"Susan! Wait for me, damn it! You're not going to believe what I just—"

That was when Susan screamed. Loud, shrill, and painful, and the sheer terror in her voice made Wilson actually fumble the gun in his hand, dropping it onto his foot. His nerves were raw and he was lucky he hadn't shot himself. He quickly gathered it up and leaped across Edith's broken body, running for the kitchen ready to defend his wife, but in his heart knowing it probably wasn't her who was in trouble. In his mind, he could already picture bursting into the room and finding Amanda tied across the kitchen table, naked and gutted like an animal from neck to belly, her intestines spilling out onto the slippery floor, still steaming from the fresh kill . . .

"Susan! I'm coming!"

Wilson kicked open the swinging kitchen door, expecting the worst, but inside he found no bloody mess, no eviscerated little girl, and no killer lying in wait. All he saw was Susan standing ramrod straight, alone over on the other side of the big island in the middle of the room. Her face was as white as a fresh snowfall, and she was staring down at something on the floor, out of Wilson's view. "What is it Susan? Are you all right?"

She refused to speak, refused to even look up at him and his heart started to break. *Oh my God! It's Amanda. She's dead on the floor over there!*

Not wanting to, but having no choice, Wilson walked over to his wife on unsteady legs, but was surprised to find there was no body lying at Susan's feet like he'd feared. "What happened? What made you scream like that?" he asked, somewhat relieved. "Are you okay?"

Susan still wouldn't answer him, but she lifted her head to look into his eyes and with a shaking finger pointed down at the ground beside the island cabinet. On the ground, Wilson saw two things: a white sheet of paper with several lines of handwriting on it, and beside it, in a small puddle of blood, lay something magically pulled from his darkest dreams.

The Heatseeker had left them another note.

And he had cut off Amanda's pinky finger.

Chapter Twenty-six

The Midnight Meeting

"That bastard!" Wilson said, a sudden rage overtaking any fear he'd walked into the room with. He hoped the Heatseeker was stupid enough to still be in the house somewhere. Wilson was going to tear him to shreds if he'd killed his little girl. "Read the note, but don't touch anything else," Wilson said. "I need to check the house to see if . . . anyone is still here." He'd almost said *to see if Amanda's body is here*, but thankfully he'd bit his tongue. Susan looked ready to scream again at any moment and the last thing he needed right now was her getting hysterical. "Just stay here and . . . and maybe get some ice. For her . . . ahh . . . hell, I'll be right back."

Wilson literally ran through the house, upstairs and down, gun ready in hand, the whole time praying Amanda was somehow still alive but not willing to let himself get his hopes up too much. He very nearly shot the full-length mirror in the master bedroom, thinking the Heatseeker was running toward him, but realized it was only his own crazed reflection just in time.

"Wilson!" Susan called out downstairs, her next words breaking down into sobs. "You won't find anyone. He's taken her. The son of a bitch has . . ."

Wilson returned to the kitchen to find Susan holding

the handwritten message from the floor, reading it while tears streamed down both her cheeks. "Here, let me have a look at that."

Taking the note, Wilson read through it twice, just to be sure he hadn't missed anything. The Heatseeker had taken Amanda to what must be his hideaway here in town, a house over on Leamon Avenue. The note was brief. It said:

> If you want to see Amanda alive, the Iceman will meet me alone at 44 Leamon Ave. at midnight to-night. Don't be late. Show up and she lives. Call the police and she dies screaming. The choice is yours. I'll be watching.

"What are we going to do, Wilson?" Susan's voice was actually quite calm now, cold and distant as if she'd already given up hope of ever seeing her daughter again. "We have to call the cops, right?"

"No way. You have to be kidding me. That's the last thing we should do. You read the bloody note."

"We have to take the chance. We have to. You're going to need help. Please!"

"Absolutely not. You're not thinking straight. He'll kill her if we go to the cops."

"He's going to kill her anyway. Oh God! I can't live without her, Wilson. I swear I can't!"

"You won't have to. I'll get her back. I promise."

"You promise? How can you say that? She's probably already dead and you know it. He's probably already—"

"No, he hasn't," Wilson cut her off. "It's me he wants, not her. He's only using her as bait, so trust me. I know he won't hurt her."

"Won't hurt her!" Susan screamed, slamming Wilson in the chest and knocking him backward in anger. She pointed at the severed finger on the floor. "He's already started to cut her to fucking pieces! Look what he did to Edith and Earl, for Christ's sake! Don't tell me he won't hurt her . . . he already has!"

"I know, Susan, sorry. I meant he won't . . . he won't kill her. He needs her alive to lure me into his trap. Don't you see that?"

"And you're just going to walk in there and save the day, are you? That's just fucking great! My daughter's life is in the hands of a hopeless drunk. That what you're telling me?" She regretted the words the moment they were out of her mouth but there was no way to take them back. The stinging insult hung in the air between them like a poisonous cloud.

"I'm not drunk . . . and I'm not hopeless! You think that bottle means more to me than my daughter does? Do you? Answer me, damn it!"

"No," Susan said, crying again. "I'm sorry. I don't know why I said that. I'm just so afraid. I don't want to lose you either. I need you, Wilson. I need both of you!"

Her honest words dissipated the poison between them, calmed Wilson down enough that he stopped wanting to fight with the woman he loved, and let him channel his anger where it needed to be. On the Heatseeker— the maniac who dared to stand between him and his family.

"I've spent the last three years letting you down, but it stops tonight. I won't fail this time. I won't! I'm going to walk in there by myself, but I won't be alone. I'll have Amanda and you on my side . . . and this in my pocket." He showed Susan the gun he'd picked up out of Earl's hand. "I'm gonna send the Heatseeker back to hell where he belongs, and then bring our daughter home to you. Okay?"

"Okay," Susan said, and ran into her husband's arms, burying her head in his chest and holding him so tightly he could hardly breath. She looked up into his eyes, saw the determination in them, and said, "I trust you."

"Thank you. I needed to hear that." Wilson pulled her close and kissed her. "Let's get out of here. I have some things to do before midnight." He bent down and carefully picked up their daughter's finger and walked over to the big stainless-steel refrigerator. He swung open the freezer compartment and gently placed the bloody digit on top of the ice cube tray. He closed the door and shrugged at his wife, unsure what else they could do with it. If there was ever a hope of the doctors reattaching it, her finger had to be kept as cold as possible. First, they had to rescue Amanda though, or none of it would matter.

"We'll come back for that . . . when she's safe."

"Shouldn't we tell someone about the Hendersons? I mean, we can't just leave Edith and Earl lying here, can we? We should call . . . somebody, right?" Susan asked.

Wilson considered it, but shook his head no. Tomorrow there might be a hell of a lot of explaining to do, but for tonight only Amanda and the midnight meeting were important. The dead would have to look after themselves.

"Come on. Let's go."

CHAPTER TWENTY-SEVEN

WATER IN A BOTTLE

Wilson drove the Honda Civic to Susan's house. It was the first time he'd been behind the wheel of an automobile in a very long time. He didn't have a valid driver's license, had lost that several years ago for repeatedly drinking and driving under the influence, but that was the least of his concerns tonight. He made it safely to Derby Hill, parked in the driveway, and walked his trembling wife into the house. She was fading on him, going into an emotional state of shock worrying about her baby girl but unfortunately there wasn't much Wilson could do about it. He couldn't take her to a doctor or even a friend, because there would be far too many questions asked that would only lead to trouble. The best he could do was wrap her up in a big fluffy comforter on the couch and get her a hot cup of Earl Grey tea.

"You going to be okay?" he asked. "It's nearly nine thirty Susan, and I have to get going."

"You're leaving now? Why?"

"I have some things to do. I can't walk in there unprepared or I'm a dead man. Just stay here and keep warm. I'll be back with Amanda as fast as I can. If we're not back by one A.M., call the police and give them the note. No wait, make it one thirty, just in case. Okay?"

"You come back to me, damn you. You hear me?"

"I will. With Amanda. Promise."

They hugged and Wilson thought she might never let him go, but in the end she kissed him and lay down on the couch, trying hard not to break down completely until after he was gone. "I'll wait up for you," she said.

"Do that. And try not to worry. I'll see you soon."

All Susan could do was nod her head and as soon as Wilson left the house she buried her face into the throw pillow and cried like she'd never cried before. Inside she was breaking, on the verge of losing the two most important people in her life, and there wasn't a thing she could do about it. She wept for both of them, holding on to the dream of seeing them safe, but in her heart of hearts sure they were lost to her forever.

Wilson could hear his wife sobbing as he closed the front door and he hated leaving her like this, but what choice did he really have? Tonight would either reunite his family or destroy it for good. He'd either bring back Amanda alive, or die trying himself. It was all or nothing, and sitting around comforting Susan wasn't going to help get their daughter back. To do that, he needed some help; an edge that might swing the balance of fate in his favor.

And time was running out.

He jumped in the car and headed for his house as fast as he dared. The last thing he wanted was to get stopped for speeding tonight. That would bugger things up royally. Luckily there were hardly any cars on the road tonight, and none of them had little flashing lights on the roof. Back at his bungalow, Wilson headed inside to gather some things and to change his clothes. Within minutes, he was back in the kitchen and ready to roll. He'd put his gun, a sharp knife, and an empty glass container he needed inside an old canvas bag and was headed for the door when he spotted a half-full bottle of vodka sitting on the countertop near the sink. The sight of it stopped him dead in his tracks, glued to the floor as every nerve in his body screamed at him to take a drink.

Just one maybe, that's all, to take the edge off and calm my nerves. Just a little sip to make my troubles go away for a second, and then I . . .

"No!" he shouted. "Not this time. Not tonight and never again. I don't need booze to make me feel good. All I need is my family!"

As corny as it sounded, standing alone in his rundown kitchen talking to a vodka bottle, Wilson knew he was right. Felt it deep in his heart and the feeling of peace that came over him let him breathe again and start moving. He walked to the counter and dumped the bottle down the drain, smiling as he did it. There were other bottles around the house but he'd have to worry about them later. For now, he had someplace he badly needed to go.

Feeling strangely empowered, Wilson grabbed an old but warm Pittsburgh Steelers jacket out of the closet and ran for the car. Quickly backing out onto the street, he wanted to get over to St. Michael's church to see Father Harris as fast as he could. Putting his foot to the floor, Wilson was totally oblivious to the fact he was being followed at a distance by an old red Ford pickup truck.

As rushed as he was, Wilson couldn't help but drive by the big two-story house on Leamon Avenue, hoping by some miracle he'd get a glimpse of his daughter through a window, or better yet, perhaps see her bolting out through a door or window and being there to whisk her away to safety without the inevitable confrontation set to happen later tonight. No such luck. The Heatseeker's house lay in darkness, entombed within the branches of several old oak trees and set way back off the street where neither the streetlights nor his straining eyes could make out more than several different layers of shadow.

Part of him wanted to stop, hide the car farther down the street and go in looking for Amanda right now. Maybe he could catch the Heatseeker by surprise, unprepared for an early assault. That was crazy talk though; wishful thinking and Wilson knew it. His old friend would be ready for him no matter what time he showed up, so it was best to stick to the game plan for now, or at least appear to. Amanda would be safe enough for the time being. Besides, he really wanted to see Father Harris about something before it was too late. Smacking the dashboard in frustration, Wilson gunned the engine away from the dark house heading for the Catholic church.

St. Michael's appeared to be in darkness too, but Wilson knew enough about Father Harris to know he'd be there somewhere. He parked the Honda out front and headed around the side of the huge brick building to where there was a small but tidy cottage attached to the church. Patrick Harris had lived there for as long as Wilson could remember and he was always telling his congregation he took pride in being available to each and every one of them at any hour of the day. If they needed him for anything at all, spiritual or otherwise, just go ahead and show up at his door. Wilson wasn't 100 percent sure the priest had meant it, but he was about to put that promise to the test.

Susan would have thought him mad for coming here, which was precisely the reason he hadn't told her. After all he had explained and shown her, Susan still didn't believe they were up against a supernatural enemy. A maniac, yes, but not an evil man-monster reborn from hell. She might believe Earl Henderson's gun would be enough to kill the man who'd taken their daughter, but Wilson wasn't nearly as convinced. To kill a demon, he figured you needed more than man-made weapons; you needed to battle on a spiritual level as well, which was why he'd decided to come to St. Michael's tonight. If anyone could help him and his family, it was the fiery Irishman Patrick Harris.

Wilson took a deep breath and knocked on the cottage door. It took several minutes and a few more raps, but eventually he could see the priest approaching the door through the panes of glass. Father Harris didn't look particularly happy to see him, but opened the door to greet him anyway. The Catholic holy man looked tired, sweaty, and disheveled, like maybe he had the beginnings of a fever and was coming down with something.

"Wilson? What in blazes are you doing here? Are you hurt? Susan and Amanda okay?"

"Ahh . . . um, no, actually. Ahh . . ." Now that he was here, he had no idea what to say to the intimidating priest. How could he possibly say his family was being stalked by a dead man? Maybe it *had* been foolish to come here.

"Come on, out with it man," Father Harris scolded him. "I haven't got all night. What's wrong?"

Wilson could only think of one thing to say, one way to start this conversation. "Bless me, Father, for I have sinned. Sinned a lot, actually . . . and plan on sinning more before the end of the night."

Father Harris was taken aback by that comment, not sure what to think. He looked Wilson up and down, trying to size up the situation. "You been drinking again?"

"No, sir. Not a drop. I need your help."

"Then you'll have it. Get in here."

The priest took Wilson's football jacket, hung it in the hall closet, then stepped aside to wave Wilson past him into a small room near the front of the cottage he used as his office. It was a bare bones kind of room, with no pictures on the walls and furnished only with an old rolltop desk and two wooden chairs. "Have a seat, Wilson. Tell me what's going on."

Wilson sat down and considered where the best place was to start. "Okay. The man the police are looking for, the one who left the skeletons at the bandstand in the park . . . I know who he is. He came to Billington to kill me."

"My goodness. Who is it?"

"This is just between us, right?"

"You, me, and God, Wilson. Out with it."

Wilson took a deep breath and then just started talking. He told Father Harris everything, condensing things a little to save time, but told him all about growing up and training to be an escape artist and about the death of his partner, Douglas Williams. Then he told him how he'd gone into hiding in Billington and how the guilt had driven him to the bottle and ruined his marriage to Susan. Before he lost his nerve, he told the priest about how he thought his one-time friend had returned from the dead, tracked him down, and about the notes from the Heatseeker he'd been sent since his arrival. Eventually Wilson made it to the part about opening his partner's empty coffin in Jamestown, then speeding back home to find Edith and Earl Henderson dead and his daughter abducted. He explained how he had no choice but to face the Heatseeker tonight at midnight, and that he planned on sending him back to hell if that was what it took to get Amanda back.

Father Harris listened to Wilson's tale with a blank expression on his face. Wilson had no idea whether he was even listening half the time, never mind believing anything he was saying. He still seemed sick to Wilson, clammy-looking and much paler than the usually rosy-cheeked Irishman normally was.

"I take it you won't be going to the police with this information, even though you should?" Father Harris asked when he was sure Wilson had nothing further to say.

"I can't. The Heatseeker said he'd kill Amanda if I do and I believe him. I have to face him alone."

"Why are you here then? What can I do to help?"

"I'm not sure, to be honest. All I know is the man I used to know isn't human anymore, Father, and I just hoped maybe you could pray with me and maybe give me something to take with me. I . . . I brought this glass bottle. I don't know . . . I was thinking maybe you could bless some water for me and that it might help."

The priest sat quietly for several minutes, thinking about everything he'd just heard. It was a crazy story and Wilson was sure Father Harris was about to stand up and toss him out. He didn't though.

"Tell me, Wilson. Do you believe with all your heart what you've told me is the God's honest truth? That this old partner of yours died and has somehow escaped the chains of hell to return for you?"

"I know it's true, Father. As crazy as it sounds, in my heart I know I'm right. I'm scared, but I know I have to make a stand and face him."

"I'm scared too, Wilson, for you and for your daughter. I don't know if I believe your story, but I know you believe it, so you'll have my help, son. And God's blessing too. Give me that bottle . . . and let's pray."

Ten minutes later, Wilson walked out of Father Harris's office with a bottle filled with holy water and a heart filled with renewed hope and dare he even say it . . . faith. Facing the Heatseeker alone was going to be the hardest thing he'd ever done in his life, but it felt good—no, it felt *right*—to have Father Harris and God on his side. Whether they ultimately helped would have to wait until later.

Walking down the hall toward the back door, Wilson was just opening the closet door to retrieve his jacket when Father Harris literally ran into him and bumped him out of the way.

"Oh, sorry, Wilson. Here, let me get that for you."

Wilson was startled, having thought the priest was still back in his office but he smiled and accepted his coat with thanks. "Okay. Thanks for . . . well, everything."

"Be careful, Wilson. Godspeed to you."

Wilson nodded, then left the cottage to return to his car parked out front. As soon as he was out of sight, Patrick Harris slumped down against the door of his cottage, tears starting to flow down his sweaty cheeks. "Oh God, what have I done? Why have you let me become so weak . . . so useless to you?"

Struggling to stand, the priest walked to the hall closet and fully slid open the door. Inside, and clearly visible if Wilson had managed to open the door, was Father Harris's black mask, dark clothing, and the replacement red flashlight his alter ego used while prowling the dark streets of Billington night after night. He'd tried so hard over the years to ignore the urges, to resist the change, but they kept beating their drums inside his head, breaking him down physically as well as spiritually, transforming him into the pervert who reveled in peeking into people's bedrooms and liked to call himself Tom.

Father Patrick Harris hung his head in shame.

CHAPTER TWENTY-EIGHT

PERVERTED PEEPING PRIEST

Sitting parked out in his red pickup, the Stranger was curious. Intrigued even. Why had Wilson gone to see the priest? Were they friends, or was he trying to pull a fast one, have the priest secretly rally the police, perhaps? No, he was stupid, but not crazy. The Stranger knew Wilson well enough to know he wouldn't jeopardize his child like that. No, it had to be something else.

Wilson had been inside the priest's cottage for nearly half an hour, and had just pulled away in his wife's silver Honda. The Stranger had started to follow, but instead, he'd pulled to a stop in front of the church, perplexed and not liking the idea he wasn't sure what his adversary was up to. Was he planning something? Plotting some way to bring him down, or enlist help in the coming battle?

Hmmm . . . what's he thinking? Better stop thinking of him as just a hopeless drunk. Be on guard for anything . . .

That was the problem though. He hated not knowing Wilson's plans, loathed the thought of not being prepared for every contingency. Of course, there was always a way to find out what was going on.

Risky but perhaps worth it. Yes?

Yes. He shut off the truck.

* * *

The urges were calling Father Harris again. They beat their drums in his head and he felt their fingers roaming all over his body like he'd stepped on a nest of hungry army ants, probing, biting, and crawling inside his mouth and ears. "Noooooooo! Leave me alone!"

Patrick tore at his clothes to try get them off but they were on his bare skin now, scratching and clawing to the thump of the drums. "Please, God! Help meeeeeeee!" But God wasn't there. Not for him. Not for a man who'd fallen so far from grace, and Patrick knew it. He understood he was getting exactly what he deserved. He also knew Tom was anxious to take over, to bury him in the dark again, where he had no control, no choices to make, no consequences to face, no guilt to endure—at least until he woke up in the morning. What used to be a prison was now starting to become a place of refuge, a place he almost looked forward to. Down in the dark corner of his mind where Tom put him was the only place he ever felt at peace. He could just slide away into blessed oblivion and let Tom deal with the problems of the world. It was the coward's way out, and Father Harris knew he should fight for his sanity but it was just getting too hard. His mounting sins getting too heavy a burden to carry . . .

Tom stood up straight and looked around. He smiled, cracking the knuckles of his right hand into the palm of his left. He reversed it and cracked his remaining knuckles, enjoying the sound as they went *pop*, and relishing the feeling of power flowing back into his body. Why the priest chose to live life the way he did was mindboggling to Tom. Why slither on the ground like a worm when you could soar in the clouds with the eagles? It made no sense.

Tom discarded the torn shirt he wore and stripped off the rest of his clothes. At the closet he quickly redressed, his black mask the last to go on. *Crawling like a worm . . . bah!*

There was no way Tom was crawling anywhere. He was a predator, the hunter, the black panther, and tonight he would hide no more. He was going out to do more than just peek in a few windows tonight. Being a voyeur was child's play and he was tiring of it. It was time to ramp things up a notch or two. Time to start becoming the nightmare he truly was and show the people of Billington what fear truly was. To do that though, he had to rid the town of the imposter who had come to take his place—this Heatseeker Wilson Kemp had told the priest about. He'd watched him before and yes he'd felt fear in the dark man's presence but not anymore. Never again.

From the top shelf of the closet, beside the red flashlight, Tom took down the toy he'd been wanting to play with for a very long time—a folding boa knife he'd stolen from the garage of a local hunter he knew. Tom thumbed the release and the four-inch blade glided open. It was made from heat-treated hardened stainless steel but coated all in black, even the blade. The knife was beautiful, like him, and he'd longed to take it along on his nocturnal adventures but until now, never had. Tonight was different though. Tonight he would evolve again, take out this Heatseeker while he was occupied dealing with Mr. Kemp. Wilson had told the priest where his daughter was being held and Tom was heading there tonight to take care of this intruder once and for all.

From there, the city was his, and the first place he might go was back to that sweet little Irish schoolteacher with the red hair, the alabaster skin, and the hard, delicious body. *The things I could make her do at the end of this knife! The way she'd beg . . . oh the way she'd scream . . .* His penis swelled in his pants, thinking of how powerless she would feel. How completely at his mercy she would be. And not just her; the entire town. Billington would be his for the taking.

Tom felt a sharp pain in his hand, the boa knife dropping to the floor, and a larger blade pressed into the flesh of his neck before he even realized he wasn't alone in the cottage anymore. Someone had entered the house, crept up, and disarmed him without Tom hearing a thing.

"Move and you're dead," the intruder said. "Okay. Now turn around. Very slowly."

Tom did as he was told, trying to remain calm and in control but fear exploded in his belly when he saw who held the dagger at his throat. *Him! Oh my God! How? How did he know I was coming?* "Please," he mumbled through the mask. "Don't hurt me."

The dark man slowly shook his head, amazed at what he was seeing. "What kind of fucking freak show are you? Huh? I saw you once, up on the trellis, when I killed the dog. Who the fuck are you, and what have you done with the priest?" When Tom didn't say anything, the man screamed in his face, "Answer me, damn you!"

Tom slowly reached up and pulled off his black mask, revealing himself. "I . . . I am Father Harris. Please . . ."

The tall man looked shocked for a second, but then started to laugh. "You've got to be kidding. You're the priest here? Wilson's priest is a fucking nutcase? Ha! Doesn't that just figure."

Tom could think of nothing to say.

"Why was Wilson here? Tell me or I slit your throat!"

He pressed the serrated edge of the dagger harder into Tom's throat, ready to slice.

"Wait . . . don't! He was here telling me about you. About his daughter . . . asking me for help."

"Help? How in hell could a broken down nutter like you help anyone?"

"He asked me to forgive his sins and bless him. And he asked me to bless a jar of water. Seemed to think it would help against you. Please don't . . ."

"Holy water? Ha! From you? That's perfect! You can't bless anything, Father. Not without faith. You stopped being a real priest a long time ago, my friend. Probably even before you put on that silly little mask and went out looking at titties. Wilson's big secret weapon is a dud, and he doesn't even know it. He put faith in you, Father, and you let him down big-time, didn't you? You're nothing but a worthless piece of shit."

Tom wanted to stand up to this man, to show him who was boss in this town, but he couldn't summon his body to lash out and defend himself. He couldn't do anything except stand there and be humiliated, tears starting to run now, which made him feel even worse. Where was the predator? Where was the hunter? Where was the panther? Nowhere, of course. They never existed, just like Tom. All of them just parts of a failed priest's disturbed mind; figments of Patrick Harris's perverse imagination.

The drums stopped beating.

The urges faded away.

Tom fragmented into shadows and was gone.

Father Harris was left all alone, standing in front of a real-life predator, a real killer, and knew deep in his hammering heart he would prowl the streets of Billington no more. The thought brought the first genuine smile to his face in years.

The dark man put his knife away.

"You like looking into windows, do you? Makes you feel tough spying on people? You make me sick. Damn your eyes . . ." he said and forced Patrick to his knees. With savage strength, he plunged both his thumbs into the fallen priest's eyes, mercilessly digging in until the eyeballs exploded and sprayed outward like a massive squeezed pimple. The priest screamed in agony, but the dark man dug his thumbs in deeper, pressing through the optic cavity and shoving through the membrane into his brain. Something deep inside the priest burst. Father Harris began to shudder, his legs spasming, his bowels and bladder letting loose as he slumped against the closet door. When the Stranger pulled out his thumbs, they were covered in blood and sticky clear gore. Gray matter was visible through the gaping holes in the dying man's face.

Father Harris was silent now, still gasping for breath, but blood poured from his mouth and nose, his damaged brain misfiring, his systems quickly shutting down. He felt warmth spread through his body and a calming peace finally coming to claim him and put an end to years of self-loathing and suffering. With his dying breath, he managed to say to his killer, "Tha . . . thank you."

The Stranger bent down close to his ear and whispered, "You're welcome, ya sick son of a bitch. You're welcome."

CHAPTER TWENTY-NINE

HOOK, LINE, AND SINKER

Wilson repacked his bag and was finally ready to go confront the Heatseeker. He was back at his house again, having changed his mind about a few things and realizing he'd forgotten something that might be vitally important if things played out the way he hoped they might. Ready now as he would ever be, Wilson headed for the door.

In the driveway, just as he was reaching for the handle on the Honda's driver's-side door, sirens started to blare and red and blue flashing lights illuminated the night sky from both ends of the street. Two black-and-white Billington police cruisers skidded to a stop behind Susan's car, blocking him in, and four large bodies piled out to change Wilson's plans about driving anywhere. They shone large bright lights in his face and carefully closed the distance between them.

"On the fucking ground, Wilson," one of them shouted, but with the lights in his eyes and all the sudden confusion, Wilson didn't recognize the voice. The police weren't in the mood to wait for him to think this all through either. Before Wilson knew what was happening, he'd been seized, spun around, and slammed to the ground in the wet grass beside the driveway. All he could see were three sets of black boots in front, and knew one of them was on his back, a heavy one, crushing the breath from his lungs. The officer pinning him to the ground roughly slapped a pair of handcuffs on him and said, "Don't move an inch, man. Dig?"

This time, Wilson did recognize the voice. "Mack? What the hell is going on? I haven't done anything!"

"Maybe you have . . . maybe you haven't," Officer Byron MacKenzie spoke into Wilson's ear. "But someone made a mess of Edith and Earl Henderson and we have an eyewitness says they heard loud noises that might have been shots, but they weren't sure. Then they saw a man leave with a little girl and they weren't acting very friendly. It took them way too damn long to decide to call us and might not even done it, but apparently a few other people showed up and there was more yelling and screaming going on. Eventually we got on the scene. Turns out the Hendersons just happen to be your daughter's babysitters and she was with them today, so how about you tell me what the fuck is going on? Where's Amanda, Wilson? What'cha do to her?"

"What? Nothing! I haven't done anything to her."

"Where is she then?"

"Ahh . . ." Wilson had no idea how to answer. He couldn't tell him about the Heatseeker or they'd cart him off to the rubber room. "Trust me, Mack, she'll be fine but you've got to let me go. Please!"

"Trust you? Hardly," Big Mack said, then addressed the other officers. "Two of you search the house . . . Daniels, help me get this drunken piece of shit into the car."

Footsteps headed off in the direction of the front door of the house, and Wilson was dragged painfully to his feet and shoved toward the waiting police cars parked on the road. A tall, dark-haired officer with a goatee and a rather large belly hanging over his belt walked ahead of them carrying Wilson's supply bag and opened the back door of Mack's cruiser. Presumably this was Officer Daniels, but Wilson had never met him before so he continued to plead his case to the big man he'd known for years. "Come on, Mack! You know me better than that. Look, I'm stone sober tonight, honest, and I didn't do anything to Amanda . . . or to Edith and Earl."

Big Mack unceremoniously frisked Wilson to make sure he wasn't armed, then tossed him into the backseat. "Save it, clown-man. I'm really not interested in listening to your bullshit." The door was slammed shut and Officer Daniels climbed in the front to keep an eye on him while Mack went to see how the search was going inside the house. He returned ten minutes later with a foul look on his face. "House is clean," he said, more to Daniels than to Wilson, but he looked back once to grit his teeth in either frustration or perhaps anger. Neither boded well for Wilson and the predicament he found himself in.

"See, I told you I didn't have her. Can you let me out now? I'm late . . . for an important meeting. Seriously!"

"And I *seriously* don't give a fuck, so shut your mouth, Wilson, or I'll come back there and gag you." Mack was madder than Wilson had ever seen him, the powerful black man looking stressed out and haggard. The Heatseeker had been causing everyone in town to lose sleep but none as much as the members of the Billington Police Department. They'd been chasing shadows and bad leads for a few days now, never getting any closer to the man who'd brought such violence and fear to their once-peaceful little town. The strain of that pressure was starting to show but Wilson didn't think this was the time to bring up the matter. He decided for now it was best to do just as he was told.

The other officers returned from the house and approached Big Mack's cruiser for instruction. Wilson recognized the blond-haired one as his friend, Jacob Jackson, but even he wasn't looking particularly friendly tonight. "You guys get back over to the Hendersons' house and help the coroner out. He's on his own and will need to gather a shitload of evidence from the scene. Make sure no one else gets inside there. Gimme a call if you need anything. Got it?"

The partners nodded, and got into Officer Jackson's cruiser. Mack started his engine and pulled away from the curb, presumably heading for the station. Wilson couldn't get locked up for the night. That just wasn't an option. If he didn't show up to meet the Heatseeker, Amanda would be killed. Wilson considered telling the truth to Big Mack. Maybe he could somehow reason with him but he didn't see how. Mack would never believe his fantastical story about dead magicians returning from the grave, and even if he did somehow get through to him the danger Amanda was in, Mack still wouldn't let him go. He'd want to go to the Heatseeker's house too, and that was also against the orders Wilson had been given. He had to show up alone, not with the entire police force in tow, sirens blaring.

Wilson shuddered at the image of it, and what it would mean to his little girl. No, there was no way he could tell Big Mack anything. He'd have to figure out some other way of getting out of this mess.

"Holy shit, boss," Daniels said, his head peeking into Wilson's canvas bag in his lap. "I've got the gun right here in the sack! Looks like a .38, Mack. I don't want to touch it, but what are the odds it's got some bullets missing that'll match up to the ones fired over at the Hendersons' house?"

"Pretty good, I'd say. What do you think, Wilson?"

I think I'm screwed, Wilson thought. If there were bullets fired over there, almost for sure they'd be from that gun. *Fuck!*

Things were quickly moving from bad to worse but there wasn't much he could do about it. He was still trying to come up with a plan when Big Mack pulled the cruiser into the police station parking lot and he was pushed, pulled, and shoved out of the backseat and into one of the holding cells at the back of the precinct. They hadn't even removed his cuffs. They'd just shoved him in the door, slammed and locked it tight, then started walking away.

"Mack!" the radios on both their hips blared in stereo. "Come in, Mack. We've got more trouble."

The voice belonged to Jacob Jackson, and it was easy to tell he was pretty fired up about something. Big Mack grabbed his radio and responded.

"What's happening, Jake? I don't need any more trouble."

"Well, we got it, big guy. Bad trouble. Father Harris has been found dead at the Catholic church. Mrs. Chapman, the neighbor, ran right out into the road in front of the cruiser to stop us. He's been murdered, Mack, and it's not pretty. His eyes are gone!"

"His eyes are *what*? Has this town gone freakin' crazy?" Mack stopped walking and turned back toward Wilson's cell. "Hey, Kemp . . . you weren't at St Michael's tonight by any chance, were you?" Wilson just looked down at the floor. Yes, he had been, but he wasn't about to tell Mack that. "Yep, about what I thought," the big policeman said, nodding his head and returning his attention to the radio.

"Listen, Jackson, stay there and lock down the scene. I'll send Daniels over to the Henderson house to help there. When the coroner is done, we'll send him your way. Don't let anyone into that scene, dig?"

"Roger, Mack. Over and out."

Daniels took his cue as well, dashing out the door and leaving Wilson alone with Officer MacKenzie in the station. "Please, Mack," Wilson tried. "You've known me for years. I didn't have nothing to do with—"

"I told you to shut your trap, Kemp, and I bloody well meant it. Not another word, hear?"

Wilson reluctantly took his advice and sat down on the cot to try thinking this through. As soon as his butt hit the lumpy, uncomfortable mattress pad, he thought back to the last time he'd spent the night here, just last Friday. He also remembered the loose steel slat in the mesh framework of the cot he'd slept on and anxiously tried to remember if this was the same cell he'd been in that night. There was a one in three chance and, although Wilson had been drunk and unconscious for most of his stay, he was pretty sure this, indeed, was the same cell.

If it is, and that slat is still there . . .

Wilson jumped off the mattress and squatted down to lift it out of the way. It wasn't easy with his hands still cuffed behind his back. It took him a few unsuccessful attempts but he eventually found the loose slat and, just like last time, he found he could wiggle its entire six-and-a-half-foot length free of the rest of the steel cot.

He laid the slat under the mattress to keep it hidden, then sat back down to think. Last time he'd had the same idea but had been too chicken to try it. He could remember thinking that back in the day he could've pulled it off easily, but he wasn't the man he'd once been. He'd been wrong though. He could be any type of man he chose to be. All he had to do was believe in himself and he could pull this off.

Maybe.

A little sleight of hand, a lot of deception . . . get Mack looking the wrong way. It just might work!

It had to work. His daughter needed him and there were no other options. He had one shot at this and if he blew it, Amanda might pay the price for his failure. To start, he had to get out of these handcuffs.

"Wilson?" Big Mack said from the other side of the bars, scaring the hell out of Wilson, who'd thought he was still out in the main office.

Regaining his composure, Wilson stood up to talk to the large man. "What do you need, Mack?"

"You be a good boy. I've gotta go to the bathroom, Wilson, and I just wanted to remind you to play nice. If you can stop being a pain in the ass for five minutes, I'll get those cuffs off you when I get back from the can, okay?"

"Sure. No problem. Go ahead."

"I wasn't asking your permission, fool. Just telling you to behave so I don't have to crack your head, dig?"

With those warm words, Big Mack headed back out into the main office and Wilson watched him unbuckle his heavy work belt and put it inside the sliding desk drawer before heading out of his view, toward the toilet.

It was going to be now or never, and Wilson steeled his nerves for it. With a deep breath, a practiced flick of his wrists, and a quiet *snap* sound, he dislocated both of his thumbs and was out of the handcuffs within seconds. It was child's play for any decent escape artist and far easier than the illusion he was about to attempt, but at least his hands were free and it would shock Mack a little off his guard when he returned. Sometimes that was all it took to make a trick work.

Wilson hung the shiny handcuffs through the bars on the cell door, where Mack couldn't help but notice them. Then he removed the long steel slat from beneath the mattress and grabbed his thick wool blanket. He practiced the move quickly once but at this point he either knew it instinctively or he didn't. Good magic was about technique, sure, but it came from the heart too. You had to *believe* you could do real magic, or you'd never convince your audience. And tonight Wilson believed he could work miracles. He had no other choice.

Wilson waited for Mack, and tried to relax.

Officer MacKenzie came back into the main office a few minutes later, and grabbed a ring of keys off his cluttered desk. He was whistling quietly as he approached the cells, but stopped midnote when he saw the handcuffs hanging on their chain on the bars of the door. "What the . . . ?" he started, then looked in to see Wilson standing up beside his spilled-over cot with his blanket held up high in front of him. All Mack could see was Wilson's head and shoulders, and damned if he wasn't smiling to beat the band. Mack was furious.

"You little bastard! I leave you for a minute and you trash your cell? I ought to hammer you silly. How in blazes did you get out of the cuffs, anyway?"

Wilson ignored his question. It was *SHOWTIME!*

"I'd like to chat, Mack, but I already told you I'm late

for an important meeting. Like it or not . . . I'm out of here, big guy."

"You're what?" Mack asked, a nervous laugh spilling out of him, but stopping when he glanced back at the handcuffs. "You're going to just walk through the bars and out the door, are you?"

"No. Where I'm going . . . I don't need doors. I'll check in with you tomorrow, Mack, to clear all this mess up. See you later."

With that, Wilson smiled and lifted his wool blanket up over his head and out of Big Mack's view. He paused for dramatic effect, then dropped silently to the floor using the steel slat to keep the blanket upright. From Mack's view it would appear as if he hadn't moved yet, and once he slid in behind his turned over bed, he released the slat and laid it flat on the floor. The blanket would fall on top of it and conceal it and if he'd done it fast enough, it would appear to Mack as if he'd instantly vanished into thin air before his eyes.

"Holy fuck!" Mack shouted, having fallen for the illusion hook, line, and sinker. One second Wilson had been standing there hiding behind his blanket, the next he was gone and the blanket was lying on the cell floor. He quickly unlocked the cell and rushed in to grab the wool blanket, his heart racing at the impossible feat he'd just witnessed.

Wilson waited until he was deep into the cell and then he burst out from behind the overturned mattress and ran for the cell door, slamming it shut and locking the bewildered officer inside before he could do anything to respond. "Sorry, Mack. Had to be done."

"You little shit! Let me out of here, damn it!" Mack reached for his firearm but it wasn't there anymore. He'd taken off his belt before going to the bathroom and put his weapon in his desk drawer. Mad as hell, Mack rushed over and was pounding on the cell door, but he knew it was pointless and soon settled down. "You're only making things worse for yourself, man. Give up now before you do something really stupid."

"I can't, Mack. You don't believe me yet, but I didn't have anything to do with any of those deaths. You'll believe me once they collect and test all the evidence from the Hendersons' and from the church. I was there tonight, both places, but I didn't kill anybody. I'll gladly turn myself in tomorrow for blood tests and DNA samples, but tonight I've got to go save my daughter. I'm sorry I have to leave you here but there's no other choice. I gotta go."

"Wait, Wilson. What about your daughter? Maybe we can help? Just let me out and I'll—"

"Not gonna happen, big guy. I can't risk it, even if I thought you believed me, which I don't. Someone will let you out soon. Sit tight and please don't try finding me tonight. I know you will, but I need this one night to try and make things right. I'll face whatever consequences there are tomorrow. Promise."

Leaving Big Mack fuming in the cell, Wilson went to the front office and was thrilled to find his canvas sack of supplies waiting for him on top of Officer Daniels's desk. He quickly checked to see his gun was still inside as well as everything else, then dashed for the front door and out into the night. So far his luck had held up, but the night was far from over. In fact, it was only beginning. Wilson ran across the parking lot, disappearing into the darkness beyond.

WEDNESDAY, SEPTEMBER 23

A SNOWBALL'S CHANCE IN HELL

CHAPTER THIRTY

FINALLY FACE-TO-FACE

The house on Leamon Avenue waited for Wilson with open arms. Every light in every room was on now, including two exterior spotlights: one shining on the driveway and garage, and the other illuminating the front door. Although midnight, the house looked anything but a comfortable haven ready to settle in for a peaceful night. It looked more like an enormous mutant spider hiding among the large oak trees waiting for some unsuspecting person to be enticed into its glow-in-the-dark web. Even from the street, Wilson could see the front door was open about a foot, clearly tempting him inside but not open enough to allow a view of what might be waiting inside. To go inside the house was surely suicide, and deep down Wilson knew it.

He headed for the door.

By the time he hit the front steps, Wilson had his gun drawn and ready. He was a rank amateur with a firearm but he'd seen enough bad police movies to know he should check to see if the safety was in the off position. He had no desire to die from such a foolish mistake but as far as he could tell, the gun was ready to fire.

Just point and shoot, Wilson. Point and shoot. The gun's

just an extension of your arm. Point your arm then, not the
gun. Point . . . Shoot!

But first he had to find someone to shoot at.

Wilson paused at the door, wanting to charge in, but
wondering if he was walking into a trap. The Heatseeker could be waiting with a gun ready to shoot him
point-blank as soon as he stepped inside. This was the
easy way inside, sure, but would it be better to find another way in? Maybe he could get in through a back window and surprise the Heatseeker. No, that wasn't going
to happen. The Heatseeker knew he was coming and
had things all planned out. He'd left this door brightly
lit up and open simply to speed things along and get
Wilson inside. It wasn't a trap; it was arrogance. The
Heatseeker didn't see Wilson as any real threat to him
so he was playing games, mocking Wilson's fear by leaving the door open for him.

Better be careful, old friend . . . your arrogance might
just be your downfall.

Wilson opened the screen door and shoved the heavy
wooden inside door out of his way as he stepped inside.
The door was hard to move, and when it bumped to a
stop a full ten inches away from the wall, Wilson knew
there was something—no, make that *someone*—hiding
behind it. Adrenaline pumped through his system and
he almost took a shot through the door, but a stale,
nasty, rotting smell hit him then and instinctively he
knew it wasn't the Heatseeker behind the door.

With great trepidation but needing to find out, Wilson pulled back the door and looked around the other
side. An older woman with silver hair was there to greet
him, a long-bladed knife pinning her in an upright position through her head and into the wood behind her.

Her flowery dress was drenched in dry blackened blood and she still wore a pair of white slippers on her feet. Her wrinkled skin was turning a shade closer to purple and sagging badly on her ruined face and upper body but her chubby legs were stretched tight, the blood in her body having settled in her lower extremities, bloating and swelling them until they looked ready to burst. Worst of all, the flies had found her open eyes and head wound, with dozens of them swarming over her eyeballs, moving in unison and looking like bulging pupils, making it appear as if the poor old lady were still alive and gazing around.

Wilson turned away, gagging. He had no idea who this woman was, but he guessed it was the original owner of the house before the Heatseeker had decided to move in. Leaving her there for him to find was just another twisted ploy to frighten Wilson and show him how futile it was to resist what the Heatseeker had planned for him.

Yeah, well, fuck you, old buddy. You're not going to do that to me. Wilson nearly added, *I hope*, but choked that negative thought off and headed farther into the house. As scared as he was, part of him wanted this confrontation, needed it, and there was no sense in delaying it any more than necessary. This evil sicko had taken his beautiful daughter, hurt her badly, and threatened her life. He had caused Wilson to go into hiding for more than two decades, wasting away his life at the bottom of a liquor bottle, and wanted to destroy his family. Wilson wasn't going to let it happen. No way. As screwed up as life had become, Susan, Amanda, and he had found something special with each other and no one had the right to take that away. Wilson was frightened, of course, but he was definitely ready to kill to protect his family. If the Heatseeker believed he didn't have it in him, he was in for a big surprise.

Through the main floor he crept, moving as quietly as he could, investigating the living room, dining room, and kitchen, but knowing he wasn't fooling anyone. His attempt at stealth was far from perfect and he even bumped into one of the dining room chairs, sending it screeching across the floor about eight inches, but he just kept moving, kept searching, and trying to be ready for the inevitable attack.

The tension was incredible, the pressure making him sweat. It pooled on his forehead, dribbling down his face. The gun in his right hand, the canvas bag in his left, it was hard to wipe away. The sweat trickled into his eyes, stinging painfully and blurring his vision. The gun was getting heavy too, heavier than he expected anyway. It was tough to keep it held out in front of him, ready to fire. His right arm was shaking, ready to cramp from the effort, and he was forced to let his arm drop to his side every now and then, to let it rest. Wilson was sure that was when the Heatseeker would pounce, when he was most vulnerable, but the attack never came. On and on, room after room he searched, but didn't find a damn thing.

Wilson was starting to think maybe the Heatseeker was playing a trick on him, that maybe he wasn't even here and was using this meeting as a distraction so he could easily go kill or kidnap Susan while he futilely stumbled around here. But then he heard a noise coming from above him, a floorboard creaking and what might have been a quick yelp of pain. *Amanda!* Wilson thought. *Upstairs. He's got her hidden on the second floor. Is he up there too?* Impossible to know and there was obviously only one way to find out, so Wilson headed for the staircase. *Easy now . . . don't charge up there like a fool. That's what he'll be expecting. Stay focused. Stay in control.*

Wilson wanted to shout up to Amanda he was coming, that Daddy was going to save her and everything was going to be all right, but it would be a pointless, silly thing to do, so he bit his tongue and stayed quiet. There was no sense giving his position away for what amounted to false hope.

Up the stairs he went, slowly, alertly, gun raised and pointing toward the landing above. Wilson kept his wits about him, making sure to keep a watch behind him as well, just in case the attack came from below. None did though, and he reached the second-floor hallway unimpeded. It was a central corridor, with two rooms off to each side and one at the far end of the hall, which Wilson could clearly see was an empty bathroom. That left four rooms to check, all of which were presumably bedrooms. Inside one of them would be his daughter and his gut told him the Heatseeker would be with her. It was possible he was hiding somewhere else, or not in the house at all, but Wilson was sure he'd find the two of them together, the Heatseeker using Amanda as cover or at least as leverage in what was to come.

Which door? he wondered. And what shape would he find Amanda in when he saw her? *Please let her be okay. Please!* Now wasn't the time to be thinking like that. Now was the time for action, so Wilson threw caution to the wind and charged into the first room on his right. As luck would have it, Amanda was there in front of him, sitting on the threadbare carpeted floor eight feet away, a tall dark-haired man in full magician's garb standing above her with a knife held to her trembling throat. Behind them, a wall-to-wall bloodred velvet curtain hung, the words FIRE AND ICE stitched into the cloth in big golden silk letters.

Wilson gasped in shock, not because he'd burst into the correct room to find them on his first try, but because he was so amazed when he finally stood face-to-face with his enemy and saw who it was that had hold of his daughter.

You've got to be fucking kidding me!

It wasn't the Heatseeker.

No, it wasn't his old partner, Douglas Williams, but Wilson knew the dark man just the same. He was older, sure, but it was hard to tell on first glance, especially with his hair dyed jet black. "Lucius? Is that really you?"

The Stranger smiled, and gave a little wink. "Long time no see, Wilson. Now back up and toss the gun."

"Not a chance. How about you drop the knife or I'll blow your brains out. I don't know what your problem is, but let the girl go. None of this is her fault. It's between you and me."

Lucius Barber, the man who'd taught Wilson everything he knew about magic, his mentor and one-time manager, only laughed, not in the least bit intimidated. "You always were a moron, Wilson. You have no idea what is going on here, do you? Drop the gun or I cut her throat. You might get off a lucky shot and take me out, but you'll be swimming in your daughter's blood before I'm dead. I should have killed you years ago after you let Doug die and destroyed all our careers but I'll take Amanda with me if it's all I can get. What do you say, hero? Feel like calling my bluff? Come on. Do it! See what it gets ya!"

Lucius tightened his grip on Amanda, pressing the serrated edge of the blade deeper into the tender flesh of her throat. "Daddy, *nooooo!*" Amanda squealed.

"No, wait! Stop! Okay . . . okay. I'll do what you say. Just don't hurt her. Do what you want to me, but leave her alone, okay?"

Wilson's head was spinning, thinking this through. Last he'd seen Lucius Barber, he'd had gray hair and a beer belly, but not anymore. He'd lost at least forty or fifty pounds, leaned down to solid muscle, and was now tall and wiry, looking like he'd hardly aged a day. In fact, in some ways he looked younger than Wilson remembered he had twenty years ago. Surely in his sixties now, Lucius was in much better shape and looked as strong as a bull.

"Do what I tell you then," Lucius said. "The gun has to go, tough guy. Make it disappear."

Wilson, thinking fast, did just as he was told. He dropped the canvas sack down onto the floor and said, "Sure. Whatever you want. You're the boss." Wilson put the gun flat against his chest and covered his right hand with his left. With a flourish of gestures that looked like he was rubbing his hands together, he suddenly spread his hands palms out to show they were both, indeed, empty. The gun had miraculously vanished.

"Bravo, Wilson. Nice try . . . but it was I who showed you that trick a long time ago. You used to practice with hard-boiled eggs, remember? Then you moved on to bigger stuff. Looked good. I barely saw you slip the gun into your jacket. Now take it out and get rid of it for real."

Wilson knew it wasn't worth his breath protesting, so he unzipped his Pittsburgh Steelers jacket and sure enough, the gun was inside just as Lucius had known it would be.

"Okay. Now back up into the hall and toss it down the stairs. Do it!"

The shock of seeing his old trainer was finally behind him and Wilson actually breathed a sigh of relief. As insane as this situation was, at least things could be rationally explained now. There was no supernatural demon from beyond the grave stalking him and his family. No vengeful devil escaping from hell to make him pay for the mistakes of his youth. No, it was Lucius Barber, a bitter old magician who'd clearly gone off his rocker and convinced himself Wilson had to pay for what happened to Doug back in the past. It didn't make things any easier, but it gave Wilson great confidence to know he was fighting a man and not some sort of monster. Wilson reluctantly did as he was told, backing up a few steps into the hallway and heaving his weapon down the staircase and out of sight.

"Good boy. If I tell you to sit up and bark, will you do that too? Ha!" Lucius bent over to speak to Amanda. "Isn't your daddy a good boy, sweetie? Why don't you give him a hand for that amateurish little trick he did for us? Go on . . . clap for your worthless father."

Amanda tried, just to keep the madman holding her happy, but her right hand was swollen and bloody from where her finger had been severed and she screamed when she tried to put her little hands together, fresh tears of pain sliding down her flushed cheeks. "Daddy, it hurts! Please . . . help me. I wanna go home to Mommy."

Lucius laughed harder, clearly enjoying the young girl's suffering.

"You vicious, rotten bastard!" Wilson screamed, blinding rage taking the place of good sense, and he charged across the room. Lucius appeared about to speak—maybe to explain why all this was happening—but Wilson didn't want to hear any more. He didn't give a shit why this lunatic had targeted his family and the people of this small town. All he wanted to do was make him pay for the sadistic things he'd done, and still planned to do. He was taking a huge risk and putting his daughter's life in grave danger but he just couldn't stop himself. He'd crept through this house of horrors like a tightly wound coil of nerves and fear and now that he had the source of his misery in sight he had an overpowering need to explode into action and smash his ex-manager's face in, to inflict at least some of the pain this deranged man deserved.

Wilson's reckless gamble paid off.

The last thing Lucius had been expecting was for Wilson to go postal on him, and before he could react, they were crashing to the floor and rolling around, fighting for control of the knife. Lucius was obviously the stronger of the two combatants but Wilson had the strength of fear and desperation to aid him. Amanda screamed and rolled out of harm's way, but she'd distracted her father enough that Lucius was able to regain his feet and land a hard, swooping punch to the side of Wilson's head. Wilson nearly blacked out, but he bit down on his tongue and his vision cleared in time for him to block Lucius's dagger hand as the razor-sharp blade jabbed toward his unprotected belly.

The fight spilled out into the hallway, both men landing a few decent punches, but this was more of a grappling match than boxing, both more concerned with defense rather than trying to land a knockout punch.

Wilson snuck a lucky uppercut into Lucius's jaw that would have dropped a lesser man, then took advantage of his temporarily disoriented enemy by repeatedly slamming his knife hand into the railing at the top of the staircase. Lucius screamed in anger as well as pain and let go of the knife, which bounced away down the stairs and out of both fighters' reach.

Wilson thought he might just win this fight, but then Lucius drove his knee up into Wilson's groin and dropped him to his knees. Instead of pummeling Wilson with his fists, which he probably could have done easily, Lucius used the time he'd gained for himself to dash down the stairs in search of his knife.

Wilson got shakily to his feet and saw Amanda worriedly peeking out at him from the bedroom door. "Stay inside and close the door," he told her. "Don't worry. I'll be back to get you soon."

Wilson didn't stick around to make sure she obeyed, he had to go after Lucius and had already given him too big of a lead as it was. He'd managed to get the knife away from the madman once, but he'd be damned if he wanted to push his luck a second time. Wilson flew down the stairs in pursuit but Lucius was nowhere in sight. At the bottom, Wilson could see the shiny steel dagger he'd knocked out of Lucius's hand and he wondered why his ex-mentor had run right past it. Wilson stopped and bent over to retrieve the weapon, and as soon as his head ducked down, a gunshot boomed loudly in the house and Wilson felt the bullet's hot breath pass by right where his head had been only seconds earlier. If he hadn't stooped over to pick up the knife, he'd be dead right now.

Oh shit! He's got the bloody gun!

There was no time left to think. Wilson lowered his head and took off running.

Upstairs in the bedroom, Amanda heard the gunshot and started to cry again. She'd closed the door just like she'd been told and was sitting back on the carpet waiting for her father to come back. Amanda didn't know what was going on downstairs but she was deathly afraid her dad was going to get hurt, or worse yet killed, and that awful man was going to come hurt her again. She cradled her injured hand in her lap and tried to wish the bad man away, completely oblivious to the fact that behind her, the red velvet curtains silently began to open, revealing the old wooden magic trunk that had been secretly hidden from view.

A second bullet flew toward Wilson's chest as he dashed from the foot of the stairs and headed for the living room, but miraculously didn't hit him. Lucius Barber had once been an incredible magician but he certainly wasn't much of a marksman. Still, at this range, he wasn't going to miss many more shots. He was finding his aim and a bullet would tear into Wilson's flesh at any moment. Wilson made it safely to the living room, putting a wall between them, but not feeling any safer. He needed to get that gun away from Lucius or somehow sneak around behind him.

Sneak around him . . . that's it! Wilson thought, spotting a handmade multicolored quilt folded over the back of the love seat. He grabbed it on the fly, continuing on into the adjoining dining room. Lucius would be on top of him in no time, but he'd be somewhat cautious, so Wilson thought he might just have enough time to set this up. He had to—there would be no chance at a second try.

Magic was all about deception, and at the heart of all good illusions was the cardinal rule: you had to fool the audience into believing they were seeing something they weren't, or getting them to focus and concentrate on something else, so they never noticed the big picture of what you were really doing. Confusion and misdirection were the magician's greatest weapons and Wilson knew it, even more so than the knife he had in his hand. It was this knife he'd use to trap Lucius, this deadly weapon that would surely catch the tall killer's eye more than anything else.

Wilson quickly went to work.

Fuck . . . Fuck . . . FUCK! Lucius repeated over and over, still amazed he'd been unable to shoot Kemp with the two wide-open attempts he'd had. *Bloody guns! I should have used my knife . . . or better yet, my bare hands.* He'd dreamed for years about getting this chance to kill Wilson and he wasn't about to blow it. No way.

"I'm coming, coward!" Lucius screamed. "Run all you want, but I'll find you. You could have saved Doug and you damn well know it. He was the son I never had, you rotten whore, and you were never half the man or magician he was. You hear me, Wilson?"

Lucius crept slowly across the living room floor, ready for and half expecting another foolhardy charge by Wilson, like he'd tried upstairs. Only a madman would attack someone who was holding a loaded gun, but he stayed alert, prepared for anything.

"They locked me up after Doug's funeral. Locked me up for twenty years. Partly 'cause I lost it, couldn't handle you taking him away from me, but partly 'cause I learned to kill in the hospital. Took one of the interns and gutted him with a kitchen knife. Killed the fat fuck of a security guard that tried to drag me off him too. More crimes I lay at your feet, asshole. Your fault . . . all of it. And now you're finally going to pay."

Lucius moved on to the dining room, and immediately saw Wilson hunkered down in front of him, ready to lunge with his dagger, but fortunately out of striking distance. He'd never cross the floor in time. Lucius smiled in triumph and fired two point-blank shots into his enemy's chest.

Amanda Kemp heard the second gunshot, but then everything went silent again. Her heart sank, thinking the worst, and she was about to shout for her dad but then the bad man started yelling, blaming her father for things she didn't understand. His angry voice frightened her but at least it meant her dad was alive and might still rescue her. Another two gunshots rang out beneath her and Amanda screamed, clapping her hands over her ears to shut out the noise. *Make him stop . . . Make him go away!*

Behind her, the trunk of secrets slowly began to open.

Lucius Barber charged into the room, sure he'd finally killed his one-time student. He was wrong. When he pulled away the colorful quilt he thought Wilson had been foolishly hiding under, he uncovered a dining room chair with his long-bladed dagger fixed to the arm with a man's leather belt. He'd seen the knife sticking through the blanket and had just . . . *Oh my God!*

Wilson attacked from behind, jumping on Lucius's

exposed back and wrapping his arms around his head and throat and his legs around his foe's arms and waist. Like a giant boa constrictor, Wilson squeezed with all his strength, not allowing Lucius to breathe, much less try to do anything with the gun.

"Drop the gun, Lucius. Do it now or I'll rip your fucking head off!"

Lucius tried to speak but Wilson had him in a guillotine choke and had it cinched in tight. The gun clattered to the floor a few seconds later and Wilson let up on his hold just a little, hoping to talk some sense into this obviously disturbed man. As stupid of a thought as Wilson knew it was, maybe he could convince Lucius he was wrong about all this. Wrong about whose fault Doug's death was too. It was a mistake though, and as soon as Lucius felt him relax, he started bucking and thrashing around, trying to shake Wilson off his back. Wilson sunk his hooks in deeper and hung on for the ride. There would be no talking to this madman. No negotiating. Lucius was years past any type of calm, rational thinking. Death was all he understood now and it was clear to Wilson that it would either be Lucius's or his. There was no middle ground here.

Wilson let his anger build, let it pour into his arms and legs to strengthen them. This lunatic had blamed him for things he'd never done, killed his friends, threatened the lives of his family, and cut off the finger of his sweet little girl. For that alone he deserved to die and Wilson had no cold feet about being his judge, jury, and ultimately, his executioner. *Fuck you*, he thought and drove Lucius forward, pushing him down onto the dining room chair and the cruel blade of the knife that waited there.

The dagger sank into Lucius's belly, sank deep, and must have torn through some vital organs because blood sprayed like an angry river, splashing onto the seat cushion and running down the legs to pool on the floor. Through it all, Lucius remained silent. There was an initial grunt of pain as the blade entered, but after that, he'd gritted his teeth and cried out no more. Perhaps he couldn't believe Wilson had actually bested him, or maybe closer to the truth, perhaps he was actually happy the way this ended and silently looked forward to the peace he might find behind death's door.

"I'm sorry, Lucius," Wilson whispered in his ear, still holding him tightly and forcing the knife deeper still. "I loved Doug too. Honest I did. He was my best friend but I can't change the past and I couldn't let you kill my little girl."

Wilson thought Lucius was already dead, but he turned his head a little and opened his eyes. "You're a dead man, Wilson . . . and it's not me your family has to worry about."

A thick stream of blood poured out of Lucius's nose and mouth, and he died choking on his blood, his body collapsing into the chair, eyes still wide-open. Wilson released his body, thinking Lucius might sag down to the floor, but his body remained in place, pinned to the chair ironically by his own knife.

Wilson staggered over to another chair on the far side of the table, his strength draining from his legs, now that the danger was over. Part of him was appalled and nauseated thinking about what he'd just done. He'd only done what he'd needed to do—it was kill or be killed—and he'd taken the only option presented to him, but the level of violence he'd been capable of was still shocking and surprising. His other half rejoiced in victory, elated he'd somehow succeeded in defending his family against all odds.

Speaking of family, Wilson knew he should try the phones here and see if they were working. Susan would be worried sick and he should try calling to tell her things were going to be okay. He should get moving, but for the moment he was just too damn bone-weary to do anything, and Lucius's final words were still haunting him, replaying again and again in his mind. What had his ex-mentor meant that he wasn't the one they needed to worry about? Prophetic words or dying gibberish?

Does he know something I don't? What am I missing?

Upstairs, Amanda began to scream . . .

CHAPTER THIRTY-ONE

THE BOUNDARY BETWEEN

LIFE AND DEATH

Amanda's scream went on and on, nearly stopping Wilson's heart and causing him to teeter and fall backward off the chair he sat on. He crashed painfully onto his back and rolled to his feet as quickly as he could. Not having a clue what was wrong, but not wanting to find out without a weapon in his hand, Wilson quickly searched the room. There was the knife, of course, but there was no way he was going to drag Lucius's dead body off and untie his blood-drenched belt to free it. Just the thought of doing that repulsed him. He spotted the gun on the floor, grabbed it, and ran for the staircase.

He took the stairs two at a time, his exhaustion forgotten again, another surge of adrenaline-fueled dread carrying him upward toward the unknown. He was praying Amanda was only screaming out of fear or panic and everything would be all right, but when he threw open the bedroom door it took Wilson less than a second to realize things weren't okay and might never be again.

Wilson began to scream too.

A monstrous *thing* (the only word that came to Wilson's wildly spinning mind) stood inside a huge wooden steamer trunk on the far side of the room, holding a meat cleaver to Amanda's throat, a scrawny, disease-ridden nightmare that was half man and half rotted corpse. It was tall and bony shouldered, and despite its frail appearance and obvious gruesome afflictions, seemed quite powerful—perhaps even supernaturally strong. On its upper body, it wore a gaudy red and black tuxedo jacket, which was ripped and filthy around the frayed edges, but was completely naked from the waist down. It looked like some sort of carnival freak, or failed lab experiment, a beast that was all cancerous growths, varicose veins, and pus-filled weeping sores, but was trying hard to stand upright and pass for a human being. Its penis was gone, rotted away, leaving a huge flabby testicle sack the color of bruised meat hanging below a still-bleeding hole.

It was *Elephant Man* meets *Night of the Living Dead*.

It was pink healthy tissue meets black putrid flesh.

It was life meets death.

It was . . .

The face . . . the eyes! Sweet mother of God . . . the EYES!

Wilson screamed again, this time not because he was shocked to see something so hideous on the waking side of a dream, but simply because he finally recognized this fiend for who it was.

It's him! The Heatseeker!

Doug Williams was in the room, or something that had once been him more than two decades ago, back before he'd died in that horrific accident onstage. Even though he'd believed the Heatseeker was behind the trouble all along, Wilson was so in shock at the sight of his deformed and decaying old partner, all he could do was stand there with his mouth hanging open, his feet seemingly glued to the floorboards. It was Amanda who broke the trance.

"Daddy! Help! Get this . . . this monster off me!"

Wilson snapped out of it and raised his gun to chest level, aiming up at the spongy head of his ex-friend. He took two steps forward into the room, trying to show he wasn't afraid but also to improve the odds of hitting his target easier without putting Amanda at risk.

For the second time in the last twenty minutes, Wilson found himself saying, "Let Amanda go, Doug. I don't know what the fuck has happened to you, but it has nothing to do with her."

The Heatseeker smiled, or half his rubbery mouth did, pleased Wilson had recognized him. A thick, syrupy line of drool ran down the left side of his cheek as he said in a deep, terribly raw voice, "What's the matter, Wilson? Don't you like the way I look? Aren't I good enough to meet your precious little girl?"

"Let her go now or I'll deflate that fucking balloon head of yours." Wilson meant it too. He'd already crossed the line once tonight in the name of his family. The killing would get easier from here on in, not harder. And besides, killing this monstrosity would be doing the world a favor.

"I don't think so, little man. I'm not done with her yet and it's been way too long since we had a chance to kick back and chat. Don't you think?"

In answer, Wilson took careful aim and pulled the trigger. He'd heard and seen enough to know killing the Heatseeker was his and Amanda's only way out of this madness. He'd never allow either of them to leave this house alive.

CLICK . . .

Nothing happened.

CLICK . . . CLICK . . .

The Heatseeker began to laugh. It sounded like the rumble of approaching thunder and sent a chill down Wilson's spine.

The gun was empty. Impossible. Or was it? Wilson could clearly recall the four shots Lucius had recently fired, and now that he thought about it, Officer Daniels and Big Mack had said something about bullets fired at the Henderson house when they'd had him in the back of the cruiser. Wilson had never actually checked to see how many bullets were left in the gun. Never even knew how many rounds a .38 caliber like this could hold. Obviously the answer was six. *Fuck! Of course it holds six, idiot!* Wilson tossed the useless weapon away into the corner of the room. Now what was he going to do? What could he do?

His eyes found the canvas bag he'd dropped on the bedroom floor earlier, before his fight with Lucius. He'd packed a knife inside of it. Other useful things too, if only he could get his hands on them. The bag was less than six feet away, but right now that seemed like an awfully far distance to travel. It wasn't like the Heatseeker would just stand there and simply allow Wilson to rummage around in the bag to find another weapon. He'd carve a red smile in Amanda's throat with his stainless-steel cleaver before Wilson could even get the bag in his hands. No, it was too much of a risk. There had to be a better way.

"Do you have any idea how long I've waited for this moment?" the Heatseeker said. "Decades filled with loneliness and pain, endless suffering beyond your wildest imagination. All worth it though; every excruciating moment just to see that hopeless look on your face."

There were a million questions running around Wilson's head but he asked the most obvious one first. "How did you get here? You died in front of my eyes. How did you ever escape . . . ?" Wilson couldn't find the words to properly express his bewilderment.

"Escape what? My coffin? Death? Hell?"

Wilson could only nod his head, but took a casual step sideways, moving closer to the canvas bag near his feet.

"It wasn't easy, but not as hard as the endless horde of people who die think. The borders between life and death are thin, Wilson, paper-thin in places, depending on time and circumstances. People on both sides of the threshold are constantly testing the walls, probing for weaknesses every single day. Psychics, fortune-tellers, mentalists, magicians, and even madmen knock on doorways from here on earth, but just as frequently spirits, demons, angels, ghosts, and other entities knock back from the other side. If you've ever experienced a vision or out-of-body experience, a lucid dream, or even déjà vu, then you've stepped across the line. Temporarily, of course, but you've been there. I searched the darkest pits of hell for years to find a more permanent crack, a way to visit this realm but not get sucked back down into the dark."

"And Lucius? Why drag him into this?" Wilson inched closer to the bag, trying not to be obvious but unsure if the Heatseeker was onto him or not.

"Lucius was a means to an end. Nothing more. A link I had to this world I needed to complete the transfer. He was in an asylum when I contacted him through dreams. I helped him plan an escape and he eventually met me at the cemetery in Jamestown and freed me from my place of rest. There wasn't much to me then, only powder, bones, and a few tufts of hair sticking to my crumbling skull—I'd left the rest in hell. But Lucius gathered all that remained and took me home to the house he'd trained us at all those years ago.

"It wasn't his anymore, naturally, but he killed the man who lived there and moved in. The house was a wreck, a junkyard of things new and old, even an entire storeroom filled with Lucius's and our old props. This travel trunk was in there and it became my home, my sanctuary here on earth while Lucius fed me and let me grow stronger."

"Fed you?"

"Blood, Wilson. To start with, anyway. Blood gives you life, old friend, and it did me as well. Lucius cut himself to feed me and soon flesh began to grow around the bones and my body began the slow process of knitting itself back together. The more Lucius fed me, the faster I recuperated, but it was still an excruciatingly slow process.

"Blood was soon replaced with flesh and I was fed the bodies of hundreds of dogs, cats, and, yes, men and women too. Lucius would bring them to me so I could feast . . . and grow. And all that time, we searched for you, searched half the country carried inside a rotted wooden box. I have no idea why I couldn't locate you as easily as I had Lucius, but maybe my hatred blinded me. It wasn't until I was in fairly close proximity that I felt your presence and brought Lucius to this decrepit town. He was a necessary evil for me, but ultimately an expendable one. I'm strong enough now to deal with you myself. You and the rest of your family, starting with this little animal here."

Amanda struggled against the man-monster but she was no match for his strength. She squealed in pain when he yanked hard on her hair, fresh tears rolling down her cheeks as she silently pleaded with her eyes for her father to help her.

"But why, Doug? Why do you hate me so much?" Wilson said, curious but mostly to keep the Heatseeker talking. He was standing right beside the canvas bag now, only a knee bend away from his knife. "I was your friend . . . your best friend. I never asked for any of this to happen to you. I didn't want you to die."

"You didn't do much to prevent it though, did you? When that drill bit was spinning toward me that night, and I finally realized I wasn't going to be able to get out in time, I looked over and there you were with this big stupid look on your face. For a fraction of a second I was filled with hope. You'd shaken off the drug I'd given you and were going to run out onstage and save me. Yeah, right! You just stood there licking your lips and looking forward to seeing the blood fly."

"That's not true, Doug. In fact, you couldn't be more wrong. I was in shock, horrified at what was happening. My head was still cloudy from the knockout drug and I was ready to pass out again. When I saw you onstage, I froze up. Couldn't move a muscle. I've thought of and dreamed of that night a million times since then and wished I could go back and change things but I couldn't. I'm not proud of the way I acted but it still wasn't my fault. You were the one who drugged me and took my place. You were the one who wore my mask and tricked the stagehands into thinking you were me. You chose to take the risk performing an escape you weren't qualified to do. How the hell is any of that MY bloody fault?

"I've suffered too, you know? Everyone blamed me for your death. Lucius . . . the fans . . . the media . . . hell, even myself. I spiraled down into a life of alcohol and bitter failure. There were days I wished it had been me who died that night. Years I thought I'd be better off dead, but I made it through all that. My wife and daughter helped me and *damned* if you have the right to blame me for living. You have one person to blame for your suffering, Doug, and that's yourself. Your greed, ego, and jealousy are what caused your death, not me!"

Everything went quiet in the room after Wilson's passionate outburst. Too quiet. The Heatseeker's fleshy lips trembled, his thin, deformed body literally shaking with rage and Wilson knew he'd gone too far; said things he shouldn't have, even if they were the truth. A cold fear spread through his body then, an icy certainty he'd just issued Amanda's death warrant. At any second, he expected the Heatseeker to chop or rip the cleaver across her tender skin and helplessly watch as her blood sprayed in twin geysers against the faded walls. If he was going to make a move for the canvas bag, it had to be done now.

"Your little bag won't do you any good, Wilson," the Heatseeker whispered, catching him glancing down. "It's too late for heroics. You took everything from me, you fucking coward. My fame, my fortune . . . my life, and now I'm going to return the favor and take what you care about most."

"Noooo!" Wilson screamed, sure the Heatseeker meant to kill Amanda. Unexpectedly, instead of slitting her throat, he dragged her backward down into the large wooden trunk on top of him and reached out to pull the heavy lid shut, trapping them both within.

Amanda screamed but it was more in surprise than pain. Wilson immediately grabbed the canvas bag at his feet, quickly fished out the knife, and cautiously approached the closed and eerily silent trunk. Psyching himself up to strike as soon as the lid was open, Wilson reached down and tugged on the thick leather handle. He expected resistance, a tug-of-war to get the lid open, but there was none. The trunk lid raised easily on well-oiled hinges, and as soon as the lip cleared his arm, Wilson gritted his teeth and started to swing . . .

His knife swished through open air.

The trunk of secrets was empty. Empty of people at least; the Heatseeker and Amanda both mysteriously gone, vanished along with the wooden bottom of the trunk and the floorboards and house rational thought dictated should be beneath it. They were all gone.

In their place was a spiral staircase leading down into pitch darkness. From somewhere far below, Amanda screamed and the Heatseeker began to laugh.

CHAPTER THIRTY-TWO

DOWN INTO THE DARK

No way! This can't be happening. Impossible!

Wilson couldn't believe what he was seeing, but recognized the spiral staircase instantly. It was the same stone steps as in his recent recurring nightmares, the one where the Heatseeker stopped every now and then to cut off . . .

"Amanda!" he screamed, shutting that thought off before it crippled him. Clutching the knife in one hand and his canvas bag in the other, fear overriding his skepticism, Wilson stepped inside the trunk and began to descend. "I'm coming, honey! Don't be scared. Daddy's coming. Hold on, baby."

Below, the Heatseeker laughed again. "That's right, Wilson. Come down to the devil's playground. We'll have us . . . pardon the pun . . . a hell of a time."

When Wilson had made it down seven steps, the lid on the trunk above him suddenly slammed shut, plunging the staircase into absolute blackness. There was no light whatsoever, and Wilson felt immediately claustrophobic, trapped within these circular stone walls. He felt like he were in the throat of a mile-long snake, slowly being swallowed and pushed downward toward the serpent's acidy stomach, every blind step leading him closer and closer to a hideous death.

He desperately wanted to run up and let the light of the bedroom back into the shaft, but he knew there was no time to waste. For all he knew, that bedroom in the dead old woman's house was no longer even there. This had to be just an incredibly realistic illusion the Heatseeker was performing, but there was always the chance it was all real, and Wilson was following his nemesis through a rip in the fabric between worlds, a portal between the boundaries of life and death, and down into the pit of hell.

One thing was sure, wherever he was it was certainly getting hot. Wilson peeled off his jacket and dropped it on the stairs behind him without looking back. It helped a little, but not much; sweat started to dampen his forehead and body.

Wilson picked up his pace, always shuffling down and curling to his right, moving as fast as he could by feel alone. He scratched his elbows and shoulders repeatedly but he ignored the pain, ignored the claustrophobia, and ignored the rising temperatures. Every now and then he'd hear the Heatseeker chuckling or Amanda sobbing, but no matter how fast he tried to move, Wilson could never seem to catch up with them. It was the opposite, in fact, every time he would catch a noise from below, it seemed the Heatseeker was getting farther and farther away. It wasn't long until he heard nothing at all. Nothing in front of him, nothing behind. Just deafening silence and the ever-present black curtain of darkness. Wilson wanted to scream, just to know he still existed, to know he hadn't gone stark raving mad.

"Amanda! I can't find you, baby. Say something. Anything. Where the hell are you?"

"Exactly!" the Heatseeker whispered, his deep, gravelly voice so close Wilson jumped, smashing his head on the rough stone wall in his panic. "She's in hell, coward. Same as you! Here . . . see for yourself."

Ahead of Wilson, down around the next bend in the staircase, a light flared, and out of the darkness a monstrous deformed shadow was cast on the wall, nearly close enough to touch. Wilson raced down the stairs, too frightened to actually let it affect him now. He was on cruise control, reacting on instinct alone, dreading the confrontation with the Heatseeker but knowing it was inevitable.

A flaming torch appeared in front of him, set into a wall sconce high above his head in the stone. The Heatseeker was nowhere in sight. The small passageway smelled of kerosene and the heat coming off the torch was incredible for such a small flame. It was so hot down here already that any additional heat was uncalled for and definitely unwanted, but the blessed light the torch gave off more than compensated for it, and Wilson slid the torch out of the sconce and carried it with him farther down the staircase. He grasped the torch in his left hand, the same hand he carried the canvas bag with, keeping his right free in case he needed to use the knife.

Now that he could see, Wilson's imagination was working overtime. He jumped at every shifting nuance of the light, every flickering shadow, tensing for potential attacks, but none came. He was stressed to the max and the heat and pressure were starting to take their toll on his body. Worse still, he started watching the stairs ahead of him, certain his recent nightmares were about to come true and he'd start finding Amanda's fingers chopped off and one placed every ten to fifteen stairs. He wasn't prepared for something that horrible and thought his mind just might snap if he had to stop to gather up more parts of his daughter.

Thankfully, it didn't happen, and Wilson eventually made it to the bottom of the long, winding staircase without incident. The staircase opened up into a wide dirt-floored corridor. The hallway was completely bare, straight ahead, a sturdy wooden door its only exit. He couldn't help but notice the sign secured to the oak panel. It said: WELCOME TO HELL.

Just like my dream . . .

With no other options open to him, Wilson pushed his way through the heavy oak door and found himself standing in the familiar large circular chamber with a high-domed roof formed out of solid rock and its entire area—floor, walls, and roof—painted bloodred. Unlike his previous nightmares, the Heatseeker—or what must have been some monstrous dream version of him—wasn't standing across the room ready to lop off Amanda's head the moment Wilson ran to save her. Neither she, nor the Heatseeker were anywhere in view, but the room most certainly wasn't empty. The skinless man was there, once again shackled to the wall with silver chains to Wilson's left. As he'd done before, the walking wound who'd once been a man licked his exposed teeth and saluted to Wilson, silently bidding him entry into the room with a sweep of his mutilated arm. Across the massive chamber, illuminated by bright white spotlights, stood a steel and wooden apparatus that chilled Wilson to the core, despite the intense heat of the room.

It was one of his old escape tables; the machinery and

restraints set up and ready to go. Not just any escape trick either. It was the Devil's Drill Bit.

Holy fuck! Why's that here?

Directly behind the escape table, on the opposite side of the chamber, another wooden door led out of the room. The door was closed and Wilson could only presume the Heatseeker had taken Amanda through it, so he made his way cautiously forward, trying his best to ignore the skinless sentinel who watched his every step with rapt attention, but did nothing to stop him. To reach the door, Wilson had to go around the magic apparatus, so he was drawn near it out of necessity as much as curiosity. Up close, the Devil's Drill Bit looked more ominous than he remembered it from his youth. It looked hard and uncomfortable, cruel and deadly, like a medieval torture device custom-made by the Spanish Inquisition, or better yet, Vlad the Impaler. Wilson shuddered and tried to walk on by.

Something grabbed his left hand.

Wilson screamed and dropped the canvas bag and the flaming torch to the floor. He was shocked to see a shiny stainless-steel handcuff firmly looped around his wrist, chaining him to the table. *Weird. How did that happen?*

He was in the process of removing the cuff when the chain suddenly went taut and he was yanked hard across the table to land on his back in the center of the apparatus. Another shiny handcuff slithered across the table like a metallic snake and latched onto his right wrist, then quickly pulled back tight to stretch Wilson painfully across the mysterious table, holding him firmly in place.

What the fuck! Wilson thought, then heard the door behind him squeak open and knew he was in big trouble.

The Heatseeker walked passed him dragging Amanda by her hair and never even acknowledged Wilson until he'd bound the girl to the wall with thick yellow ropes beside the skinless man. The Heatseeker no longer carried his nasty-looking meat cleaver, but was now wearing his white leather theatrical mask, the vivid gold, green, and red image smiling grotesquely on his misshapen head.

"There you go, kiddo," the masked magician said. "Stay here and play with old Peeler. He's friendlier than he looks . . . I think. The two of you can get ready to watch your daddy die. You never know; it might be fun. I know I'm sure gonna enjoy it."

"Leave him alone," Amanda said, bravely ignoring the skinless freak beside her. Tears were running down her dirty cheeks, and her eyes were wide and pleading but the Heatseeker only laughed and walked over toward Wilson. He easily removed the knife from Wilson's trapped right hand and casually walked to the head of the table.

"Well, well, well . . . what do we have here? Got yourself in a heck of a bind now, don't you, old friend?"

"Don't you dare hurt her, you bastard. If you or that . . . that thing over there touches her, I'll—"

"You'll do nothing," the Heatseeker interrupted, clearly enjoying this. "And don't worry about her new pal, Peeler's been with me for years. He was an old friend of Lucius's actually, back in the day, a lunatic who thought he could escape his troubles by shedding all of his skin. Instead . . . he ended up finding me. Peeler's not important. I just thought you might like a little audience for your big trick. You ready to put on a show?"

"Let me out of these cuffs right now!" Wilson screamed,

ignoring the question. "What's the matter with you? And why are you wearing that damn mask?"

"Because I like it, and I don't know . . . it just seemed so damn appropriate. Just like the good ol' days, don't you think? Oh . . . nearly forgot. I have one of yours too." The Heatseeker reached into his tuxedo jacket and pulled out another leather mask, roughly pulling it over Wilson's head and down over his face but didn't bother trying to tie it in back. Wilson's mask showed the sad version of the dual tragedy image, its smiling demented twin gazing down on him from above.

"Jesus, Doug. Stop it, man! Why are you doing this?"

The Heatseeker leaned down inches from Wilson's face, his rancid breath nearly making Wilson gag. "I'll tell you why," he whispered. "Because I want to. Because I can. What other reasons do I need? You killed me on this machine . . . now I'm going to repay the favor. Tit for tat, ya know?"

With that, the Heatseeker moved to the end of the table near Wilson's feet, and hit a button out of view that brought the deadly machine roaring to life. Amanda started to scream, Peeler started to clap, and the Heatseeker started to laugh as the huge drill bit began to spin faster and faster, but Wilson didn't hear or notice any of them. He was too busy concentrating on the steel auger slowly descending toward his chest.

You can get out of this thing, Wilson. Easy. Just relax and do it.

If memory served him right, he should have about fifty seconds to get off this table—a minute tops—which was more than enough time to slip a few handcuffs. Back in the day, he'd have pretended to struggle and delay things long enough that the crowd would be screaming and thinking he was in trouble when actually it only took seconds to get out of danger. There were no crowds to please here though, and Wilson had no desire to push his luck, so he dislocated his left thumb and slipped out of the cuff. He was about to reach across and free his right hand too, but suddenly his left wrist was trapped again. The handcuff was possessed or had a spell cast on it, seemingly having a life of its own, reattaching to his wrist as soon as he pulled free.

Oh shit! Wilson thought, getting worried now, trying to slip the cuff a second time. He did, but just as easily, the cuff grabbed his hand again, pinning him back in place.

The drill bit spun closer.

The Heatseeker laughed louder, loving every second of his sadistic revenge plan. "Not so easy to get out, huh? Been there, done that, big guy. Better hurry, Wilson . . . time's running out!"

Wilson didn't waste time pointlessly arguing with the monstrous man who'd carefully planned his death. There had to be some way out of this. *Concentrate, man. Think!* Maybe if he was quicker. The possessed handcuff could move like a snake and it was fast, but he could be faster. *The cuff's on a chain and will only be able to reach so far, right?*

Right. Or at least Wilson hoped he was. This time he slipped the left cuff and immediately rolled hard to his right, clearing the drill and standing up beside the table, where he quickly slipped the right cuff too. On the table, both handcuffs bucked around, writhing as if angry and in disbelieve he'd broken free. They weren't the only ones either. The Heatseeker was livid, hitting the kill switch on the drill to bring the deadly auger to a grinding halt. Wilson thought he was going to charge him, but even in his rage and disappointment at not seeing Wilson torn to pieces, the Heatseeker was smart enough to realize he still had the advantage over his enemy.

He had Wilson's daughter.

And he had Wilson's knife.

The Heatseeker retreated over to where Amanda was tied to the red wall. He simply placed the tip of the shiny blade against the side of her delicate throat and waited for Wilson to make the first move. There was no fear in his eyes, and he was still smiling, almost looking forward to whatever Wilson decided to try. One way or another, he was sure he'd get his revenge in the end, even if his plans had been so rudely changed.

Peeler whimpered and moved as far away from his master as his chains would allow. The skinless man curled into a ball and cowered against the wall, wanting no part of whatever was about to happen.

Wilson ripped off his ghoulish stage mask and tossed it on the floor. He moved to the other side of the table, and being careful to avoid the reaching handcuff on that side, he bent over and picked up the canvas bag. Inside, he had no other weapons to choose from, so he pulled out the Teflon-lined glass bottle; thankful it hadn't shattered when the bag had fallen to the hard stone floor. It was time to see if God were on his side. He uncapped the bottle and raised it reverently above his head.

"Bless me, Father," Wilson said in prayer. "Give me the strength and courage to strike down your enemies. Let this water cleanse the evil from this place in your glory."

The Heatseeker began to laugh again, a deep, rumbling, terrible laugh that echoed through the vast chamber. "You pathetic fool, Wilson. You bring a glass of water to the gates of hell? Have you lost your mind entirely?"

"This isn't just water, Doug. It's holy water, blessed by a priest earlier tonight. I'm not as stupid as you seem to think."

"You sure about that, big boy?" the Heatseeker sneered, releasing Amanda and walking slowly toward where Wilson stood. "Might want to rethink things a little. Lucius followed you to the church tonight, and after you left he went in and killed your so-called holy man."

"What? Father Harris? But why would—"

"Seems the good priest wasn't quite as honest with you as he was with Lucius. Turns out he was a fucking pervert, a coward like you who roamed around in the dark peeking at titties and pussy through the windows to get his jollies."

"That's a lie. Patrick Harris was a good man and a—"

"He was a sicko, Wilson. Bug-shit crazy, in fact, and any semblance of faith in God he might have once had was gone long ago. Your little jar of holy water is useless. Well . . . not entirely, I guess." The Heatseeker reached out and easily plucked the glass container from Wilson's trembling hand. "It is rather hot in here . . . Cheers!"

The evil magician winked, a contented look on his oversize, deformed face, and smugly tipped the bottle up to the mouth slit in his mask to drink it dry. The pain hit him right away and now it was Wilson's turn to smile.

Fuck you, old friend. I got ya!

The Heatseeker dropped the knife. He also dropped the bottle. His mask, mouth, tongue, and esophagus burned away almost instantly, the skin of his throat disintegrating and splitting open like a peeled juicy fruit. The ghoul started to scream, frantically tearing off the top half of his gruesome mask but his vocal cords were being eaten away and all he managed to do was blow out a wet, gurgling slosh of bloody foam through the gaping wound. His eyes locked onto Wilson, frantic and wild, clearly bewildered as to what had just happened.

"Hydrochloric and nitric acid. Every magician's best friend. Can burn the fuck out of you but might just save your life; remember? I've kept a bottle of it around my house for years. You're not as smart as you think either. I went back to ask Father Harris another question to-night . . . and I heard the conversation between Lucius and him. At the time I thought it was you, but I didn't dare go close enough to look. No matter. I knew my holy water was useless but thought it might be something I could use against you all the same. I went back home and switched it for my acid, hoping you might be stupid enough to try something like this. Worst case I could have at least thrown it at you, but I like this much, much better."

The Heatseeker's face and neck were a ruin of bubbling flesh, and he was staggering around in a daze. Before he could make a move for Amanda or the knife again, Wilson maneuvered around him and when the timing was right, launched a flying kick at his chest that knocked the grievously injured magician backward onto the sturdy wood table behind him. Before the Heatseeker could re-act, the possessed handcuffs slithered across the table and latched onto his wrists, pulling the chains tight and pinning him in place. He struggled against the restraints, still trying to scream, but Wilson had heard quite enough out of this freak to last a lifetime.

"Save it, Doug. It's over. My life and my family are all I've got in the world, and like it or not, you aren't taking them. I win. You lose!" Wilson reached down and put his hand on the green start button. "Ready for the limelight again? All set to wow the crowd, tough guy? It's what you always craved, isn't it? Well, you got it. Do your thing, motherfucker! It's SHOWTIME!"

Wilson punched the button and the Devil's Drill Bit roared to life once again. With the razor-sharp auger already partially descended from earlier, it meant the Heatseeker only had about thirty seconds to attempt an escape. Though Doug had been and still was a great magician, Wilson knew it wasn't going to happen—he wasn't an escape artist and never had been. So just like the first time, the Heatseeker thrashed around on the table and tried his best, but he wasn't going to be able to slip out of the possessed cuffs.

The drill bit continued to descend.

Wilson retreated over to his daughter, worried he might have to fight the skinless freak chained beside her, but Peeler was still shivering against the wall and didn't even look up when he approached. Wilson untied Amanda from the ropes, careful not to bang her damaged hand. They'd have to get her to a doctor as soon as possible, but for now, Wilson held her close and told her to close her eyes. She didn't need to see what was about to happen and truth be told, Wilson wasn't sure he did either. He wasn't leaving though. Not yet. Not until he was sure the Heatseeker was dead.

Dead again, he thought, and the maniacal laughter that threatened to burst from his lungs scared him a little and he cut that thought off quickly. *Hold it together, Wilson. Don't lose it, man.*

On the wooden table, the Heatseeker had stopped thrashing around, resigned to the fact he couldn't get out of the cuffs that bound him in harm's way. Instead of watching the rapidly descending drill bit, he turned his head to the side to stare over at Wilson. His face was an open wound, a ruin of foamy blood, melting skin, and exposed teeth and bone. The only parts of his face still remotely human were his eyes and Wilson had never seen anyone stare with such cold, calculated hatred. In those eyes, Wilson saw death, grueling despair, and the specter of such cruel, intense, eternal suffering he was forced to look away for fear of being sucked into their darkness. Where the Heatseeker was going, Wilson had no desire to follow.

And then the spinning blade bit into the Heatseeker's red and black jacket and the tender meat of his reanimated chest beneath. The razor-sharp auger mercilessly drilled through diseased skin and bone, sending a shower of gore fifteen feet in the air and covering the near walls with a fine red mist and chunks of sticky, rotted flesh. The whirling blade chewed down through the Heatseeker's black heart and effortlessly tore his spinal column into shrapnel, quickly coring all the way through to the blood-drenched wooden table below.

Having reached its preset mechanical limit, the Devil's Drill Bit shut down, grinding to a halt, leaving the vast chamber Wilson and Amanda stood in deafeningly silent and smelling like death. Wilson had seen enough. He felt no victory at the moment, no joy. All he wanted was to get away from this awful place and take his daughter home to Susan. "Come on, honey. It's over."

Staying well out of reach of the docile, skinless man, Wilson quickly retrieved the still-flaming torch from the floor, ignoring the warm red juices on the handle, and led Amanda out of the room. They began the long, arduous climb back up the winding staircase, Wilson holding his little girl in his arms for as long as he could, but he was too exhausted to carry her very far. Eventually he had to set her down and let her climb the stairs herself.

A few minutes later, the ground beneath them shifted unexpectedly, the entire staircase swaying as if becoming unmoored from its foundation. *What on earth?* Wilson thought.

"Daddy . . . look!" Amanda yelled, pointing back down the stairs, fear in her voice again.

Wilson turned and his breath caught in his throat. The staircase was starting to dissolve behind them. Not melting, no, it was slowly fading away to nothing, disappearing before their very eyes. With the Heatseeker dead and gone, this powerful grand illusion he'd created was now crumbling, the passageway between earth and hell he'd opened slowly closing its door. Wilson couldn't understand any of it, but he knew enough to know they were in big trouble. Wilson grabbed Amanda and shoved her forward. "Run, Amanda. Run as fast as you can!"

Together they bolted up the stairs, taking them two at a time until they were no longer able. Even when they were nearly spent, they forced themselves onward and up, the magic staircase evaporating behind them and the pitch-black void closing in on their backs. Just when Wilson was sure they were doomed, envisioning the stairs vanishing beneath their feet and them falling endlessly down into the bottomless dark chasm below, they found the lid of the old travel trunk and dove out onto the threadbare carpet of the second-floor bedroom where they'd started from.

With Amanda safely in his arms, Wilson watched as the trunk of secrets started to tremble and shake, then suddenly it vanished from the room. One second it was there, the next it was just gone. *Good riddance*, Wilson thought and kissed Amanda on the forehead.

"You okay, sweetie?" he asked. "How's your poor hand?"

"It hurts, Daddy, but not as much as before. Thanks for coming for me. I knew you would."

"You're welcome. I love you, Amanda. Always have . . . always will."

"I love you too, Dad. Can we go home now?"

Wilson smiled and hugged her tight, thrilled and amazed they were all going to be okay. Actually, they were going to be something better—they would be together.

"Sure we can, angel. Let's go."

SATURDAY, APRIL 17

SEVEN MONTHS LATER . . .

CHAPTER THIRTY-THREE

SOME NIGHTMARES NEVER END

The winter had been brutally cold, with more snow burying the town than in the previous five years combined. Most of the citizens of Billington had grumbled and complained through the entire season, but not the Kemp family. They'd used the long, quiet months to rest and work on mending not only their family life but also their previously close-minded way of thinking. The events of last September had changed them. Changed all of them, Susan and Amanda perhaps even more so than Wilson.

Wilson had always believed in the power of magic—whether to heal, destroy, or simply to entertain—but Susan and Amanda had needed a crash course, whether they'd wanted one or not. The Heatseeker had altered their outlook on life, made believers out of them, and although life had been hell for a while it had brought their family together and prepared them to stay vigilant and on guard. Amanda had lost her baby finger, of course, but it had never really fazed her. She was a tough kid and had even given herself the nickname of Stumpy to her friends and classmates. Wilson and Susan were amazed by her resiliency and incredibly proud of her for helping their family return to at least a seminormal way of life.

Without Amanda, they'd be lost.

At least the police left them alone now, usually anyway. A few of the police officers still looked at Wilson funny and would whisper among themselves that he must have been involved in the murders, but for the most part they were left in peace. Wilson had been arrested the day after he'd rescued Amanda, had voluntarily turned himself in to Officer Jake Jackson, in fact. He'd been locked up with an extra guard posted outside his cell, just to keep a twenty-four-hour eye on him to make sure he didn't pull any more of those fancy disappearing tricks. Wilson had given blood, urine, saliva, and hair follicle samples, and graciously submitted to a polygraph test twice in the following week.

Wilson had altered his story radically from the truth, of course, but stayed close enough that things went remarkably smooth. He'd told investigators how his old mentor, Lucius Barber, had escaped from a mental institute and came to Billington on a killing spree aimed at Wilson and his family. He explained about his ex-partner Douglas Williams's death years ago, how Lucius must have blamed him for the terrible accident, setting up an elaborate scheme to torment and frighten Wilson, then eventually kidnap his daughter, Amanda. Wilson had gone to the house on Leamon Avenue to rescue her and had been forced to kill Lucius in a heroic act of self-defense. DNA evidence from the Leamon house, Edith and Earl Henderson's place, St. Michael's Catholic Church, the red Ford pickup truck (belonging to a missing farmer named Duke Winslow, who would later be identified by his dental records as the human skeleton left on the bandstand in the center of the park), and various other crime scenes around town, all traced back to Lucius Barber, confirming Wilson's farfetched tale and forcing the authorities to release him back to his family. In total, Wilson spent twenty days in jail, waiting on lab results to be confirmed and the murder investigation to be closed.

Thinking back on the events of last fall, Wilson was still confused about a lot of things. He'd staggered home that night, Amanda asleep in his arms, thinking he'd forever be wondering if the staircase to hell had been real or simply just an elaborate illusion. Unfortunately, he'd learned the answer less than an hour later. When he finally made it home to Susan's house, it was the middle of the night and Susan was standing in the front yard with a frightened, dazed look on her face. He'd assured her their problems were over and that besides Amanda's finger, they were both okay, but still she seemed afraid. "What the matter?" he'd asked her, but all she could do was point to the house.

Inside, Wilson had been astonished to find something big sitting in the middle of the living room that had never been there before. It was the trunk of secrets, the old wooden travel trunk they had so recently watched disappear from the second-floor bedroom over on Leamon Avenue. How it had gotten there was anyone's guess. Susan said it had just appeared there right out of the blue.

Not really wanting to but knowing he had to look, Wilson cautiously opened the lid, half convinced that some nightmares never end and the stairway to hell would be open once again. Thankfully, it wasn't. In the bottom of the wooden trunk were a ripped red and black tuxedo jacket, half a leather mask with its colorful smile disintegrated off the bottom of it, a stainless-steel meat cleaver, and a pile of dust and bones. *He's finally at rest*, Wilson had thought, but also knew in his heart that this had been real magic. Real power. Somehow his old friend had accomplished what no other before him, magician or madman alike, had ever succeeded in doing—he'd found a way back from the grave. It was a frightening endeavor, but amazing at the same time.

Susan hadn't cared, of course, and ordered Wilson to get rid of the box before the police found it. He agreed. He already had his simpler version of the story ready for the authorities and there was no need to complicate things by dragging the withered remains of Douglas Williams into this. Some secrets were better off kept.

So Wilson had tried to get rid of it—three different times. The first time, Wilson had buried the Heatseeker's remains in the backyard, and busted the trunk into burnable-size pieces with a sledgehammer. Before he could even light the fire, they found the trunk back inside the house, intact in the living room again, the dust and bones back inside. Thinking maybe it had some sort of spell keeping it together, he and Susan had tried again, digging a sizable hole in the backyard to bury the entire crate without damaging it. Covered in dirt and exhausted from all the digging, they'd returned to the house only to find the magic trunk once again inside waiting for them.

The sun had been rising by that time, and Wilson knew the police would be searching for him, so for the time being, Susan had helped him drag the trunk down into the basement, where they left it sitting under a paint-covered drop sheet. Susan had taken Amanda to the emergency room at the hospital while Wilson showered and then eventually turned himself in to the police, the trunk staying hidden in the basement until his return nearly three weeks later. Once the heat had settled down and the eyes of the town were no longer constantly watching, Wilson had tried once more to get rid of the Heatseeker's accursed wooden box.

Susan had borrowed a friend's pickup truck and they had driven the trunk all the way back to Jamestown, New York, and under the cover of darkness had broken back into Doug Williams's mausoleum and returned the Heatseeker's remains to his empty casket. They then threw the wooden trunk into the nearby lake, watching it sink out of sight and hoping that by returning his body to his final resting place, whatever curse they were a part of, the spell would be broken.

Impossible as it seemed, the magical trunk was waiting for them back at the house in Billington again. Resigned to the fact they were never getting rid of the damn thing, Wilson had taken the box back down to the basement again. He used six long steel chains to wrap around the box and six brand-new heavy-duty steel locks to make sure no one would ever open up the trunk of secrets again. Then he covered it with the drop sheets and tried his best to forget about it.

Winter had set in and the Kemp family had bunkered down to start putting their life back together. Months passed and so too did their fear. Wilson stayed true to his word and never touched the vodka bottle ever again. He'd briefly considered restarting his career as a magician but for the welfare of his family he decided to just put the past behind him and start fresh. Once he'd sobered up, he'd found a decent job down at Pridmore's Hardware Store on Main Street. The pay wasn't great and Wilson had to cover for the owner every second weekend, but it was honest work and he was thankful for it.

February turned to March, and March to April, spring melting away the ice and snow and the grass and flowers began to grow. Wilson and Susan were like happy teenagers, their family united again and seemingly without a care in the world. Amanda no longer had nightmares and on Saturday, April the seventeenth, for the first time in ages, she decided to sleep in her own room again, finally getting tired of Mom's nagging and Dad's snoring. Not that Wilson or Susan minded her sleeping with them. She'd been through a lot—they all had—and the past seven months of sticking together had forged a bond between them that would never be broken.

With Amanda tucked safely in bed, Wilson made love to Susan and drifted off to sleep with her wrapped in his strong arms. After years of guilt, shame, and alcohol abuse, his life was back on track and finally perfect. Well, perhaps not perfect, but as far as he was concerned, after everything they'd gone through, it was close enough.

CHAPTER THIRTY-FOUR

FOOTSTEPS

Wilson's contented snores echoed around the second-floor bedroom for over an hour, but then he slipped into the REM stage of consciousness and the buzz-saw noises suddenly stopped. Wilson dreamed of a dark place, and of a strange, skinless man covered in blood and open sores, who constantly licked his teeth to keep them wet. It was his first nightmare in over a month but although it was a disturbing sight, it wasn't horrific enough to wake Wilson or make him toss and turn in his bed. Within minutes, his dream shifted and Wilson was enjoying a family drive in the country with Susan and Amanda happily singing along to the radio as they drove along.

Wilson smiled in his sleep, and a hush fell over the house, a peaceful calm that was rare for the Kemp family, lulling them all into a deeper level of sleep.

If they hadn't been so far into dreamland, one of them might have woken up at the sharp noise that came from the basement. There was a loud bang followed quickly by two more, and then things quieted down again. Not totally though. There were more thuds drifting up the basement stairs but they were softer now—steady, rhythmic noises coming from deep inside the antique magic trunk sounding more and more like distant footsteps echoing up a long and narrow staircase. The noise was building.

The footsteps were getting louder.

The footsteps were getting nearer.

Upstairs, Wilson, Susan, and Amanda Kemp peacefully slept on, believing their private nightmare was finally over. They were wrong. Douglas Williams had died and been sent to hell twice now, but like all truly great magicians, the Heatseeker still had a few tricks left up his torn and rotted sleeve . . .

Keep reading for an advance look at the next horrifying
novel by Gord Rollo . . .

Valley of the Scarecrow

Coming Soon!

CHAPTER ONE

Oak Valley, Iowa—September, 1936
Miller's Grove

Killing was something new for Angus Tucker. He'd
never even considered it before, never dreamed he was
capable of such a heinous cowardly act, but if the truth
be told a dark anger had crept into his heart lately and
whether he liked to admit it or not, murder was on his
mind. For the big Scottish man, the golden rule of "do
unto others as you'd have them do unto you" was much
more than just a friendly verse from the Good Book;
they were words of wisdom to live by, solid advice from
the highest authority. Up until tonight, Angus could
confidently say he'd done just that, lived his entire for-
ty-one years of life as a God-fearing Christian who tried
his best to keep the peace and always help his fellow
man.

That was going to change tonight.

Cold-blooded murder, he thought, tasting the sound
of it in his mind and finding it bitter. *You'll be damned,
Angus. Damned for what you're about to do.*

Probably true, but it was a chance he was prepared to take and at least he wouldn't go to Hell alone. Angus gazed around the clearing at the other dozen men gathered in the woods bordering the cornfields, brooding silently while they waited for the others to arrive. They were all hardworking men, strong hearty immigrants from Scotland and Ireland for the most part, with a few first generation Americans tossed into the mix who were already in the valley when they immigrants had settled Miller's Grove a decade ago. Angus had a long mane of ginger- colored hair and was bigger than most of the other village elders. He was tall and broad shouldered from years of hard physical labor in the fields, so naturally they looked up to him for guidance. His physical stature as well as his calm, intelligent personality made him a perfect leader in times of turmoil and stress. Times like tonight, when the future of their community was at stake.

Not to mention their souls.

"Should we get goin', Angus?" Charlie Magee asked, another Scot whose brogue was as thick as the day he'd arrived in America. "Looks like we're a' here."

The small crowd of men moved closer, anxious to here Angus speak, but he waited for the last few stragglers to circle around him so he wouldn't have to shout. "Best wait another few minutes, lads, just to be sure. We dinny want to move until he's started his sermon. Are they in the church a'ready?"

"Aye," Davey Leask answered from the back, short of breath from having just arrived in the clearing from where he'd been scouting the church. "Only Joshua and three others. If we're gonna do this, tonight's the perfect night."

"If we're gonna do this?" Angus asked, curious. "Are you and the others having second thoughts? I canny do this alone ya kin?"

Most of the elders nodded their heads in agreement, but there were still murmurs in the back and too many people whispering among themselves for Angus's liking. Singling out Jim Hancock, the oldest and most respected elder present, Angus asked, "What is it Jimmy? Out with it. We need to stand together or not at all."

"Agreed," the diminutive Irishman said, his shoulders slumping. "It's just that he's a reverend for Heaven's sake. A man of God. How can we even think about . . . ?"

"He stopped being a man of God a long time ago," Angus interrupted. "We a' know that. You, Jimmy, more than most. With your own eyes you saw him meet with the Man in Black, right?"

At the mention of the Man in Black, the crowd went silent. It was a name no one in Miller's Grove ever said out loud and all eyes turned towards the little man in the front row. "Aye, Angus. I did. He appeared out of the shadows . . . out of nowhere in the middle of the corn and I watched Joshua walk right up to him and kneel at his feet. I'd never been more scared in a' my life."

"And you're no' the only one. I've seen him too, and we a' know how Joshua's changed in the last year. Reverend Miller was a good man, no question. The best of us maybe, which is why we named the village after him. He was our guiding light here in America, but that was before the hard times. He's been turned from God . . . corrupted by the Man in Black into a greedy, evil monster who'll drag us a' to Hell with him if we don't make a stand. You've a' heard him speak . . . a' heard his blasphemous sermons. He's out of his mind and walks hand in hand with the demons now. For our sake, for our families', we have to stop him. I dinny wanna do this either, but there's no other choice. God has put this task in front of us and we canny look the other way any longer. Tonight we end this, once and for all. Are you a' with me?"

There was a chorus of "Aye" from the Grove's elders, and everyone joined hands in a display of solidarity. Angus was pleased and more than a little relieved. He had no idea what he'd have done if they'd given up and went back to their homes. "Good. Then let's get going and by the grace of God we'll do what needs done, but first we should pray." The men huddled together, going down on their knees in a circle around Angus. He knew none of them were prepared for what lay ahead, but they were as ready as they'd ever be. "Forgive us, Lord, for what we are about to do . . ."